133 HOURS

ZACH ABRAMS

OTHER FICTION TITLES BY ZACH ABRAMS

You can buy Zach's fiction books at Amazon by linking to:

Alex Warren Murder Mystery series:

Made a Killing - http://mybook.to/madeakilling

A Measure of Trouble - http://mybook.to/ameasureoftrouble

Written to Death - http://mybook.to/writtentodeath

Ring Fenced - **http://mybook.to/ringfenced**

Source - **http://mybook.to/source**

Twists and Turns - **My Book**

You can find out more about Zach's publications from his Amazon
page at http://author.to/zachabrams

O HOURS

I STEP FORWARD ONTO THE MAIN CONCOURSE OF GLASGOW Central station to find the not uncommon feature of a wet and greasy surface. As I rush forward, my foot skids on the tiles and I totter for a second or two, trying to regain my balance. For a moment, I marvel at the thought of a city with Glasgow's pedigree for science, art and culture accepting some genius's idea to floor their principal railway station with tiles. My years of teenage ballet training serve to no avail when a surge of rushing commuters jostle past. Clutching my handbag to my chest, my other hand reaches out, seeking a hand, an arm, a shoulder... anything for support, but it's not to be. I yelp as my hip thuds against a bench whilst my ankle twists under me, my torso spiralling to the ground. I notice one heel of my stilettos is twisted out of shape.

Crowds of passengers pass me in a blur in the moments I take to nurse my wounds and regain some composure. I realise I've scraped my thigh, but more concerning is my throbbing ankle.

Once I've confirmed there's nothing broken, I apply a gentle massage to ease the pain then try staggering to my feet.

"You alright, luv?" I hear the man's voice, an English accent, as my elbow is supported, lifting me upright. He's gone before I can consider a reply. A literal case of too little, too late, I think.

Biting on my lip to deflect my attention from the pains in my leg, I shuffle forward a few paces. I feel strange, disoriented. It's not the fall. My head is fuzzy; I can't seem to think straight. It isn't only my throbbing ankle; my limbs are sore, disjointed almost, and I have an ache from my nether regions. I must be coming down with something.

I glance upwards towards the enormous destination screen. At first, all I see is flashing lights, too painful to focus, but I make out the time showing on the digital clock; it's 8.56. I'm going to be late.

Something else is wrong. I'm never late. I'm diligent. In the four months since I started at Archers International, I haven't ever arrived less than fifteen minutes early. Mr Ronson, the regional director, told me he was impressed by my work and my commitment. He said I would have a great future with the company. Now, here am I, requiring a five-minute brisk stroll to the office and I'm struggling to walk.

1 HOUR

IT'S ALMOST 9.40 BY THE TIME I EXIT THE LIFT ON THE seventh floor. I push through the double doors, entering the expansive open plan section, stumbling towards my desk.

Seeing me, Margaret steps from her private room. She asks, "Where the hell have you been?"

I'm aware of everyone in the office turning to look at me. Then their heads go down. They're pretending not to listen but their ears are primed. The tension is palpable. Margaret Hamilton is my department supervisor. She's had a love-hate relationship with me ever since I joined the company. It isn't personal; she hates it whenever Mr Ronson gives credit to anyone for their work, unless it's her, and she loves any opportunity to put someone down, no matter who. Particularly when it's one of the younger or newer female members of staff who she feels she can bully. Margaret is tall and thin with a face which, on better days, looks like a chewed toffee. The girls in the office joke that she must be a reincarnation of her namesake who played the Wicked Witch of the West in the original version of *The Wizard of Oz*. It's cruel, but then so is she. Margaret's in her fifties, married with grown-up children who've fled the nest. I've been told that she lives a bitter existence with a nasty, cruel beast of a husband, only relieving her angst by lording it over her subordinates at work. If it's true, then maybe I don't grudge her the release, just provided I'm not the victim. Unfortunately, right now, I'm in her sights.

"I'm sorry. I know I'm late, but I had a bit of an accident on the way here. I tripped and I've injured my ankle, broken my shoe, too. I came here as quickly as I could." I chance a smile, in the hope my pain and distress might trigger a hint of sympathy.

"Don't talk nonsense, Briony." She scowls at me in a most disarming way. "If it was only a matter of you being a few minutes late, then I'd have let it go with a reprimand, but you can't get away with this kind of behaviour. You've really let us down. It's not only me. Mr Ronson was livid."

I'm genuinely taken aback. I can't understand where this is coming from. Maybe it's a trick, and she's trying to put me off my guard. "What do you mean? I'd never let you down. I love my job. Tell me what you mean."

"You can't be serious. You've been absent with no explanation for three days. You didn't tell us why, or let us know where you were, and you didn't answer our calls. You missed the major client presentation on Tuesday. The one your team's been working its socks off to prepare, the client we've been courting for three months to pull off, and you think that's acceptable?" She looks me up and down. "Now you swan in here looking like a tramp. Your makeup's blotchy, your hair's a mess and you look as if you've slept in those clothes." Her eyes harden. "It looks like you've been on one almighty bender. Or are you on

4

drugs and just come out of a trip? I don't know what you've been up to and frankly, I don't care."

What does she mean? I don't do drugs. Admittedly, back in my university years I tried smoking weed a couple of times, but that was years ago, and it did nothing for me. As for alcohol, I'll sometimes have a glass of wine or three, but it's only ever social drinking. I may occasionally challenge the official government guidelines for the maximum number of units recommended for healthy consumption, but I don't get drunk and I've never been, or want to be, 'out of my mind' with drink.

My head spins and I think I might faint. I can't make sense of what she's just said. "Three days? But, but... it's not true. I... I ... wait a..." I try to speak but my thoughts are jumbled. I can't form a coherent sentence. I grasp the back of a chair for support, fearing I may otherwise collapse.

"Mr Ronson's in a meeting so he can't deal with you now. I can't imagine any way he'll consider letting you continue in employment as you're still on probation. For now, you can consider yourself suspended. I suggest you go off home and clean yourself up and then come back at 2pm. We have already put any personal stuff you had in your desk in a box, because we'd no idea if you were ever coming back and we needed the space. You can take it with you if you like." Margaret's face is stern, but I suspect there's a self-satisfied smile lurking behind the impassive exterior.

I'm hardly surprised by her verbal onslaught, but the prospect of losing my job hits me like a stone. I meant this to be my chance to build my career. After four years of hard graft to achieve my first-class honours degree and two years further work experience, I landed my position as junior marketing executive at Archers International. I draw in a gasp of breath and hold it. I know my eyes are welling up, but I'm determined not to cry in front of this bitch. I gaze down at the floor. To my relief, she turns and strides back into her room.

I half-run, half-stagger, back out of the main office. To my left is the ladies' toilet. I push the door and rush in. I now feel dreadfully ill and realise I'm about to throw up. Barely in time, I barge open a cubicle door, collapsing onto the floor with my head over the white porcelain as I start to retch. My chest heaves and saliva drips from my mouth. My face is perspiring. I want to be sick, to clear my system of whatever's poisoning me. Nothing's coming up. I'm desperate. I need to make myself feel better. I try forcing two fingers down my throat. It makes me retch again and heavier this time but, save for a thimbleful of liquid, nothing comes up.

I'm exhausted. My mouth and throat have a nasty acidic taste and I feel pain and discomfort all over my body. I flush the toilet and then, with difficulty, I drag myself off the floor and haul myself up using the worktop in front of the wash-hand basins. I cup cold water in my hand, then bring it to my mouth to gulp, trying to remove the bad taste. I gag when the liquid hits my throat and instead try to slowly sip the water.

I glimpse myself in the mirror. No, it can't be me. The face staring back looks considerably older than my twenty-five years. If this was what Margaret was talking about, then I can hardly blame her. I look dreadful; it's all that she said and more. My cheeks are hollow, my eyes are sunken, with the pupils looking like pinpricks and my skin's like parchment, decorated by clown-like blotches of mascara. My rain jacket is dirty, probably after my fall, and my dress is creased almost beyond recognition. How can I have come to work looking like this? I take pride in my appearance; I'm normally immaculate. What's happened to me?

I must be ill. Margaret said I'd been AWOL for three days, but surely not? I couldn't have been ill and slept all that time; I'd have known, wouldn't I? Whatever, I must do something about it now. I pull off some paper towels from the dispenser and soak them, rubbing the makeshift cloth over my face, trying to clean myself and remove any caked cosmetics. I want to make myself look human again. I run my fingers through my hair hoping to restore some kind of order. I'm fishing in my handbag, looking for lipstick, when I hear footsteps. The door opens and in walks Alesha.

Alesha started with the company a month or two before me. She's one of the secretarial team, not a marketing graduate like me. She's young, twenty-one, I think, and she's very pretty. She has perfect skin, dark in shade, almost black. She's a little above medium height, has shoulder length, poker straight, jet-black hair and a figure to die for. 38-23-36, if I'm not mistaken. She should have been a model. She likes to be noticed and tends to wear low-cut tops. All the men in or visiting our company, Mr Ronson included, are guilty of furtive glances at her cleavage. Hell, if I was that way inclined, I'd be tempted. In the time I've been with Archers, Alesha and I have rarely spoken other than the conventional pleasantries.

The moment she sees me, she rushes across and places her arm around my shoulder. "Briony, whatever's happened to you? We've all been so worried."

My eyes well up again at this gesture of kindness. I try to think how to answer. "I don't know. I really don't know," I reply.

"Ignore Margaret. Everyone knows what a cow she can be. Tell me what happened."

I try to think. Much as I could really use a friend just now, I suspect her motives. I hardly know Alesha and now she's here with this sudden outburst of companionship. I don't know if she's naturally kind, or if she's merely seeking some juicy material for gossip. Irrespective, I've nothing to lose. "I don't understand any of it. I came into work not realising anything was wrong. I've not been able to come to terms…"

"Sit down. Let's talk and see what we can work out," she offers, leading me to a chair. I see no reason not to comply.

"To start with, what can you tell me about today?" she asks.

I try to think, but nothing comes quickly. "The first thing I remember is being in Central Station and realising that I was running late."

"What about before? You were in the station, but how did you get there? Where did you spend last night? Were you at home or staying with someone else? Did you walk to the station, or get a train or even a bus?"

The questions make sense but, much as I rack my brains, I can't think of the answers. I remember being in Central Station, but not how I got there.

She sees my troubled expression and gives my shoulders a squeeze. "Don't worry. It will come back to you. Now, what's the last thing you can remember doing before coming alive in Central Station?"

I'm struggling to think, and I plunder my memories. My mind seems so blank. Pondering some more, I say, "The last thing I remember is working late on Friday. I knew I didn't have time to go home as I'd planned to meet my friend Jenny, at Alfredo's. We planned to have a couple of drinks before going out to dinner. I didn't get changed and instead went out dressed in my work clothes. I went to the bar, as planned."

"Okay, that's a start," Alesha replied. "What about the friend you were meeting? Why not contact her? She might be able to fill in some gaps. She may know where you've been."

"Of course! That makes sense. I don't know why I didn't think of it myself," I reply and truly I don't. I'm meant to be smart. My brain feels fuzzy and I'm not thinking straight. "I should have met Jenny at 8pm. I'll try to call her now." I open my handbag and rummage for my mobile.

"Just a thought. Can you remember what you were wearing on Friday?"

I pause and close my eyes, trying to recollect. "Yes, it was my navy, linen, Jaeger dress. I'd chosen it because I had an important meeting with the MD of Carson's, a new client and I wanted to look smart."

Alesha's jaw drops and I follow the direction of her eyes. "Oh my God! That's what I'm wearing. I'm in the same dress I was wearing last Friday and I've no idea where I've been or what I've been doing since."

My knees buckle, and I again think I might faint. I'm saved the further indignity as Alesha props me up and then guides me to a cubicle and puts down the toilet lid so I can sit.

"This can't be happening. It must be a nightmare. I can't account for anything that's happened since last Friday evening."

"That's what... five and a half days... one hundred and thirty-two hours," Alesha calculates, "perhaps more."

"Maybe I'm ill and I passed out somewhere. Could I have been unconscious all this time? Christ, aliens could have abducted me for all I know." My pathetic attempt at dark humour does nothing to lighten the mood.

"Or worse." Alesha blurts the words then she covers her mouth, shocked at having voiced her thoughts.

Neither of us speaks as her words hang heavily between us. Her facial expression is deadly serious, and I suspect that she, like me, is contemplating however else, and for what purpose, I might have been abducted. I don't panic. I feel a strange detachment, almost as if I'm on the ceiling looking down at Alesha and myself having this conversation.

My brain wanders. I visualise myself lying naked. Hands are touching me, lots of hands, touching everywhere, stroking, caressing, probing. Is this my imagination or my memory? I feel dirty, so dirty. Bile is rising.

"But why can't I remember anything?" I ask.

"I don't know. Perhaps it's trauma. Maybe you're ill with something. I know little about these things. Then again, someone might have drugged you."

"I must get home. I need a shower." I feel a compulsion to cleanse my body and maybe it will clear my brain, too.

"No, not yet. You mustn't. You have to speak to the police first," she replies. "It may be nothing. I truly hope it's nothing, but you will need their help to find out."

"You're right. I will have to do that." My eyes well up again and this time I can't hold back the tears. It escalates and, within seconds, my whole body convulses with racking sobs. Alesha steps in and holds me close, cradling my head. I grasp her tightly as if my life depends on it. Maybe it does. At first, my mind is frantic, visualising images, horrible images of what someone could have subjected me to. My body shakes, and I screw my eyes tight shut, but the images are still tormenting me. I gulp in deep breaths, realising I need to calm myself down or face a full panic attack. Gradually, my breathing evens out as I come to terms with my predicament.

Alesha says nothing, but she holds me close, stroking my head. Some time passes before I can wrench myself away. I know I need to be tough to get through this. I feel stronger now, more able to face what's ahead.

2 HOURS

"Alesha, I know what I have to do now. I can't thank you enough for your help, but I don't want you to get into trouble because of me. You've been away from your desk for ages. You'd best go back."

"I will not let you face this alone. You need someone to stay with you, and unless you have any better ideas, then I'll be the one, for now at least. But you're right, I can't just walk out from the office without saying something and I need to pick up my bag and jacket at any rate. Will you be okay if I leave you for a few minutes while I tell the witch what's happening?"

I nod.

"I don't care if she likes it or not, I'm coming with you," she adds. "So, don't go anywhere until I come back. I won't be long."

"Okay, thanks, I really appreciate it," I say, forcing the edge of a smile. It's meant to reassure her, but I fear it may make my face look more like a horror mask, thereby having the opposite effect. "While you're away, I'll try phoning Jenny to see what she knows."

Alesha gives my shoulder a squeeze then rushes out the door.

I stand again, placing my handbag on the worktop and I rummage, looking for my mobile. I lift out the phone case and open it only to find that my phone has been dismantled. The back of the case has been removed and the battery and SIM card are lying loose in the case. As my thinking is becoming more coherent, I realise the implications. Being ill and passing out somewhere causing me to sleep off the last few days is no longer a credible possibility. It wasn't likely in the first place, but it was preferable to the alternative. Someone has dismantled my phone, which means what's happened to me over the last few days has been inflicted on me by someone else. To avoid dwelling on what else they might have done, I try to consider why they took the phone apart. Perhaps it was to stop me making calls or sending messages, or to avoid receiving any, but surely, they could have achieved the same result by switching it off? The action was more deliberate; it must have had a purpose. Of course, I think, it would deactivate the GPS to stop the phone or its location being traceable. If that was the intention, then why not destroy it or just dump it? It makes little sense.

I reinsert the SIM and battery and switch the device on, being met by the standard start-up chimes. Good, it seems to work. Next, I notice the icons. The low battery warning is flashing, but it's also showing there are four voicemails, nine text messages, six WhatsApp messages and an indeterminable number of emails and Facebook, Twitter, Pinterest and LinkedIn notifications. The latter five don't concern me as I normally receive loads of notifications every day. They must have accumulated as I haven't logged on for almost a week; there might be hundreds. I need to prioritise the other messages; maybe they will tell me something about what's happened.

I want to call Jenny, but first I need to do this. I click on messages and thumb through the chronological list. I want to start with anything that's come in since last Friday.

The first three on the list are all from Jenny, all written in text-speak.

Timed on Friday at 7.55pm. *So, so, sorry, running late, will explain later, should be there by 8.30.*

Next, Friday 8.42pm. *Where are you?*

Then 9.03. *Looked everywhere, you're not here! What's up, you pissed at me being late? I'll call tomorrow when you cool down.*

Does this help? I wonder. It confirms my arrangement to meet Jenny and, from what she's said, I know she turned up late, and I'd already left, but it doesn't actually confirm that I was there. I try to concentrate and visualise what happened. I can see myself sitting at a table, on my own, nursing a glass of Merlot. I've been to Alfredo's often enough so I can draw a clear picture but, try as I might, I can't be certain if it's a memory from Friday or a mental reconstruction. If only I could be sure, then I'd have a solid starting point.

The next message is from Dad, timed at 9.21 on Saturday morning.

Mum and I are having a wonderful time. We celebrated actual day of anniversary yesterday with a fabulous dinner on board. Thanks for the champagne and flowers, delicious and beautiful in that order. We docked in Naples this morning and we're about to leave on a trip ashore to visit Pompei and Vesuvius. We'll keep you updated. Don't work too hard. Love Mum and Dad xx

I'm pleased their holiday is going well. They've been planning it for months to celebrate their thirtieth wedding anniversary. A memory returns. I made arrangements online to send flowers and champagne to their cabin on their special day, but then I realise that as I set it up days beforehand, it doesn't fill in any gaps for me.

Timed at 10.27, there's a spam message warning me time is running out for me to make a PPI claim.

Then Saturday at 10.51, Jenny texted again. *Tried calling and left message. Are you still pissed? I'm sorry, please talk to me!*

I must call her back, I think. I guess she suspects I've cut her off because she let me down. We've been best pals since secondary school. I must confess, over the many years we've been close, there have been times when I've lost it with her and gone into a strop. She'll think that's why she hasn't heard from me. I need to let her know what's happened, or, more to the point, I need her to help me find out what's happened. The battery is showing only 2%; I can't call now, or it will almost certainly cut off. I must get the phone recharged as soon as possible. I need to go home to get my charger. I'm desperate to get some fresh clothes, too. I'd better check if I've cash for a taxi.

I rummage again in my bag and pull out my purse. Opening it, I think there's something odd. I see no paper money in the wallet section and only some smash in the change pouch, £2.33 in total. The five pound note I keep behind my business cards is still there and so is my travel Zone card, driving license, gym membership and credit Mastercard, but my bank debit card isn't there. I always keep it in the same place and it's missing. Oh shit, have I lost it or has someone taken it? I normally keep between twenty and sixty pounds in notes, so where's that gone? Have I spent it or has someone has taken it? I feel unsteady and I can again taste the acid from my stomach. I clutch the worktop for support as I digest this new information. This keeps getting worse and worse.

I hear the door as Alesha returns.

"Well, here's a surprise for you," she announces and her voice is cheerful.

"I don't think I can take any more surprises," I reply, unable to share her glee, my voice bitter.

Undaunted, she continues, "You won't be troubled by this one. I marched into Hamilton's office to tell her I needed to take time off to look after you. I was assertive and would not take no for an answer. She told me to sit down and tell her what it was about." Alesha smiled. "You won't believe this – she told me, of course I must go! She said she'd have preferred to come herself, but she was running late for a client appointment which she couldn't get out of.

"She said she wanted me to keep her informed and would call you later. She gave me this card for you. It has her personal mobile number, and she said to call any time. She also handed me twenty pounds and said to use it for taxis or anything else you needed. She added that I should say nothing about any of this to anyone else in the office." Alesha raises an eyebrow. "What do you think, has the ice queen melted?"

"I don't know what to say," and truly I don't. Have we misjudged Margaret, or is she just trying to cover herself in case

I make a complaint? I don't care; the state I'm in, I'll take whatever help is offered.

"Let's get out of here," Alesha suggests, guiding me out of the toilets and towards the elevator.

"I've tried to check my phone but the battery's nearly out. I must go home for my charger so I can see the rest of my messages. I've only just started."

"Where is it you live? I didn't think to ask before. Do you have family who can help you?" Alesha asks.

"I rent a flat on the South-Side. It's in Langside. I only took on the lease a couple of months ago, after I started this job. I lived with my parents up until then. The only family I have are my Mum and Dad and my gran. She has dementia and needs full-time care. She lives in a nursing home now. Mum and Dad are great but they're not around at the moment. It was their thirtieth anniversary the other day and last week they left to go on a Med cruise to celebrate. They're not due home until Sunday, or Monday more like. They've been looking forward to this holiday for months, so I don't want to tell them anything until they're home. I probably couldn't get hold of them easily anyway, 'cos they keep their phones switched off most of the time and Dad told me the broadband is practically non-existent. I reckon I'll just have to brave it out until they get back."

I think for a couple of seconds before adding, "Maybe I could move back into their house for a few days. I know my room hasn't changed at all since I left."

Alesha looks pensive. "Are you sure? Don't you think they'd prefer to know sooner, rather than later?"

I hadn't considered this. I don't know what to do. Mum and

Dad need this holiday, particularly after Dad's heart scare last year; they deserve it. They ought to be able to celebrate their special occasion without me spoiling it. On the other hand, if they knew that I was in trouble, then they'd want to be here with me. They'd rush home early, doing whatever it took to be here beside me. They may feel hurt that I hadn't told them, or feel I didn't trust them, but it isn't true. I wouldn't want to harm them for the world.

Lurking at the back of my mind is also the thought that I don't know how they'll react when they hear what has happened and I don't want to be a disappointment to them, either by letting them know, or by holding back information. It seems like I'm damned if I do and I'm damned if I don't. Although I don't yet remember what's happened to me, whatever it is, I'm okay now. At least, I think I'm okay now.

I convince myself not to tell them. I argue that if they're given the shock of being told something's happened to their daughter while they've been away enjoying themselves, then it could be harmful to their health. If they were told I'd been abducted, or I'd been raped, then they'd be traumatised. The shock could kill them. However, if I were to wait until they come home to tell them, then even if they are angry because they hadn't been informed sooner, they at least will be able to see me and know I am okay. Besides, there's nothing they can do, other than hold my hand and worry, so what's the point of spoiling the last part of their holiday?

"You're right, Alesha, they probably would want to know. But, all things considered, there's nothing they can do, and it would do them more harm than good to be told now."

Alesha chews on her lip, clearly not convinced, but she says no more on the subject.

"I've started looking at texts, but I would like to check the rest of my messages, or at least as many as I can before my battery runs out."

"What have you found so far?" Alesha asks.

"Nothing major," I reply. "I've confirmed my recollection that I was due to meet Jenny at eight. She didn't turn up until late and I was gone."

"Well, at least you know you were there, so you have a starting point."

I think about this before replying. "Not really. I know I was meant to be there but don't yet know whether I actually arrived."

3 HOURS

THE ELEVATOR DOOR OPENS OPPOSITE TO THE BUILDING'S reception area. I breathe deeply, welcoming the gust of fresh air coming in from the street as people pass through the front entrance. "I'm going to take a seat for a couple of minutes," I say, pointing to the sofa in the main lobby. "Let me see what else I can check," I hold up my phone, "and while I do, can you speak to the man at the security desk to see if there's any record of when I left this building on Friday?"

"Good idea. I'll get right onto it."

The last three texts are social messages from acquaintances and are of no further relevance. I switch onto my voicemail. Of the four messages, the first one is electronic spam seeking to know if I need help resulting from an accident I had that wasn't my fault. I'm so sick of these calls. I wonder if I should reply to them and ask them to sort out my current dilemma? I feel myself grimace, thinking I've not totally lost my sense of irony.

I find the second message rather concerning. It's from the

letting agent I rented my flat through and it's asking why the rent payment due on Monday hasn't been received. That's odd, I think; I pay by standing order and there ought to have been more than adequate funds to cover the payment. I must investigate this. I'll call my bank at the first opportunity, but there are a few priorities I need to attend to first.

The third message is from Jenny, asking if I've cooled down enough to talk to her and finishes by asking me to call her back.

The fourth message is from Mum and Dad, calling from Palermo in Sicily, while on another excursion from their cruise. Hearing their voices, I wish they were here. At this moment, I'd love nothing more than to be enveloped in a family hug, to feel safe and protected in their care. Their voices are joyous; they're clearly enjoying their holiday. They've raised me to be strong and independent and this thought confirms my determination not to say anything to them until after they return home. As it happens, I only hear the start of their call before the phone falls silent, its battery dead.

Alesha returns, having confirmed that I left the building at 7.23 on Friday evening. "You ready to go?" she asks.

"As ready as I'll ever be."

She clicks a few buttons on her phone, then looks up to tell me the taxi will be at the front door in five minutes.

"Let's go straight to the police. The nearest station is at Baird Street," she suggests.

"I'd prefer to go home, so I can get my battery charger. I need to phone Jenny and I'd like to change into other clothes."

"I think the sooner you get the ordeal over with, the better. You can call your friend now using my phone, if you like. Everything else can wait," Alesha replies.

Much as I want to go home, I can see the logic. Once I'm back at my house, I won't want to go out again. I nod my agreement

Alesha hands me her phone just as the cab arrives. We get in and I dial Jenny's number. Only when I hear it ring, does it occur to me how easily I recollected her number, despite rarely using it because it's on autodial on my mobile. My memory is working so my thinking can't be too muddled

Before the fourth ring, I hear her voice announce, "Jenny Douglas." She sounds cautious, obviously not recognising the number.

"Jenny, it's me, Briony."

"Briony, really. You've finally come down off your high horse and consider I'm worthy to speak to again."

"Jenny, stop; it's not like that. I wasn't pissed, and I wasn't avoiding you. It's... it's... it's just that..." I struggle to think what to say.

"It's just what?"

"Jenny, I'm in trouble. I can't remember a thing that's happened to me since Friday."

"Is this some sort of joke, Briony? What are you on about?"

"It's no joke, Jenny. I wish it was. It's more of a nightmare. I think I might have been abducted."

"Are you serious?"

"Totally serious."

"Oh my God! What's happened? Where are you? Where are you calling from? I don't recognise the number."

"I don't know what happened – that's the problem. I'm in a taxi, along with Alesha from my office. I'm calling on her phone as I've no charge in mine. We're on our way to the police station to see if they can help."

"You don't remember seeing anyone?"

"No. I remember nothing between Friday evening and this morning."

"My god. That's nearly a week! I don't know what to say. Do your mum and dad know?"

"Listen, Jenny, I need your help. The only thing I know is that I left work about half past seven on Friday and I was meant to meet you at eight at Alfredo's. I've seen your texts. I read them before my phone's battery died. I need to know what else you can tell me."

"Of course. I'll help you any way I can, but I don't know if there's anything I can add. I got delayed and didn't arrive until, I don't know, maybe half eight, going on nine o'clock and you weren't there. I thought you must have got fed up with waiting and left."

"That's it? You didn't see me, or speak to anyone who knew when I'd left, or if I was with anyone?"

"I'm sorry, Briony, I didn't. I just made the assumption. It was already late, and I was famished so I headed home and picked up a kebab on the way. If only I'd known."

I take a deep breath. I'm disappointed and exasperated, realising I won't learn any more from her.

"What police station are you going to? I'll come and keep you company. I just need to tell the boss I'm taking some time out."

"You don't need to. Alesha's here with me."

"I want to help. I'll do anything I can. Tell me where you're going and I'll meet you there as soon as I can get across."

I think for a second. "There is something you can do. We're on our way to Baird Street. Could you find me there and collect my keys, then go to my flat and pick me up a change of clothing? Could you also get the charger for my phone?"

"No problem. I'm happy to help. I'll be there as quickly as I can."

I feel reassured knowing I'll see Jenny soon. Although Alesha has been great, a tower of strength in fact, it's not the same. I've been close to Jenny for so long, she's almost like family.

The journey passes in a blur. I can hear the driver prattling on about something, a news item, but I can't take it in. Arriving outside the police station, Alesha settles the bill, then takes my arm and guides me through the entrance into a cavernous room.

A young-looking civilian assistant approaches us. "Hello, my name's Cynthia. How can I help you?" she asks.

I get flustered and don't know what to say. Alesha sees my hesitancy and once again comes to my aid. "My friend needs your help," she starts. "She has no recollection whatsoever of anything that's happened to her between Friday and today and we think she's been abducted, probably drugged..." She looks at me before continuing, "and it's very likely she's been raped."

"I see," Cynthia says calmly. "Please come with me and take a seat over here." She guides us to a seated area in the corner.

"The first thing I need to do is get some basic information from you." She lifts a tablet and takes details from me: my full name, address, date of birth, nationality, telephone number, email address and employment details. "I'll arrange for an officer to speak to you."

She moves away a few paces and then makes a call. I can't quite make out what she's saying but I think I pick out words... code six two... solo. She looks at me and nods. Then she asks, "Do you have a preference? Would you like to speak to a male or a female officer?"

My first thought is that it doesn't matter, but then it occurs to me that I'm likely to undergo some intimate questioning and I don't think I would be comfortable talking to a man. I won't be comfortable talking to anyone, but the idea of a male stranger seems so much more daunting. "A female officer, please," I reply.

4 HOURS

It may only have been a matter of minutes but, to me, it seems an interminable length of time before the officer arrives. "Hello, I'm W.P.C. Paula Fleming. I'm a trained Sexual Offences Liaison Officer, or S.O.L.O. for short. I'd like to take you through to what we call the comfort suite so we can get a full statement from you. We can either do this privately or, if you prefer, your friend can come and sit with you."

Before I can answer, I see Jenny arrive. She's looking around frantically until she spots us. She rushes over and hugs me tightly.

"Oh Briony, are you okay? I was so sorry to hear about your problem and I'll do everything I can to help." I fish my house keys from my handbag and give them to her. It looks as if her eyes are welling with tears and I struggle to keep my composure.

"I won't be long," she says. "You said you want your charger and a change of clothes. I'm guessing something casual like denims, tee-shirt and undies. Anything else?"

"Yes, get me my trainers please, maybe my fleece as well, in case I feel cold. Thank you so much."

"Okay, I'm on it. I'll be back in thirty minutes, an hour, tops," Jenny says as she races away.

"I was asking whether you wanted to be seen alone or with your friend?" Paula repeats.

"I'd like Alesha to be with me, please." I look to Alesha for confirmation. She indicates her assent. "Can Jenny come in, too, when she gets back?"

"Yes, no problem."

"Will you be the one investigating what's happened?" I ask.

"No, I'm the liaison officer. I'll take your statement, after which we'll decide what further steps we need to take. There's a specialist rape investigation unit who handle this type of case. They aren't in this office at present because they're handling other matters. I'll take things as far as I can and then we'll decide whether they need to be involved."

"Wait a minute," Alesha interrupts. "Are you suggesting you might choose not to carry out further enquiries?"

"Not at all," Paula replies. "Once I've taken your statement, then we'll discuss your options and I'll explain what's involved. It's entirely up to you whether we take matters forward. You're under no pressure either way."

As I don't yet know what's involved in an investigation, I'm not too certain what she means, but she sounds friendly and reassuring and I hear myself say, "Okay."

———

4.5 Hours

PAULA LEADS us through a door and along a narrow corridor. My nose crinkles; I detect the odour of disinfectant failing to conceal a more natural stench of body odour. I gag, being hit by another wave of nausea, and I choke back the bile. We pass through another entrance and through a second corridor before Paula unlocks a door to the side and beckons us in. The room is warm and looks comfortable. There's subdued lighting and the walls are a pastel colour. There are no windows, but I see a climate control unit in the corner above a kitchen area. Thick carpeting covers the floor and there are four well-upholstered seats surrounding a coffee table.

I settle into an armchair. Alesha sits to my right with Paula opposite. Paula starts off by confirming all the information already taken by Cynthia, when I first arrived. Next, she says, "I need to record this." She activates a device and then tells me she wants to be told everything that's happened to me, described in my own words. She gives Alesha a steady stare, a clear sign that while she's happy for her to attend, she wants her to stay silent while I give my statement.

"This is really difficult," I say.

"I know, but just do your best," Paula replies.

"No, you don't understand," I say. "It's difficult because I don't know what happened."

Paula raises an eyebrow. "We need to start somewhere. Please tell me what you do know?"

"The problem I have is, I have no recollection of what's happened to me for the last week. The last thing I remember is being in my office working, last Friday. The next thing I'm certain of is being in Central Station this morning on my way into work." I pause to draw in breath. "I've checked, or rather Alesha checked for me. I left the office at about 7.30 pm on Friday. I was meant to meet Jenny at eight at Alfredo's for drinks and dinner. She turned up late, and I wasn't there. As far as I know, I haven't spoken to anyone and I haven't seen anyone, and no-one has seen me since then until this morning."

Paula considers this for a second. "How do you know Jenny was late?" she asks. "Did she tell you?"

"Well yes, she did, but I first realised when I checked the texts on my phone. She'd left me messages."

"I see," says Paula. "I'd like you to leave us your phone so we can check all messages and so our telematics experts can analyse it. They may be able to track where you've been."

I lift my phone from my bag and hand it to her. She places it in an evidence bag.

"When I opened my bag this morning, I discovered that someone had dismantled my phone. The cover had been separated and the SIM and battery detached," I explain. "I reassembled it so I could check for messages."

She looks sombre. "It looks as though someone was very careful with their planning," she says, but she doesn't comment further. Instead, she nods, encouraging me to continue.

"Like I said, the first thing I remember this morning was being in Central and I didn't feel at all normal. I felt flu-like, you know, dizzy and disoriented. All my limbs ached. I felt sore all over and particularly sensitive here and here," I indicate my breasts and pubic region.

"Please explain in more detail for the tape," Paula says.

After verbalising where I feel pain, I add, "I don't know what else I can tell you."

"I understand," Paula replies, but the pensive look on her face suggests a different story. "It's not too unusual for people to have blackouts or memory loss. There's a whole range of reasons why it can happen. The brain is a very complex organ," she says, tapping her temple as if I wouldn't understand without a visual aid. Maybe I'm traumatised, but she's treating me as if I'm an imbecile and I don't appreciate it. I must have pursed my lips without realising it. Misinterpreting my gesture, she compounds her felony by explaining further. "Let me put it another way. It can often store lots of memories without you being aware that they're there."

I want to tell her not to patronise me. I have an A-grade pass in biology, but I reckon it's better to preserve my strength. Also, I'm aware I need to keep her on-side if I'm going to achieve anything. I grimace and nod.

"It's more than likely that your memory will come back, or at least some of it and it could happen in stages." Paula smiles at me reassuringly. Alesha, being aware of my discomfort, takes my hand and gives it a squeeze.

"I want to remember, at least I think I do. It's the not knowing that's tearing me apart," I say, and I mean it. How can I cope when I don't know what I need to cope with?

"I meant what I said. It's not unusual for victims of rape or abduction to suffer from memory loss, but I haven't come across a case like this before where someone has had a gap in their memory of such a long period of time."

"I have no wish to set precedents, but this situation isn't of my choosing," I say.

Paula nods in acknowledgement. "I have more questions for you, Briony. We need to know as much as we can about you, so we have the best chance of getting to the truth of the matter. Don't get me wrong, we don't doubt what you've already told us, but we need to put everything in context so we can correctly interpret any evidence that we find."

"It's okay. I expected you'd want to know more about my personal life."

"Once we've finished the interview, the next stage is to send you across to the medical unit for a forensic examination. It's next to Sandyford Clinic." Paula appraises my reaction and being satisfied I appear to comprehend, she continues. "We'll want to take all clothing you've been wearing for examination. I take it you haven't already changed?"

I glance at my wrinkled dress and manage a half smile. "You're right, I don't normally dress like this. These are the clothes I was wearing when I went to work last Friday. As far as I know, I've had them on since then. I've been desperate to change but thought it best to come and make my report first. Jenny will be back soon with some fresh clothes for me to change into."

"The medical staff will also give you a full examination. They'll take blood samples, check you over for cuts, bruises or puncture marks and they'll take photos. They'll swab you for DNA. Are you okay with all of that?"

I give a slight shudder at the thought. "I can't say I'm comfortable with the idea, but I understand it's necessary," I reply.

"Good," Paula says. "I'm pleased you feel able to cooperate. Now, I know you haven't changed your clothing, but have you showered or washed since your memory gap?"

"No," I reply. "I really wanted to, but Alesha advised me not to, not until you've had a chance to examine me."

"That's good. Alesha was correct. I understand you'll want to wash as soon as possible. It shouldn't be long. Now, have you eaten or drunk anything?"

"No, not yet. I felt sick about an hour ago. I sipped some water, but nothing else."

"Again, that's good. A little water shouldn't make any difference. You're probably starving. We can arrange some tea and toast once we have examined you."

"Thanks." It hadn't occurred to me before, but now, with the mention of toast, I feel ravenous.

"Thinking about last Friday, in the time that you can remember, did you drink anything alcoholic or did you take any drugs?" Paula asks.

"No, I was at work. I'm not much of a drinker and I never drink while I'm working. I had been planning to have some wine in the evening. As for drugs, they don't interest me. It just isn't my scene."

"Are you on any medication? Are there any prescription drugs you routinely take?"

"No, I don't take anything," I answer quickly and then reconsider. "Wait a minute. There is something. I've had a recurring sports injury which affects my shoulder. It kicked off again after I played badminton on Wednesday, that would be last week, and I took Co-Codamol on both Thursday and Friday mornings."

"That's a powerful painkiller," Paula says.

"Yes, but I needed it. Is this relevant?" I ask.

"It could be," Paula replies. "Co-Codamol contains codeine. It's an opiate. If taken along with any other drugs, the effect can be exaggerated or there can sometimes be side effects."

"But I didn't take anything else." I assert.

"Nothing that you're aware of," Paula replies. "Possibly someone else administered something to you without you knowing about it. How much Co-Codamol did you take?"

"Two tablets each morning. I think the pills are 500mg."

"Okay, that's noted. Now, can you tell me if you have ever suffered from blackouts or memory loss in the past?"

"No, never."

"How good is your memory, normally?"

"I'd say it was very good. To qualify with my degree, I had to study and retain large amounts of data. I'm good at remembering names and faces as well as addresses and phone numbers. I suppose, like anyone else, there'll be the odd occasion when I'll forget a birthday, or where I mislay my keys or my phone, but overall I've never had any problems."

"What about your family? Is there any history of dementia or Alzheimer's?"

"No, I don't think so, other than my grandmother. She has been diagnosed with vascular dementia, but it only started two or three years ago and she's well into her seventies."

"What about mental health? Do you, or have you ever had any issues?"

Before I can answer, we're interrupted by the sound of knocking. An officer pokes his head around the door. "Hi, Paula. I've a Jenny Douglas here for Briony Chaplin."

"Yes, we were expecting her, send her in," Paula replies.

Jenny comes in carrying a large bag. "I think I've got everything you asked for. It took me less time than expected. A mixture of little traffic and breakneck speed," she says, then reappraises, remembering where we are. "I didn't go over the speed limit, honest."

"Thanks so much, I feel better knowing I have this ready," I say.

Jenny gives a cautious smile, takes the seat on my left and immediately clasps my hand in hers. She looks at Alesha and says, "I'm back now, if you'd like to go."

"No, it's okay," answers Alesha. "I'd like to help if I can."

Jenny shrugs.

"You can stay if you like. It's entirely up to Briony," Paula says.

Although I haven't known Alesha for long, when I think about it, I feel comforted by having her, as well as Jenny, here with me. "Thank you for staying," I say

"Are you okay?" Jenny asks, looking at me.

"I think so, for now. Paula has just asked if I, or my family, have any memory problems or mental health issues." I look back at Paula. "Thankfully no, I haven't ever had any problems."

"And what about your family?"

"No, nothing."

"Can you really be certain?" Jenny interrupts, frowning and looking at me.

"What?" I ask, then realise what she's getting at. I close my eyes tightly. I don't want to deal with this. Without realising, I clench my fist tight and my nails unintentionally pierce the skin of Jenny's hand. I only realise when I feel her abruptly pull back. "Sorry," I offer, lamely.

"Is there something you need to tell me?" Paula asks.

I stare at the floor, not wanting to make eye contact, my voice little more than a whisper. "If you must know, I was adopted as a baby. I was only a few months old when I came to live with Mum and Dad. I have never known any other family."

"What can you tell me about your birth parents?"

"Very little. All they told me was that my mother was a single parent. She was diagnosed with a terminal illness shortly after my birth and I was offered for adoption."

"Have you ever researched to find who your real parents were, or whether you have any other relatives?" Paula asks.

I'm affronted and it's not only her questions; I find her style of asking to be confrontational and very intrusive. How dare she make assumptions or try to impress her own values onto me? I'm also annoyed with Jenny. How could she leave me open to this when she must already know my feelings on the matter?

"I know who my *real* parents are – they're the ones who've cared for me and raised me for the last twenty-five years. Just because some man and woman went through a random act of fornication, resulting in an egg being fertilised, doesn't make them parents. It certainly doesn't make them *my* parents. There's no reason why I need to, or want to, find out more about my biological mother and father."

I know I'm sensitive on this issue and I shouldn't let it get to me. Maybe it's guilt, because, if I were to be honest, I've often thought I'd like to research where I came from, but I don't want to upset Mum and Dad. They haven't ever discouraged me, but I'm concerned it might be taken as a betrayal. It's nobody's business but mine, so I won't have anyone, whether they be police, friend, or anyone else, trying to tell me what I should have done.

"I'm sorry," Paula says. "I didn't mean to upset you. The purpose of my question was to find out if there might be..."

"Might be what?" I'm trying to calm down but it's a struggle.

"If we're going to properly investigate to find out what happened to you, then you need to be completely honest with us. We need as much information as possible, so we don't waste resources looking down blind alleys *and* so we explore every relevant avenue. You may think it improbable, but we need to research whether your adoption has any relevance to the enquiry."

"In case I've inherited any mad genes," I say, my tone caustic.

Jenny places her hand on my arm. Whether it's to support and comfort me or to restrain me, I can't tell. I'm intolerant and shake her off.

"I won't pull my punches," Paula replies. "Yes, it's our job to consider every possibility. We can't rule out that your complaint might be frivolous. We also need to consider whether any family members could have an involvement, be they birth or adopted family. Statistically, a very high percentage of crimes are committed by family members, so we will want to carry out checks on your birth family. For what it's worth, I believe what you've told me. However, I'm duty-bound to follow the standard procedures."

I inhale deeply, considering her words. "I'm sorry if I overreacted. My emotions are very near the surface."

"That's understandable, given your situation." She continues, "I think it best if we can move on."

"Yes," I agree, nodding.

"Are you currently, or have you recently been, in a relationship?" Paula asks.

I frown and shake my head.

"Please answer, verbally, for the recording."

"No, nothing serious."

"Can you tell me the last time you had sexual intercourse?"

Jenny clasps my hand, and this time I don't withdraw. She knows the answer because I've told her about it. I should have expected this question. I expected to be questioned about my personal life, but nevertheless, someone I don't know quizzing me on such personal issues feels intrusive.

"Saturday night," I reply. "The Saturday before last Friday," I correct. I feel the need to explain further. "Michael and I were in a relationship for over a year. We were very close. I thought we would get engaged, but then he was offered a transfer to a big job in Newcastle. This was six months ago, about the same time as I was being recruited at Archers."

I sigh, then carry on. "I was telling you the truth when I said I haven't recently been in a relationship. When Michael moved away, we agreed to have some time apart... see how it worked as a long-distance relationship. At first, we talked daily but gradually it became less frequent. He called to tell me he was coming up to Glasgow last weekend. We met on the Saturday and it was as if we'd never been apart. We shared a meal and a bottle of wine. He stayed that night at my flat and yes, we did have 'sexual intercourse', but in the morning he admitted to me he'd found someone new in Newcastle. I was furious because he took advantage of me, acting as if we were a couple and not telling me it was a one-night stand. I threw him out and told him I never wanted to see him again."

Despite my determination that I'd never let the bastard upset me again, I feel the trickle of tears roll over my cheeks. Jenny is holding my hand reassuringly and Alesha has taken my other hand.

Much as I don't see the point, Paula takes Michael's contact details.

"I'll contact his local police force and get them to speak to him," she says. Knowing he may be inconvenienced doesn't displease me, even a bit.

"Do your mother and father know about Michael?" Paula asks.

"I didn't tell them about last weekend. They did know when we were a couple. They weren't at all upset when he moved south because they didn't particularly like him. They thought he wasn't good enough for me," I say, containing a restrained half smile.

"From what you've just told me, I think they may have been correct," Paula replies. "Now, can you tell me if there's anyone you've had an argument with, or with whom you've had a serious fallout in the recent past? Is there anyone you know who might want to get back at you for anything?"

I shake my head. "There's no one I can think of. I sometimes have the odd squabble at work over business issues but nothing out of the ordinary. There can be petty rivalries, but that's about it."

"Anything outside of work?" Paula probes.

"No, nothing. Nothing I can think of."

"Any old issues, anyone who might hold a grudge?"

I try to think but come up with nothing.

"One final question. Have you checked your pockets and your handbag? If so, was there anything unusual... anything missing, or anything there that you hadn't expected?"

I tell her my concerns about the missing money and bank card. She looks perturbed and takes my credit card from me so she can check for any unexpected purchases made using it and, as I'm able to remember my bank details, she says she will also check for transactions on the missing debit card.

"If there's nothing else, then I think we should go across to the clinic to have you examined," Paula says. "They'll take prints and DNA from your friends as well, for elimination purposes."

A shiver runs down my spine at the prospect.

Both Jenny and Alesha insist they will go along as they don't want to leave me.

---

5 Hours

JENNY AND ALESHA are asked to wait in the reception area before being called to give their samples. Meanwhile, Paula takes me through and introduces me to the doctor and her team who'll be carrying out my examination. I'm desperate to get this over with and although I'm given each of their names, nothing registers.

Paula gives me her business card with instruction to call her number if I remember something relevant, or think of anything which I'd like to add to my statement. She also tells me to use it if there's any other reason I want to contact her. She also leaves me an information pamphlet with contact numbers for local rape crisis centres and other support groups. I stare blankly at the booklet before stuffing it in my bag, not wanting to believe I'm here, doing this. She tells me to expect a call or a visit from someone from the rape investigation unit.

"But I don't have my phone. How will they contact me?"

"They'll call, or come to your home address. We have your

landline and can call it. If you're going to be away from home, then call me to let me know where you'll be and how we can contact you. We should be able to return your mobile before long, maybe even tomorrow. One other thing – the forensics unit may want to check over your flat. Are you okay with that?"

I can't make sense of it but nod my agreement.

She explains that as there's nothing more for her to do at this point, she'll leave me here.

6 HOURS

I'M DETERMINED TO STAY DISPASSIONATE. WHEN I REMOVE my shoes and my dress, the technician places them in evidence bags. I unclip my bra and hand it over, too, but I stop, frozen, as I go to remove my briefs. This isn't right.

"Is something wrong?" she asks.

I stare at her and then back at my underwear and my jaw drops, initially lost for words.

"What's wrong?" she asks.

"These undies, they aren't mine," I say.

Her look is quizzical.

"I never buy this type. I always either wear designer under-wear or else Marks and Spencer's. When I dressed last Friday, the last day I remember, I'm sure I was wearing a Victoria's Secret thong. These are plain white briefs." I tug the elastic waistband at the back to look at the label. It confirms my suspicions. The briefs are labelled *George*;

they're from Asda. I've never bought my underwear from Asda.

I feel a wave of panic. I don't know why it should make such big a difference to me when I'm already contemplating that I've probably been drugged and raped. However, the thought of a person unknown removing my undergarments and dressing me in different ones, ones I wouldn't ever normally wear, feels an intrusion too far. I try to think why. Could my thong have been ripped off? Or perhaps it became soiled in some way. Then again, it might have been kept as a trophy. Try as I might, I find no conceivable innocent explanation. My hands are shaking as I carefully remove the briefs and hand them to the technician. I'm completely unclothed. She gives me one of the health board's disposable paper gowns to wear. The room isn't cold – if anything, it's warm and stuffy – but I'm standing there shivering.

Despite the gown, I feel naked. I feel even more vulnerable and exposed as the examination is carried out. Although the nurse is friendly and chatty, I can't absorb anything she's saying. I try to numb my brain as the examination progresses. I imagine I'm detached, someone else, somewhere else, watching what's going on. She starts by taking me to a booth to give a blood sample, one prick in my arm, then she attaches a tube. Afterwards, she guides me back to the main room where I'm asked to lie on an examination table and to twist and turn on request, to enable the study to proceed effectively. The doctor makes a detailed appraisal of my body and every so often she takes photographs. If only I could have been watching this as an observer and not as the victim, I'd find it fascinating; the professionalism and attention to detail.

She's narrating a commentary on what she's doing, together

with her findings, onto a recorder. It's like I've seen on thrillers or documentaries on TV when a medical examiner is carrying out a post-mortem. The two key differences are, one, it's happening to me, not some random corpse and two, I'm still alive. She checks for bruises, abrasions and scratches and for any traces of DNA or fabric traces left by an abductor, or from clothing or furnishings. I hear her record seeing marks on my wrists which may suggest a ligature. There's some bruising to my neck and thighs but apparently nothing significant.

She asks me to lean my head over a table and brushes my hair to collect any particles that fall out onto a piece of sterile paper. Then she apologises about causing any pain before pulling a few hairs complete with follicles from my head and then some pubic hairs. She takes a skin sample from me and then scrapes the underside of each of my fingernails and toenails, as well as taking clippings, looking for skin fragments left by someone I may have held onto or scratched. On frequent occasions, she places items in evidence bags and scribbles notes against them. She takes my fingerprints and I'm asked to provide a sample each of urine and saliva. I hear from her narration that she's looking for evidence of restraints or puncture marks from needles. She takes swabs to detect any evidence or DNA residue in the form of hair, skin, sperm or saliva from an assailant. I'm asked to stand while I'm meticulously sponged over. I have to stifle my screams and my desire to run as there's an all too familiar feeling of unknown hands touching and stroking me everywhere. I pretend it's not real, not me, trying to avoid the feeling of violation as I'm examined inside and out, but it isn't working. Tears are streaming down my face.

It's an ordeal, but once it's complete, I'm told I can shower and change into the fresh clothing Jenny brought me. I doubt there's enough water in Scotland to enable me to feel clean and fresh again. I gladly accept the offer and I immerse myself under the flowing jets, but it helps little. I'm not comfortable knowing where I am and that others are waiting for me on the other side of a door. I want to be home to have a long, leisurely shower. I quickly wash, a superficial cleaning to remove any evidence of this most recent intrusion, then I dress, desperate to get away from this place.

6.5 HOURS

THE MOMENT I STEP BACK THROUGH THE DOOR, INTO THE reception area, both Alesha and Jenny jump to their feet and come over, each taking an arm.

"Are you okay? What could they tell you?" Jenny asks.

"I'm okay, I think," I say. "They didn't tell me anything. I suppose I should have asked, but my brain's a mess so it didn't occur to me."

"Do you want to go back in and check? Or, if you like, I can do it and ask on your behalf," Jenny offers.

"I don't think they'd give out any information to anyone else," Alesha says, "but if you want to go back in, then I can go with you."

"Yes, please," I reply.

"We'll all go," Jenny adds.

I'm quickly able to find the nurse who assisted the doctors' examination. I ask if there's any information she can tell me.

"There's not a lot I can say to you at the moment," she replies. "We've taken blood samples and swabs and we have various other items we've identified for analysis. There's also your clothing, which we'll test. It will take some time until we get the results. A full report will be sent to the police."

"But you also checked me over, so what did you find? I've got no memory and I need to know. It's tearing me apart imagining what someone's done to me without me knowing anything."

"I don't know how much I can help," she replies. "There is no evidence of particularly violent sex. You haven't been brutalised, but that's not to say you couldn't have been raped, particularly as there's nearly a week you can't account for. We hope to know more once we have the test results."

I think about what she's said. I don't feel like I'm any further forward. "Please tell me if you find out anything from your tests," I ask, my voice trembling, imploring.

She purses her lips and nods.

How often must she receive such a request? I wonder.

7 HOURS

IT'S ALREADY GONE FOUR O'CLOCK BY THE TIME WE LEAVE. As Jenny has her car parked outside, she offers to drive me home. She tells me she won't stay, as she can't get out of working this evening, but will drop by when she finishes. Besides Jenny's day job, she often works in the evening, assisting her brother, Philip, who opened a specialist clinic to help people get over phobias, stop smoking, or give up other addictions. Alesha insists she wants to come with me and says she won't leave me alone. Jenny claims she's happy that I'll have someone with me, and she'll check in later. However, there's something in her tone. I detect some animosity between her and Alesha.

Progress is slow, hampered by early rush hour traffic compounded by the late end of the school run. As the car crosses the Kingston Bridge, Alesha's phone rings. She looks at the screen and mouths, "Ice Queen," to me before answering. I hear her side of the conversation, "No, you won't be able to call as the police have kept her phone." She then explains to

Margaret where we are and what's happened so far, then she turns to me. "She'd like to talk to you."

I shrug and reach back for the phone.

"Hello, Margaret. Yes, I'm on my way home."

"I'd like to come over and see you," she says.

"Why?" I ask. This is the same woman who was ready to fire me this morning!

"I think I might be able to help," she says.

"What? Do you know something?" I ask. Both Jenny and Alesha turn to stare at me.

"No, I can't help there, but I'll explain when I see you."

I don't understand, but there's so much I don't seem to understand just now. She's not taking no for an answer, and I'm not up for a fight. "Okay, but please give me some time to get home and showered." I'm desperate to have a long shower.

"I'll come over in an hour or two. I have your address from the personnel files, and I know the area." She leaves no room for argument.

"What's that about?" Jenny asks

Alesha and I both shake our heads.

As usual, parking is impossible so Jenny drops us in Sinclair Drive, a short walk from my flat. Alesha and I climb the stairs and I turn the key to open my front door.

8 HOURS

THIS IS MY FLAT, MY PRIVATE PLACE OF REFUGE. IT'S A traditional Glasgow red sandstone tenement, built in the late Victorian era, well over a hundred years ago. It's been modernised and now comprises a square entrance hall with all apartments off it; a double bedroom, large bay-windowed lounge, dining kitchen and a family-sized bathroom which has a white enamel three-piece suite with an electrically powered over-bath shower. In the short time since moving in, I've upgraded all the decorations and added my personal touch of style.

I don't know why, but something feels odd. I walk from room to room, but I see nothing out of place. However, whether imagined or otherwise, I have a feeling that someone has been here. At my request, Jenny came in to collect my change of clothes, but it's something else... as if someone's been here who shouldn't have been. Maybe I'm being stupid; it's probably paranoia. After what I've been through today, it makes sense to be suspicious about everything, but maybe, just maybe, my fears are justified.

For all I know, while I've been AWOL, anyone could have taken my keys from my handbag and used them. I remember there are other sets, too. The landlord and agent each have a set to be able to access the flat if there's an emergency. Who's to say that a previous tenant didn't retain keys as well? I realise I'm probably being ridiculous. I haven't felt uncomfortable with the flat, or with the agent and landlord holding keys, in the months since I moved in, so why now? It's obvious why now, and my real fear has nothing to do with the landlord or agent. Whoever abducted me had access to my keys and they could have been in the flat. God knows what else they might have done.

Distractedly, I pick up my mail and leaf through it. There's the normal stack of advertising blurb accompanied by what looks like a utility bill and a statement about my Council Tax. I'm about to cast them aside when I spot a hand-delivered envelope with my name in bold script on the front. I rip it open to find a notification from the landlord expressing concern that my rent hasn't been paid, and it's late.

Much as I've loved the flat and I know I've spent a small fortune personalising it to make it mine, I now feel uncomfortable in it and I suspect my discomfort is not just a temporary blip. Albeit, I haven't been able to check what's happened about the rent payment; I reckon it's immaterial. Given my current concerns, if I will not feel safe and comfortable here, I'll have to serve notice to leave. I remember being given one of the new Private Residential Tenancy agreements, which allows me to end the agreement by giving only twenty-eight days notice. I must sort out the problem on the rent first, but I can't see myself wanting to continue with the tenancy.

Alesha says she's happy to sit and wait while I take a shower. I show her into the lounge where there are two large, deep button leather sofas. She sinks into one and picks up some magazines from my coffee table to leaf through. Meanwhile, I go into the bathroom and strip off. I set the temperature to near-scalding, step into the over-bath shower and stand under the flowing water. It's only been an hour since my last shower. Feeling a compulsion to cleanse myself, I spread shower gel all over my body and rinse off, repeating the exercise multiple times.

Afterwards, I stand still, allowing the water to flow over me. I close my eyes tight. I try to think... I want to remember, at least I think I want to remember. An image comes into my head, I don't know why. The picture is of a girl lying naked on a bed and I see three men standing around her. I can see them clearly; I can describe them in detail. In turn, they undress, slowly and deliberately. She seems oblivious to the men and what they do, as first one of them spreads her legs, inserts his erect penis and rapes her, followed by each of the others doing the same. She is unresponsive; her face is blank, distant, impassive.

At first, I wonder if she might actually be dead, but then I see her eyes flicker and I can discern that she's breathing. I feel sick watching this play out in my mind's eye. Why am I visualising this? Am I the girl? Am I recollecting what's happened to me? I try to concentrate on what the girl looks like. There's no question, she is more than a bit like me. Her face is more angular, but she's just about my figure. She's trim and toned, the same shape and a similar hairstyle, straight layered with a side-swept fringe, but while she's blonde, my hair colour is a cherry red, with highlights. She can't be me, surely. I try to concentrate on the images in my head. The scene replays but it's not the same; the girl remains mainly unresponsive. This time there are variations in the action. I watch in horror, seeing her manipulated on the bed with each of the men penetrating her in different ways.

My face is wet, and it's not from the shower. I realise that I'm weeping. It can't be me. Please, please, don't let this be me. It can't be a memory. Please, please, it must be a dream, a fantasy, a nightmare. My legs buckle, and I sink to my knees, then lower, until I'm lying in the bath, adopting a foetal position, my arms clutching my legs. If I can make myself small enough, then maybe I can disappear. Racking sobs overpower me and I'm having difficulty breathing. The shower jets are continuing to douse me.

In the distance, a voice is calling, then I hear a thumping sound and a crash, the sound of wood splintering. I'm aware the water isn't running over me anymore and I prise my eyes open. Alesha is standing over me. She drapes a towel across my shoulders and pulls me towards her, hugging me to her.

"It's okay, it's okay," she says. "You're safe. I'm here to protect you."

Only with her help am I able to step from the shower and pat myself dry and then throw on clothes before exiting the bathroom. Alesha's dress is soaked from holding me, but she doesn't seem to notice. I can see she looks relieved. Her face is tear-stained.

"I could hear you crying," she tells me. "I tried knocking, but you didn't answer. The door was locked, so I had to force it. I'm sorry, I've caused some damage. Are you okay now?"

I tell her about what I saw; the visions, my doubts, my fears.

"I'm sure it will only be your imagination playing tricks on you," she says. She's trying to calm and reassure me; however, she can't maintain eye contact and I know she doesn't believe what she's saying. "You said you could visualise the men clearly. Did you recognise any of them? Have you seen them before?" she continues.

"No, I'm certain, I don't know them. I haven't met any of them."

"In that case, I think you should write down their full descriptions, as accurately as you can, and give it to the police."

I tell Alesha where I keep pens and paper. She finds a pad and takes notes as I recall the descriptions.

All three aged maybe in their thirties. First man is a little above average height, about six one, I guess; stocky, not fat but muscular, shoulders like a bull, looks as if he works out a lot; round head, almost circular and no hair; he has a shaved head. Large nose with a kink halfway down; must have been broken at some point – a boxer or rugby player, maybe. Pale, pale skin; teeth are even but yellow-coloured, could be nicotine.

Second guy is smaller but not by much; he's skinny but not puny, wiry, actually. Sandy-haired and freckled; his face narrow, eyes close together, blue I think or maybe grey. A tight mouth and heavy jaw; a tuft of hair on his chin, not enough to describe as a beard.

Third guy looked older; a lot smaller, not much over five foot, I reckon. Olive skin, Mediterranean features, thinning dark brown hair and stubble on his face. Very dark eyes, almost black. When he smiled, I saw he had two broken teeth at the front.

"That's really good. It will give the police a lot to go on," Alesha says. "I'm thinking back to crime movies I've seen. What is it they ask? Did any of them have distinguishing features?"

Much as I hate to do it, I close my eyes and make myself visualise them again. The effort gives me an acidic taste; I try to ignore it. "Yes, the first guy had a large tattoo on each of his arms; a snake wrapped around a sword."

"Were both his arms the same?"

"Yes, I think so, at least they were very similar. Second guy wore a large signet ring on the middle finger of his right hand, also a bracelet, heavy linked silver. Oh, first guy again, had a diamond stud in one ear." I screw my eyes tighter shut, "the left ear. And guy three chews his nails, they're short and very uneven."

"Okay, I've got all that," Alesha says. "Now I reckon you could murder a nice cup of tea, or would you prefer something stronger?"

"Tea would be good," I answer. For just now, my brain's cloudy enough without taking anything to mix it up more.

"I'll sort it out. You just sit there and relax for a bit."

"I'll let you make it, but I'll come next door with you. I can show you where everything is."

9 HOURS

I PULL BACK A CHAIR FROM THE SOLID PINE DINING SET and sit down. The kitchen has loads of fitted storage units and appliances. I tell Alesha where everything is kept.

While the tea is brewing, she pulls open the fridge and lifts a plastic bottle towards her face. Her nose crinkles, her face taking on a distasteful frown. "Ugh, I'm afraid this milk is off." She holds the bottle at arm's length, inspecting the label. "It's well out of date. I'll pour it down the sink." Looking around her, she adds, "The bread's mouldy, too, or I'd have made toast. Can you take your tea black? I'm okay with it that way."

"I can, but we don't need to." I point to a larder unit. "There should be a carton or two of UHT long-life milk if you're okay with it. I don't feel like food just now, but I have some bread in the freezer if you would like some."

We sit across from each other at the table, with our drinks. Alesha puts her hand on mine in a friendly, comforting gesture.

When I consider, it's difficult for me to accept that I hardly knew her before today. I feel like we've been friends for years. In these last few hours, she's become privy to my situation and been present through my interview, hearing some of my most intimate secrets and witnessing my fears. She's been unbelievably supportive and a good confidante. Today has been one long nightmare, and I don't think I could have coped without her help. For now, I'm happy to sit here in her company, doing nothing.

"When we were waiting for you at the clinic, I got talking to Jenny," she starts. "She told me you've known each other since school."

"Yes, we first met at secondary. It must be..." I pause to think, "fourteen years ago now. We've been very close over the years. It's almost as if we're related. We know each other's families quite well, too. We've holidayed together often, right back to our early teens. Jenny would come with, when Mum and Dad took me on vacation, and I sometimes went with her when her mother and brother went away. It meant we had twice as many holidays."

Alesha smiled. "You were so lucky."

"We were. We did everything together. There was a small group of us who were close friends. Tony, that's Antoinette, and Karoline and Freida made up our little gang, but Jenny and I were especially close." I think back, reminiscing, "We made a great team because Jenny was really smart, and I was the daring one."

"What do you mean, daring?" Alesha asks.

"Oh, nothing significant. It was just that we liked to play practical jokes. We'd work out all sorts of pranks to play on our classmates and teachers. We'd think them up together, but more often than not it was me who carried them out."

"Why was that?"

"As I said, Jenny was smart. She didn't want to get caught."

"So, you were the one who got caught?" Alesha asks, smiling.

"No. Hardly ever, actually. She may have been smart, but I was street smart. I nearly always escaped with no one knowing it was me, and even if they suspected, I could talk my way out of just about anything."

"Sounds like good training for a career in marketing," Alesha jibed.

I'm about to defend myself before realising she's probably right. I laugh at the thought, aware it's the first time I've had something to laugh at all day.

"What sort of things did you do?"

"Nothing special. Various wind-ups, or sending folk on a fool's errand. One time, we had the entire class believing there'd been a news item about Iceland imminently sinking into the sea because of global warming. We embellished the story with add-ons like saying Bjork had been on television pleading for international aid." I chuckle at the memory. "Because Jenny went along with the story, everyone believed it. You see, Jenny was very accomplished academically, always top of the class in science, and she was considered to be a bit of a dork. Because Jenny was agreeing it was true, everyone believed it."

"How did you get away with that one?"

"It was quite easy because there were a lot of stories at the time about rising sea levels because of melting ice flows. It sounded quite credible. We both claimed someone had shown us an internet news feed which featured the story – fake news we'd call it now, I guess. By the end of the day, we had most of the class believing they'd seen the story themselves."

Alesha laughs. "You must have been very popular at school."

I take a moment to think. "I was, I suppose. I was lucky that way. Looking back, I had an easy time of it. I could achieve reasonable pass results without having to do much work. Also, my folks were quite comfortably off, so I always had the latest gadgets and fashionable clothes. Our gang was usually considered the in-group. Jenny wasn't anywhere near as lucky. Her father died when she was very young, and her mother had a bit of a struggle to bring up the two kids on her own. They had to be careful with money.

"Besides, she sometimes doesn't do herself any favours. She's not unattractive. She has a pretty face and, until recently, we were the same size and shape. She'd often borrow clothes from me. We used to share lots of things. I think she's put on a few pounds in the last few months and, as you may have noticed, she doesn't wear cosmetics. Because she was very studious, she was considered a bit of a swot and, resulting from all of that, she suffered a lot of bullying. Being part of our little group helped because we looked after each other, but she had quite a hard time as a teenager."

"Is there a reason why she doesn't wear make-up?" Alesha asks.

"She says it's an allergy thing, but she doesn't like to talk about it. This has been going on for years, back since early high school. I've tried to convince her to investigate whether there are products she'd be more tolerant of, and it would have been easy for her to do now because she's a qualified pharmacist, but she hasn't been interested. Personally, I think she's wanted to make herself different."

"Maybe it's a religious thing or a moral stance, you know, like being against animal testing," Alesha says.

"No, I'm certain it's nothing like that. She'd sometimes immerse herself in her studies, even though she was already miles ahead of the rest of the class. She didn't seem to care that some kids thought she was a nerd."

"That's sad. Was she very unhappy?"

"I don't believe so. What she did was self-imposed and there were lots of times we had great fun. We still do. She's very kind and generous and she's a great friend."

Further discussion is curtailed when we hear the doorbell ring.

I lift the security entry phone, and when I hear Margaret's voice, I buzz her in.

10 HOURS

THE THREE OF US SIT IN THE KITCHEN DRINKING TEA, exchanging small talk. I don't understand why Margaret invited herself here. However, I'm reluctant to ask, as our short conversation in the office this morning wasn't particularly convivial. I don't have to wait long, as her face takes on a more serious look, a moment before she opens the conversation.

"I expect today's been quite an ordeal for you. How are you feeling now?"

I don't know what to answer. I don't really know how I feel. Everything is so surreal. I'm no longer feeling pain or aches, but it's like my body's not my own. Like I described before, an out-of-body experience. I've spent the day answering one question after another, trying to remember and visualising horrific scenarios of what's happened to me. I've been pushed and prodded, had all sorts of samples taken and now I just feel numb. Instead of trying to explain, and risk appearing totally gormless, I merely say, "Okay, I guess."

Margaret stares at me with intensity and it's as if she can see into my very soul. "You don't need to put on a brave face for me," she says.

I remember her words when she phoned. "You said you might be able to help," I say.

"I did," she says. "I want you to know that you're not alone and that there are people around to support you."

"Thanks, I do have some good friends, but if that was all you meant, you could have said so on the phone." I bite my tongue after uttering my thoughts, remembering I'm speaking to my boss.

She doesn't appear to take offence. "There's more," she says. She lowers her eyes, unable to look me in the face. "When I said you weren't alone, I meant in what you've gone through. I don't want any of this discussed other than by the three of us, but I've gone through something similar. Well, I don't know how similar it may have been, but I was sexually assaulted several years ago."

"Really?" I gape and stare back at her, amazed. I'm uncertain if I'm more surprised at this happening to Margaret, or of her confiding in us.

"Don't sound so shocked," she says, a sparkle of humour in her eyes. "I wasn't always this age and away from work, I'm nowhere close to being as austere."

"I'm sorry. I didn't mean..."

Margaret holds up her hand to stop me. "I won't go into details, but suffice to say, I understand what you must be feeling. It's tough, really tough, but it's something you're going to get through and I'm here to help you in every way I can."

"Can I ask if they caught the one who attacked you?" I question.

"No, they didn't. He was never called to account. He got away scot-free and a lot of it's probably my fault because I didn't report him. It's one of my greatest regrets."

I can see Margaret's eyes are welling up.

"It was a very long time ago and things were different then. It was before I met my husband. I didn't have any family I could rely on and I felt alone, with no one to support me. Back in those days, the police and the courts were a lot less understanding of victims. I wasn't confident that I'd have the strength to be dragged through the system, giving evidence and being cross-examined. The awful part is, I know who it was and I'm fairly confident that he's got away with the same thing over and over because no-one stood up to him."

Margaret pauses, then adds, "Let me tell you, I'm proud of you, Briony, because you're strong enough to stand up for yourself."

"Don't be too quick in giving praise. I don't feel very strong just now, and I'm not sure if I'll be able to cope." I can feel my teardrops wetting my cheeks. "It's so difficult to handle because I literally don't know what happened to me. I'm hoping the police will find something. I've given a statement and they're looking into it now."

Margaret nods. "You've already been able to do more than I could," she says. "Would you like to tell me all that you know?"

I give a rundown on my whole day, explaining everything that

I've gone through, what's been said, my visions and my fears and trepidations. I see Margaret close her eyes when I describe my visualisation of the girl being molested.

"What are you planning to do now?" she asks me.

"I haven't been able to plan. I just couldn't. Besides, there has been no time." I try to put my thoughts into words. "If it wasn't that my parents are away until after the weekend, then I'd probably stay with them for a while. I don't feel at all comfortable here in my flat now, but I don't want to be alone."

"I can stay with you if you like," Alesha offers. "I would offer to have you back to my place, but it could be awkward because I still live at home with my mum and dad."

"Jenny's in the same position as she lives with her mum," I say. "I could stay with her, but I wouldn't want to go through explaining anything."

"If you like, I can stay with you here, or at your parent's house. I'll only have to pick up a change of clothes and let my folks know what I'm doing," Alesha offers.

"I've a better alternative," Margaret says. "I want you to come back home with me. I stay in a bungalow in Clarkston, it's not too far away. You too, Alesha. You'll be able to support Briony. I have plenty of room now that my children have grown and moved off to university."

I'm taken aback by the kindness of her offer, so much so that I speak without thinking. "What about your husband? Wouldn't he..."

"Jeffrey? I'm sure he'd be pleased to have the company."

"But I thought ..." I stop, not knowing what to say. I can hardly tell her what I've heard about her husband.

"Too much thinking and too much gossip," Margaret says. She purses her lips. "Do you really believe I don't know about the ridiculous rumours that go around in the office? I've heard at least four variations speculating that I'm married to a brute, or a criminal, or a madman, trying to explain why I'm rarely seen outside of office hours."

I feel my cheeks flush with embarrassment and, from the corner of my eye, I see Alesha is having the same reaction.

Margaret chuckles. "Jeffrey's a sweetheart. I don't think I've ever met a kinder man."

"But if you know there are rumours," Alesha asks, "why don't you set the record straight?"

Margaret shrugs. "For one thing, I don't want to feel pressured into telling people about my private life. I shouldn't have to give anyone explanations. Of course, I've told Jeffrey what's been said about him and he thinks it's funny."

"I don't understand," I say.

"I'll tell you because you're going to find out anyway when you come to my house." Margaret doesn't seem to acknowledge any possibility that I won't accept her offer. "Jeffrey is a former police officer. He was a sergeant in the serious crime unit, and he had twenty years of service. After he was injured in the line of duty, he had an operation which was botched. It left him unable to walk, and he has limited use of one arm. As a result, he needs to spend most of his waking hours in a wheelchair. He was invalided out of the force and now rarely leaves the house."

"Oh, how sad," Alesha says. I want to comment and show empathy, but I feel lost for words. I don't know what to say.

"Now, don't you dare show you feel sorry for him or he'll have your guts for garters. The one thing he can't take is other people's sympathy. It's why no one in the office knows about it. No one except Stuart Ronson, that is. Although much of Jeffrey's body is wasted, his mind is as sharp as it ever was. More so."

"I'm sorry, I didn't mean to..." Alesha starts.

Margaret waves aside the apology. "Jeffrey's brilliant on computers. He received specialist training and learned a lot when he was working on criminal investigations, but since leaving, he's had the time to hone his abilities." There's a smile on her face and her admiration is obvious. "A few years back, he started a freelance research business after a couple of private investigators asked him to do some work. Between his computer skills and the contacts he had through his former work, he was able to achieve some amazing results. He now works directly for companies and private clients as well as PI's and he's so busy, he frequently needs to turn clients away. It isn't his disability that keeps him home, it's the love of what he's able to achieve on the internet."

I'm intrigued. I don't want to be alone and although Alesha has offered to stay with me, I don't relish the prospect of staying in my flat. My parents' home would be preferable, but it isn't ideal. Particularly as I haven't worked out yet how I'm going to explain to them what's been going on and why I didn't tell them sooner. I'm sure Jenny will offer some help, but I don't know when she'll be here, or what she'll be able to do. The prospect of Alesha staying with me at Margaret's home has some definite appeal.

"Briony, why don't you put together a bag of things you'll need, so I can take you back to mine and introduce you to Jeffrey before it gets much later? I can stop off at your house, Alesha, if you want to pick anything up."

"Okay by me," Alesha says. "I'll give my mum a ring now, so she knows what's going on."

Margaret looks at me and, seeing no dissent, nods. "Good, that's decided."

The decision has been taken away from me and I'm relieved and nervous at the same time. "I'd better call Jenny and let her know what I'm doing. I'll have to call Paula as well. She said to let the police know where I would be, in case anyone needs to contact me."

I call Paula's number first, but she isn't available. Margaret provides me with her address and phone numbers, which I give to the officer who answered. He tells me he will record it on my file.

I call Jenny's number and she answers on the third ring. "Good news. I've arranged to have tomorrow off so I can spend it with you and I'm not on duty or on call at all this weekend. I'll be able to be with you, if you want. I can drive you anywhere you need to go. I'm just finishing up here for tonight, so I'll be round soon. I can be there in half an hour."

I explain to Jenny about my change of plan. Following a pause, she asks, "Are you sure you want to do that? You hardly know these people. Why would you want to spend tonight with them? Are you not already in a fragile enough state?"

I feel uncertain. Can Jenny be right? Am I putting even more pressure on myself?

Margaret calls across, "Would Jenny like to come and stay as well? Invite her. We've got plenty of room."

Jenny overhears the offer. "No, thank you," she replies. "I want you to know that I'm here for you, Briony, but I don't want to spend tonight in a strange house with people I don't know."

"You've met them before. You've come along to a couple of my office nights out. You must have seen Alesha there and I think I must have introduced you to Margaret, the time you picked me up after work."

"I might have heard you mention their names before. I can't be certain, but they're not people you know well. I do remember meeting some of your colleagues, but I don't recollect ever meeting Alesha. As for Margaret, isn't she the one you complained to me about, the first-class bitch? No, I don't think it's a good idea to stay with them tonight."

I feel confused; it's a dilemma. Jenny's correct, I hardly knew Alesha before today and my opinion of Margaret was anything but favourable. A few moments ago, I decided I'd be going, but now I don't feel so certain. I again try to consider the alternatives and it helps me choose. "I've made up my mind, Jenny. I'm going to spend tonight at Margaret's. I haven't even thought about tomorrow yet. You could come over, even if you don't stay."

I want my friends around me. Maybe I should say more, but I don't.

"If that's your decision, then it's up to you. You must do whatever you think suits you best. Call me in the morning and I'll come over." Jenny's words sound placatory and supportive, but I can hear an edge in her voice. She doesn't sound happy.

"Okay," I say. "I don't have my mobile, but I can remember your number."

After I hang up the phone, I realise my talk with Jenny has left me feeling even more drained. I'm uncertain and vulnerable. When I stand, my legs are unsteady. I make no attempt to move.

"Would you like some help to sort a bag?" Alesha offers.

"I think I can manage," I reply, but my voice must have been unconvincing, because Alesha follows me into the bedroom and helps when I go to lift an overnight case from atop my wardrobe and fill it with nightwear, a change of clothes and some toiletries.

11 HOURS

Margaret has parked her Volvo near to my flat. I place my bag in the boot and we get in to take the short drive to Simshill, where Alesha lives. Margaret and I wait in the car while Alesha dashes in to collect her necessaries for an overnight stay, together with a change of workwear for tomorrow.

Only a few minutes later, we drive through Clarkston Toll, exiting onto the Mearns Road. Half a mile further, we turn left, drive a little further, then pull into a driveway. The car's tyres crunch over the red whin chip surface, announcing our arrival.

We ascend a shallow ramp which covers the three steps to the entrance, then go through a broad uPVC glazed front door to enter a square hallway with several doors off. Margaret points, in turn, to each of the rooms on the ground level. To our immediate right is a lounge; behind this a dining room and then a study, which Jeffrey uses as his office. To our left, the first room is Margaret and Jeffrey's bedroom, followed by a family bathroom, an open stairway leading to the upper floor and a small sitting room. Immediately facing us, there's a door into a large dining kitchen, which has been significantly extended from the original property, Margaret explains. She tells us that when their children were young, they developed the house, building the rear extension as well as dormer and Velux windows in what had been the attic, to create three bedrooms and a shower-room upstairs.

She invites us to take our bags up, but before we move, we hear the noise of an electronic motor and watch as a wheelchair exits from Jeffrey's office. Approaching us with a welcoming smile and an outstretched arm, Jeffrey is very dapper, dressed in fashionable chinos and an open-neck shirt. His demeanour is cheerful. He has a jovial, round face, spectacles with heavy black rims and is clean-shaven, with a bald pate surrounded by a thin network of brown strands of hair.

He pumps our hands enthusiastically, introducing himself and saying he's pleased to have us stay.

Jeffrey asks if we're hungry, suggesting we get ourselves settled first, then meet in the kitchen for coffee and sandwiches.

Realising I haven't eaten, I gladly accept the invitation.

"Yes, please," Alesha adds.

Margaret shows us upstairs. There's one large room with twin beds and the two other bedrooms are each singles.

"Would you feel better if I slept in the same room as you?" Alesha asks.

Besides romantic entanglements, and holidays with Jenny, I haven't ever shared a bedroom with anyone. But right now, I'm fearful of spending the night alone. "Yes, please," I say.

We each deposit our bags in the larger room, then return to the kitchen.

Even before entering, we can smell the rich, enticing aroma of freshly percolated coffee. We walk into the kitchen to find a serving plate, mounded high with an assortment of rolls and sandwiches, sitting next to a large bowl of potato crisps.

"Come in, help yourselves," Jeffrey invites, smiling when he sees our reaction.

I've picked up a sandwich even before sitting down. I don't want to appear rude, but my mouth is watering, and the food looks very appetising. Desperate for sustenance, I devour a further two sandwiches, hardly recognising a flavour. Then I slow down, belatedly remembering my manners, eating slower and more delicately, relishing the taste.

"Do you feel any stronger now?" Jeffrey asks.

"Yes, much," I reply. "I hadn't realised how hungry I'd become – not until I started eating. It's just what I needed."

We sit around, drinking coffee and making small talk. It seems natural and uncomplicated. Following a lull in the conversation, I'm brought back down to earth when Margaret asks me if I'd like to tell Jeffrey about my police report. Seeing my shocked expression, she apologises. "I'm sorry, I shouldn't have said anything. I thought maybe he'd be able to assist. You're under no pressure to talk about anything. It was only because I thought he may be able to help you find some answers."

"No, it's all right. You caught me unawares. I don't want to appear ungrateful, but..."

"You don't have to explain," Jeffrey says. "We invited you here so you'd feel safe. There's nothing you have to do or say. If and when you want to talk, then I'll be happy to listen and again, only if you want, then I'll try to help."

"I would like you to help me, if you're prepared to take it on. But I feel really drained. I don't feel up to going over everything again just now." I hesitate before continuing, "Another thing is, I don't know if I can afford to pay you. How much is it you charge?"

"Pay me? What are you talking about, lass? If there's anything I can do to help you, then I'm happy to do it. There isn't any charge," Jeffrey says.

"But earlier this evening, Margaret told us you had a business carrying out research, and that you were so busy, you were turning clients away," I say.

"Yes, that's all perfectly true, but it's work I do for commercial clients. Friends are different. If I can help a friend of Margaret's, then it's not business, it's because I want to. I wouldn't dream of making a charge."

I'm about to speak, to ask why he thinks Margaret and I are friends, but I stop myself. I look at Margaret and she nods her agreement. She is smiling. Margaret considers me a friend. I'm overwhelmed by emotion. I want to express my gratitude, but my tears are flowing and my voice catches in my throat, stopping me before I blurt out a simple, "thank you".

Both Margaret and Alesha come over to me and we embrace in a group hug.

12 HOURS

I WANT TO ASK MARGARET ABOUT THIS MORNING WHEN I arrived at work. She was very aggressive, her attitude so different to how she's been since. Although I don't want to risk imperilling the closeness we now seem to have, I need to know.

"You were very angry with me this morning," I start, speaking with caution.

"Yes, I was, and you want to know why, don't you?" she says.

"I do," I answer, trepidation showing in my voice.

"I suppose you deserve an explanation. I believe you have real talent. It was me who recruited you." She can see I look puzzled. "Yes, Stuart was the one who carried out the interview and the formalities, but it was me who picked you out. There were other candidates who had more experience, but I convinced him to go with you. What's more, you didn't let me down. Your performance, your commitment and your skill have all been first class."

"But I thought you didn't like me! At no time did you ever give me credit for my work. Nothing I ever did seemed good enough."

"That's my management style. I want to get the best out of all my staff. From experience, I've found if I push for bigger and better results, I usually get them. I've tried the soft approach in the past and found it doesn't work in our line of business. Praise often makes people soft and complacent, particularly when the praise is for something barely adequate and not special."

"So, you weren't unhappy with my work?"

"Anything but. In your first four months, you've shown more promise than any other junior executive we've ever recruited. At least, that was the case until last week."

"You thought I'd let you down?" I ask.

"When you didn't turn up for work on Monday, we were concerned. More so when we didn't hear from you. We thought you might be ill. We tried calling both your landline and mobile but there was no reply and no response to voicemails, texts or emails. Your parents were listed as your next-of-kin and we got no answer there, either. We were on the verge of having you listed as a missing person when we received an email on Monday afternoon."

"An email? I don't remember sending you an email. What did it say?" I ask.

"All it said was, *Won't make it in today.* There was no explanation and no apology." Margaret continues. "We didn't know what to make of it because it seemed so out of character for you, but we reckoned there must have been a good reason and you'd be back on Tuesday to explain.

"You'd been working with Dwight and Chrissie, preparing the presentation for Archchem. Although Dwight is the team leader and therefore the senior and meant to be managing the project, we knew it had been predominantly your ideas coming forward. When you didn't come in on Tuesday, Dwight met the client and I'm sorry to say, he didn't have a clue. I'm not convinced he understood the concept, and he botched it. For us to win preferred supplier status with Archchem would have been a major step forward. Instead, we're left scrambling around, trying to salvage what little scraps of work we can get from them."

"I'm so sorry."

"Of course, you must already know, Dwight is the nephew of Carlton Archer, the founder of the company and still the group's president. We know Dwight is fairly useless, but he was foisted on us, supposedly to gain international experience. Dwight blamed you. He claimed he didn't have all the material because he didn't know where you'd filed it. Stuart was livid, and you weren't around to defend yourself."

"But it should all have been there," I say.

Margaret nods. "Then you didn't come in on Wednesday and returned this morning looking as if you'd been on a bender."

"I can see why you'd be angry," I say.

"I was! I was furious and I felt you'd let me down, personally. It was only when Alesha came to see me that I realised you weren't to blame. I don't believe it was you who sent the email."

"I'm sure I didn't," I say.

"If someone had access to your phone..." Margaret starts to suggest.

I think about this. "My phone had been dismantled when I found it this morning. I don't know when it happened."

"The most likely explanation I can think is that whoever had the phone, wanted to avoid it being traced," Jeffrey suggests. "They may have taken it apart, then either used the Sim in another device, or temporarily put it back together to be able to send the message. I'm sure the police will check all the phone's parts for prints and to see if, and when, they've been used. However, we need to make sure that whoever's investigating knows about the email."

"I'll call them in the morning," I say.

"Something else is bothering me, too," Jeffrey says.

"What?" I ask and my question is echoed by both Margaret and Alesha.

"This may make you uncomfortable," he says. "Do you want me to go on? This could keep for another time."

"I doubt if anything could make me feel much more uncomfortable than I already am," I say.

"Fair comment," he says. "I ask myself why someone would feel the need to send that email. The obvious answer is, they didn't want anyone to think you were missing. More to the point, they didn't want anyone looking for you."

I nod, not quite understanding where this is going.

"A random abductor isn't too likely to be concerned if you were reported as missing. It's not absolute, but I believe this considerably increases the probability of the abductor being someone you know, or who has some connection to you."

Much as I thought I wouldn't feel any more uncomfortable, I now have a terrible heaviness in my chest. Up until now, I've been trying not to think too much about being abducted and what treatment I may have been subjected to for the last week. However, Jeffrey's conjecturing, I may already be acquainted with the abductor forces me to confront the question. Who do I know who might have done this to me, and why?

17 HOURS

ALTHOUGH THE SUBJECT IS QUICKLY CHANGED AND WE SIT around the table talking about anything and everything for hours, I don't feel any more at ease. I'm exhausted and have been for hours, but I prefer to be sitting in the company of friends rather than trying to sleep. After the visions I had earlier in the day, I'm fearful of what nightmares await.

Jeffrey, Margaret and Alesha have been wonderful. Although I can see they, too, are tired, they've made no suggestion of going to bed. Their eyes are heavy and there are intermittent rounds of yawning. It's now passed 1 a.m. and I know I'm fatigued; I can hardly remain seated upright. I've been leaning on the table when my elbow suddenly slips and I almost fall.

Margaret looks at me. "You've had a very difficult day and I can see you're exhausted. I think you need to try to get some sleep."

"Yes, you're right," I accept. I suspect tomorrow won't be a walk in the park, either.

"I've already made up the beds, but I'll show you where we

keep spare bedding if you need it. You've already seen where we keep everything in the kitchen, so help yourself to beverages or food if you feel like anything if you wake early, or through the night. You too, Alesha," Margaret says. Then, looking at Alesha she adds, "I'm up about 7 o'clock and I leave for the office at eight. If you can be ready for then, I'll drive you in."

"Thanks. I'll set the alarm on my phone," Alesha replies.

While we're walking up the stairs, Margaret turns to me and says, "There isn't anything you need to get up for. You should try to get as much sleep as you can as it will help you regain your strength. You've seen where Jeffrey and I sleep. If you need anything through the night, anything at all, just call us. Although I'll be gone at eight, Jeffrey will be here if you need anything."

Both Alesha and I thank her for her kindness and hospitality before exchanging goodnight wishes as she leaves.

We each take a turn using the upstairs shower-room to wash and ready ourselves for bed. I climb under a sheet and pull the duvet tight around me.

"Do you want to talk some more or are you ready to sleep?" Alesha asks. I hear the exhaustion in her voice and know the offer is well meant. I want to sleep, although I don't know whether I'll be able to. Alesha needs to be awake and ready for work in a few short hours. She's done more than enough already. "Let's try to sleep," I reply.

Within just seconds I can hear her breathing has become steady and deep and I reckon she's already out for the count. I try to relax, to banish fears and dreads and images. I close my eyes. It works for a few seconds at a time before some thought enters my mind and my eyes spring open, looking around to confirm where I am and that I'm safe. I try counting sheep, remembering happy thoughts, calm and gentle scenes, but it helps little.

I toss and turn in bed. Although I want to stay silent so I don't wake Alesha, I can't lie still. One minute I feel too hot and peel back the duvet, then the next I'm cold and pull it back. I try one arm or leg out, then the other, then both out or in, each variation providing moments of comfort before I need to move again. I'm relieved Alesha seems to be in a deep slumber, oblivious to my nocturnal gymnastics.

Occasionally, I think I must have drifted off, but not for long before the whole pantomime starts over again. Periodically, I glance at the clock alarm sitting on a wall shelf. It's as if I'm in a different dimension, as I feel as if hours have passed with only a few minutes movement showing on the clock. I note passing the benchmarks of 1.30, 1.45, 2.00, 2.15, 2.30, 2.45, 3.00 and 3.15... then darkness and silence.

I've been dreaming. There were fields of corn and warm sunshine on my skin, a farmhouse, a fence, but they're all fading, becoming more distant. I open my eyes. It's dark. It doesn't feel familiar. I'm apprehensive; where am I? I'm lying in a bed, an unfamiliar bed. It's a single bed. Strange, I haven't slept in a single bed since I was a young child. My fingers run over the surface. There's a sheet under me. It's cotton, crisp, fresh and smooth. Above me is similar, another sheet but heavier. No, it's not it's the same but something is on top, a cover, no, a duvet. My hand reaches across beyond the edge of the mattress. There's a bed frame, smooth timber, I think, maybe pine. I inhale and can smell the fabric. It has been recently laundered as I can smell detergent, and something else. It's fabric conditioner, it smells of roses. I don't use fabric conditioners because some of them make me sneeze. I crinkle my nose, waiting for the inevitable. It doesn't happen. I don't sneeze. This must be one brand I'm okay with.

Where am I? My night vision is kicking in, my eyes are starting to focus. I look around me. It's a square room, there's a bedside table next to me and another bed beyond. I was right; it is pine-framed with sheets and a duvet, but it's not even. There's a shape, an outline, a body. I look closer. I see movement, rising, falling, breathing. I listen carefully. It is breathing, quiet, even breaths with an occasional nasal rasp. Someone is sleeping. Who is it? Where am I? My eyes scan the room. I see a clock. It's showing 5.32.

Without warning, it comes back to me. It's Alesha sleeping. We've spent the night at Margaret's house because I didn't feel comfortable or safe at home. First, Alesha offered to stay with me so I wouldn't be alone and then Margaret invited me, no, invited us, to stay at her house. Oh hell! The nightmare! I remember yesterday. I remember the realisation I've lost the time between Friday evening and yesterday morning, five and a half days. I remember going to the police station with Alesha, giving my statement, going to the clinic and being examined. It was all so horrible. I remember all that, but I've still no idea where I've been or what's happened to me in the last week. I feel a wave of panic, nausea, a bitter, acidic taste in my throat. I think I might faint. At least there's nowhere to fall, as I'm lying down.

I lie still, suppressing the urge to scream. My breathing is ragged. I must calm down. Deep breaths are needed; inhale, exhale, inhale, exhale. That's better. Again, again. Slowly, my reason returns. I need to be strong, I need to be logical if I'm going to get through this. I need to count my blessings, too. I'm fit and well, I think. I have friends and support. There's Jenny and Alesha, there's Margaret and Jeffrey. Mum and Dad will be home in a couple of days and the police, too, will help me find the answers I need.

While far from convinced, I've reassured myself enough to face another day. I'm tired, very tired, but I don't want to sleep anymore. I don't want to risk waking again the way I did. I'll lie in bed and rest for a while. I need to think, to try to trigger some memory of where I've been.

Today is Friday. Last Friday was the last day I can remember with any clarity. I cast my mind back. I arrived at work early, as usual. No, to be more accurate, I was even earlier, because I needed to prepare for a 10.30 meeting. It was with, what's his name? The M.D. of Carson's – Fielding, that's it. It was a short meeting, but important. I had to find out more about his requirements. I was clear of the meeting by 11.15. For the rest of the day, I was working on the Archchem presentation. Dwight, Chrissie and I worked together all day. I didn't go out for lunch. I knew I would be meeting Jenny for dinner, so I didn't want to eat much. I sent out for a tuna wrap and an apple to keep me going. I washed it down with orange juice. I don't think I finished the wrap, either; I only ate half.

The three of us worked solidly, completing research, preparing the Power-point slides and the handouts and rehearsing who'd do what. Chrissie left at about four-thirty because she had to collect her daughter from her childminder. It wasn't important, because she only had a small role to play on this project. Dwight and I worked on. I had planned to work late so I could go straight out to meet Jenny. When was it I left? Alesha checked. It was about 7.30.

What happened next is all a great haze. My next solid memory is walking through Central Station yesterday morning. I must try to remember. I concentrate. The same visions I had yesterday come back. I don't want to watch, but I feel I must. I need to find some clue. I need to know if I'm the girl. I see her lying on the bed, the men around her. I try to focus on her. Her body is naked. There are no obvious marks or scars to distinguish her. She does look very like me. The face seems a little bit more slender, longer, and I think it's harder looking, but the picture isn't clear. It could be me. Her hair's a different colour. Perhaps she's wearing a wig. A different colour could alter the perception of shape as well. I know this from my art studies. I can't be certain.

I try to focus on each of the men. The description is no different to the one I gave Alesha. There must be more. I think about the room. It's a large bedroom. The girl is lying on a bed and it's big, larger than a standard double; it could be king-sized. There's no bed frame. Instead, it's a divan with a shell-shaped headboard. The surface is plain-coloured, an off-white, it might be a mattress protector; there are no other bed coverings. There's ample space around the bed for the men to stand without the room looking cramped. No other furniture is in sight. There's more space beyond the bed, before a wall. It's painted a pastel shade, nothing definite, a blue colour I think, nothing remarkable, no pictures. There's no window, at least not on any wall I can see. Nevertheless, the room is bright. I don't feel any further forward. Am I putting myself through this for nothing?

What about sound? I wonder. Their voices, or any background noises which might help locate this place. I concentrate but I hear nothing. I see lips moving. It's as if the men are talking to each other and giving instructions to the girl, saying what they want her to do. It's like mime; I hear no sound whatsoever. No speech, no background noise;, instead there's complete silence. I don't understand why. Is there anything else of note? I don't think so, but wait, there's a smell, an unpleasant smell of stale filter coffee. It's nothing like the delicious aroma of freshly percolated beans which enticed me to Margaret's kitchen last night. It's more like the stale smell after a jug's been left sitting on a hotplate, then allowed to stew for too long, until it turns to tar.

What else can I remember? My mind wanders. The same memory I had yesterday returns. Whether it's real or imagined, it's a sensation of hands touching me. I visualise it; me lying flat and hands touching me, big hands, little hands, disembodied hands. I see no people, only hands. The memory is not only visual. I sense the hands touching my body, large hands with coarse skin, small, smooth hands, stroking, touching me everywhere, lifting me, turning me, touching my face, my body, my limbs and more, everywhere. I want it to stop. I want to be left alone.

I squirm and turn my face into the pillow. I squeeze my eyes tight shut and will the image and the feeling to stop.

I take deep breaths to clear my head. What else? There must be something else?

A series of images flash in front of me. I don't know where they're from. I don't know if they're real or fantasy, if they're relevant or a product of my imagination. The images are like a series of snapshots taken in a room. It's not familiar, I don't know where it is. There's a bookcase filled with DVDs and paperbacks. I try to focus but none of the titles are discernible. Another picture has a table with chairs set around it. It's a rectangular dining table. There's a table-cover and I see a box on top. It's the size of a shoebox and there are small bottles in the box. In another image I see a window frame, but there are no windows visible because the curtains are drawn, heavy velvet drapes. It must be daytime because there's a chink where the curtains meet, allowing in a stream of bright sunlight; it's visible coming through the gap. Other images show a wall-mounted television, a computer workstation. There is nothing remarkable, nothing to identify the location. Accompanying the images, I again sense the same rancid smell of stale coffee.

I'd hoped my memory might return and I'd know what had happened to me during the missing days. Much as I'm apprehensive of learning exactly how I may have been abused, the not knowing is tearing me apart. I'm disappointed because there's very little, if anything, to go on. That said, I also feel a slight relief thinking I seem to be having more memories coming back to me. Paula suggested this could happen and I so much hope she could be right.

22 HOURS

Checking the clock again, I see it's now 6.10. My throat is dry; I feel thirsty. I decide to get up. There's only half-light as I quietly sneak out of bed. I don't want to disturb Alesha, but I can tell she's still sound asleep. I pull a gown over my nightdress and slide my feet into my slippers before cautiously manoeuvring out of the room. A light is already switched on in the hall and I make my way down the stairs. Despite my best efforts to be silent, I find out the hard way that there's a creaky floorboard halfway down the stairs. I jump in shock as I hear the unexpected noise and this only adds to the problem. I silently mouth a profanity. Re-gathering my composure, I make my way to the kitchen.

I'm surprised to see that the kitchen is also illuminated. When I enter, I can see Jeffrey sitting at the head of the table, a steaming mug of coffee in his hand. Hearing me enter, he looks up and smiles. Without speaking, he points to his cup and raises an eyebrow, questioning.

I give an enthusiastic nod. "I was thirsty. I only came down for a glass of water," I whisper.

"You don't need to worry about staying quiet," Jeffrey answers. "It would take an earthquake to wake Margaret once she's out." He winks conspiratorially. "Toast?" he asks.

"No, thank you, coffee will be fine."

He pours a mug and places it in front of me. "Milk or sugar?"

"No, thank you. It's perfect as it is." I cradle the mug in both hands, place my nose over its edge and inhale deeply, luxuriating in the aroma before tasting some of the delicious hot liquid. "Yes, perfect," I repeat.

"Were you able to sleep?" Jeffrey enquires.

"The bed was very comfortable," I answer, circumventing the question.

Jeffrey nods, a knowing look showing on his face.

"I did get some sleep, but not much. I'm quite well rested, though," I say. "What are you doing up at this time?"

"I never need much sleep," he replies. "I woke more than half an hour ago. I lay for a few minutes knowing I wouldn't be able to sleep any longer, so I planned some work I need to do instead. Once I'd done that, I thought a hot drink would go down well, so I switched on the machine and prepared a couple of slices of toast." He points to the crumbs on his otherwise empty plate.

"And then I came down and spoiled your nice, relaxed breakfast. Sorry."

"Don't apologise," he says. "It's not as if I mean to be antisocial.

I don't mind a bit of company. No doubt I spend too much time on my own."

I try to think how to make light conversation. This normally comes naturally to me but today, it seems, I need to make an effort. "Have you a lot of work on today?"

"I have a few contracts on the go but there's nothing very urgent. One company, an existing client, is planning to set up a new manufacturing division, and they asked me to research new overseas suppliers for them. I have another client who's involved in banking. The chief exec. wants me to investigate some dubious transactions where repossessed assets have been sold off under value. It's possible there's a serious fraud going on, but he wants to handle it in-house without calling in the authorities at this stage. There isn't a rush on any of it because I'm already well ahead of schedule."

"It sounds very interesting," I say, noting the enthusiasm in his voice.

"Some of it is. It can be quite similar in concept to what I did in the police. There's a lot of straight grunt work, labouring through mountains of information and trying to categorise and make sense of it. One advantage over police work is I don't have to spend most of my time on paperwork to cover my back. True, I need to produce reports for clients, but it's not the same. The work can be fascinating at times, particularly when you discover something important, or get the feeling that your efforts are making a real difference."

"I know what you mean," I reply. "I accept the things I do are different. My work doesn't change people's lives the way yours does, but I really get a buzz when something I think of, or do, is taken seriously and becomes a key element of a project."

"I understand. Margaret's worked in marketing for decades. I know how much she enjoys it and, from what I've seen, I don't think you should underestimate the effect it has on people's lives and their habits. She's proven to me how important it can be. You don't need to sell me on the idea." Realising his unintentional pun, Jeffrey sniggers and I join in.

"What's going on here? I invite you into my home and then find you flirting with my husband in the middle of the night." Margaret enters the kitchen. I look at her stony-faced expression. There's a silent pause before she can't keep up the act and breaks into laughter. "Good morning, Briony," she says, coming over to me and giving my shoulder an affectionate squeeze. Without asking, Jeffrey pours coffee into a fresh mug and places it on the table in front of her.

Margaret doesn't sit. She stands, sipping her drink. "How are you feeling?" she asks.

Physically, I feel okay, but I can't get to grips with my situation. It's all so surreal. "I want everything to be normal again," I say.

"It will be," she reassures. "Have you had any more memories?"

"Very little, nothing meaningful,"

"It will take time, be patient."

I look down at the table, unable to meet her gaze. "What do I do in the meantime?"

"There's no easy answer," Margaret replies. "You'll need to speak to the police again today. Your test results may take a while to come through, but you should ask them when to expect to hear anything. Also, see if they can tell you when they'll have your phone back."

"That's good advice," Jeffrey says. "I don't doubt that they handle every case to the best of their abilities, but you have to consider that, with all the cutbacks, police resources are scarce, more so than ever before. They have to prioritise and they're more likely to apply resources to your case if they know you're chasing them for answers."

"Thank you. I'll keep that in mind. I remember Paula saying she'd be on duty from 8.00 a.m. I'll call then."

"Unless I'm mistaken, she's the liaison officer," Jeffrey says. "The investigation team is a different group and they ought to be assigned today, if they haven't already been. Currently, Paula is your main point of contact and you can continue to talk to her even once you're introduced to the team."

Although I want to get my memory fully back, I feel I need something else to think about. I know I can't spend all my time dwelling on my fears. I'd go crazy. Maybe I'd be better working, I think. Maybe a project to work on would distract me enough to get through this time. "When can I come back to the office?" I ask Margaret.

She looks surprised. "I thought you'd need some time to get over this, to get your head together."

"I need to be doing something," I say. "I can't claim I'd be very effective, but I need to be doing something which occupies my mind."

Margaret nods. "I understand. I believe it's too soon right now. Besides, you have things you need to do today. Let's see how you are over the weekend and we can think about whether you're okay to come back next week. You don't need to rush into anything."

Margaret looks at her watch. "I'd best get myself ready," she says, before darting out of the kitchen.

"I know you want this all to be over, but these things take time. I know from experience. I'm sorry, but nothing will happen as quickly as you would like," Jeffrey advises, "you just need to accept it."

I know he's right. However, it doesn't make it any easier for me.

23 HOURS

WE SIT TALKING AND I'M UNAWARE OF TIME PASSING. I
hear some noise of movement from upstairs. Ten minutes pass
before Alesha comes in. We exchange greetings. How does she
do it? In the short space of time she's taken to ready herself, she
looks like she's walked off a movie set, dressed to perfection and
professionally made-up. I'm instantly impressed and simultane-
ously envious.

I glance down and recollect I came straight from bed to get a
drink of water. Only now, I realise I've neither washed nor
dressed. All I'm wearing is a nightdress and a dressing gown. I
must look a mess. I've never done this before. Well, maybe my
parents or Jenny have seen me at breakfast not properly showered and dressed, but no-one else, not even Michael. Especially
not Michael. It occurs to me how mixed-up and confused I
must be. Thinking about it, another interpretation could be that
I am so comfortable in Jeffrey and Margaret's company as to be
ambivalent about my clothes and looks. Without realising it,
have I temporarily adopted them as surrogate parents? There

can be no question about how kind and understanding they've been, but it doesn't justify me being so presumptuous.

"I must get washed and changed," I say, rushing back upstairs.

I collect my cosmetics and look out some fresh clothes from my bag. Why didn't I hang them up last night? Now it will take ages for the creases to even out. I go through to the bathroom. The mirror is cloudy with steam because of Alesha's recent shower. When I wipe the condensation away, I'm shocked by my image. I appear ten years older than I should. This isn't me, is it? I look cadaverous. My cheeks are sunken and my skin is like parchment, grey-coloured except for heavy dark rings around my eyes. I'm certain there are wrinkles there I've never seen before. I run my fingers through my hair. It's lank and life-less. How could I have sat downstairs with Jeffrey and Margaret looking like this and not known? They didn't react, but what must they think of me? They are such good people.

A recollection of what Jenny said yesterday comes back to me and I feel a slight discomfort. They are good people, aren't they? How can I be certain, when I've so recently come to realise what a poor judge of character I am? I'd previously considered Margaret to be a demon and Alesha to be not worth talking to and look how they've turned out and supported me? I placed so much trust in Michael and he let me down. Worse, he betrayed me in the worst possible way.

The only thing I can be certain of is that I can't rely on my judgement. At least I haven't lost my sense of irony, I think.

Margaret and Jeffrey seem wonderful people. They've done nothing to cast any doubt, but nevertheless, I must proceed with caution, I tell myself.

Looking around me, I see a bottle of Radox shower gel and I

decide to test whether its claim to reinvigorate stands the test. I hang up my dressing gown and let my nightdress fall to my feet. Then I step into the shower cubicle. I stand, allowing the water to cascade over me, taking my time, hoping the flowing water will wash away my tarnished image.

I'm reluctant to leave but know I must. I turn the dial towards cold with the jets on full. It has the dual benefit of shocking me into alertness and giving me sufficient inducement to leave the shower.

I feel chilled and I'm dripping wet. I reach out of the cubicle and lift a towel from the heated rail, enveloping myself in its comfort. I lift a second one and towel-dry my hair before twisting it into a turban.

I clear the mirror and re-examine myself. Not great, but a considerable improvement, I think. I clean my teeth, throw on some clothes, then carefully apply cosmetics. Paying particular attention to my eyes, I mascara my lashes and use shadow to lighten the rings. A touch of rouge and I look almost human again. I spot a hairdryer attached to the wall, so I find my hairbrush, disentangle the turban and restyle my hair to its normal shape.

Another glance in the mirror; that'll do. That'll *have* to do, I correct myself.

24 HOURS

I RETURN TO THE KITCHEN. JEFFREY LOOKS UP FROM HIS newspaper, pen in hand. I see the almost complete crossword on the table.

"Can I help?" I ask.

"No offence intended, but this is one challenge I have to do myself. It's a ritual for me."

"Well, you know where I am if you get stuck," I jibe.

"Don't hold your breath." Jeffrey's sporting a broad grin. "Margaret and Alesha left a while back. They asked me to say goodbye. Margaret said to call her if there's anything you need that I can't help with. Now, how about some breakfast?"

"I don't think I'm hungry," I reply.

"Regardless, you need to keep your strength up. We've got a very nice muesli. Go on, give it a try."

I relent and I have to admit it is good and I feel stronger for it. "I'd better give the police a call. Is there a phone I can use?"

Jeffrey hands me a cordless handset and shows me into the lounge. "Sit in here so you can talk in private. I'll either be in the kitchen or in my office if you want me."

It's probably only a couple of minutes, but it feels like a long time as I sit staring at Paula's card, the phone in my other hand, preparing to make the call, thinking what I want to say.

There's no point putting it off any longer. I dial and Paula answers.

"I'm glad you called. I was about to give you a ring," she says.

I'm instantly alert, on edge. "What is it? Have you found something? What can you tell me?"

"Calm down, Briony. I've nothing to tell you, yet. We're only at the very start. I wanted to talk to you to give you an update on the procedures. The investigation team have been assigned. Sergeant Zoe McManus will lead it. She's read through my crime report and she needs to meet you as soon as possible."

"Do you want me to come back in?" I ask.

"No, something else. Because of the amount of time you've been missing, she wants to have your flat checked over. She'd like to meet you there. Would 11.00 a.m. this morning be okay? She'll have a forensic team with her as well."

I look at my watch. It isn't half-past eight yet so there's plenty of time. "Yes, no problem."

"Now, you were calling me. Was there something you wanted to tell me?" she asks.

"Yes," I say. I tell her about my visions and give her the descriptions of the three men.

"I've got that. I'll make sure it's on your file and that Zoe knows. Was there anything else?"

I tell her about the email Margaret received and Jeffrey's suspicions.

"Very interesting," she says, "but let's not jump to any conclusions."

"Can you tell me when I'll get my phone back?" I ask.

"I can't say for certain. Maybe later today, or tomorrow. It's with the telematics technicians right now. Hopefully, they might be able to clone what's on it so you can have it sooner rather than later. Check with Zoe when you see her."

I ring off and take a deep breath. Despite my determination and best efforts, tears are rolling over my cheeks. I swipe them away with my fist, thinking I'd better touch up my make-up before seeing anyone.

I know I can get a bus or cab from here, but Jenny said she had the day off and offered to drive me. It's not too early to call. I dial her number.

"Hello, who's that?" Jenny asks.

"It's me, Briony. I'm calling from Margaret's."

"Oh, sorry. I didn't recognise the number. I'm so glad you've called. I've been awake all night, thinking about you. How are you?"

"Okay, I suppose. I've been well looked after. Listen, last night you said you had the day off. You offered..."

"Anything. Just tell me what I can do."

"I've just spoken to the police. They want to meet me at my flat. I'm at Margaret's house just now."

"No problem. Give me the address, I'll be straight over."

"Thanks, Jenny. There isn't any rush. They don't want to meet until eleven." I give her the address.

"Okay, I'll be there soon. Why does she want to see you at the flat?"

"It's not the policewoman you met yesterday. They've appointed an investigation officer, and she wants to meet me and bring a team of techies to check things over."

"That's odd. Why do they want to check your flat? They won't find any evidence there. It wasn't where you were attacked, was it?"

Attacked? I can't get used to the idea of being attacked. "I guess they're being thorough. As I can't fill the gap in my memory, I truly don't know where I've been. Besides, anyone could have been in my flat. It makes sense to check."

"Yeah, I suppose. I only said it because I want to look after you. I think you've been through enough of an ordeal without being put under any more stress."

"I appreciate it, Jenny. I'll go now and get ready. I'll see you when you get here."

————

HAVING FRESHENED UP, I go back to the kitchen. Jeffrey's nowhere to be seen and, as I walk towards his office, I hear music playing, classical music, orchestral. I recognise the pulsing drum beats of Mars, from Gustav Holst's *Planet Suite*. The door is open, and I can see he's sitting punching keys on his desktop computer. I knock and wait for his attention, but he doesn't hear over the music. I knock again, louder this time and call his name.

Jeffrey gives a start, then turns to see me. Momentarily, he looks back at the screen, enabling him to click the mouse, muting the sound. "Sorry, I didn't realise you were there. I often listen to Classic FM while I'm working. Margaret complains I play it too loud. Normally, there's no one else here for me to upset and as our property's detached, we don't have to worry about disturbing the neighbours."

"You've nothing to apologise for. It didn't bother me at all, and I love listening to music. I learned to play clarinet when I was at school and I still dabble a bit. It's me who should apologise for disturbing you when you were working."

Jeffrey waves aside my protests. "Pull up a chair. What did you want to talk to me about?"

"No, it's okay. I only wanted to tell you I'm going out. I've arranged to meet the police at my flat. My friend Jenny is coming over now to pick me up."

"Good. Is there anything I can help with?" Jeffrey asks.

I shake my head. "I don't know how long I'll be."

"Don't worry, I'll be here all day. You've got the number if you need me. We normally eat about 6.30. I'm making a pasta bolognaise."

"That's very kind, but I don't want to impose."

"You'd be best to stay for a few days... until you feel more back to normal."

I smile. "Thanks," is all I'm able to say.

25 HOURS

Remembering Jenny's reluctance to come to the house last night, I think it best to wait for her outside. It's an unusually pleasant day for October, dry and warm with hardly a cloud in the sky and only a mild breeze. I sit on the wall, looking around at the garden. Other than a couple of small flowerbeds, the surface is all either paved or covered in red whin chips, allowing for maximum parking potential and minimal maintenance. I inhale deeply, enjoying the fresh air, clearing my head.

I don't have long to wait before spotting Jenny's Renault Clio approach, rolling to a halt in front of me. I have the door open and I'm starting to climb in almost before the car's come to rest.

"You're in a hurry," she says. "You must have been really desperate to get out." Jenny leans across, throwing her arms around me, pulling me into a tight hug. "Oh, Briony, I'm so sorry about what you've been through. I'm here now. I can help you."

"We're very early. I'm not due to meet the police until eleven. Can I ask you to take me on an errand before going to the flat?"

"Of course, whatever you want. Where would you like to go?" Jenny asks.

"My bank. My rent payment wasn't transferred, and I haven't been able to find my bank card. I need to know what's going on."

"You told Paula about that last night. She said she would look into it."

"I know she did, but I don't know how long it'll take. I need to see what state my finances are in now," I say.

"That's a good idea. Where is your bank?"

A good question. Most of my banking is done online now. I know the bank branch where I opened my account. I've dealt with them for years. However, it was closed some months ago as part of the bank's cost-cutting measures. I can't be certain which branch they moved me to.

"I'm not certain where my home branch is now. Let's try Shawlands," I suggest.

Within fifteen minutes, we pull into the car park of the Shawlands Shopping Mall and make our way through hordes of pedestrians on Kilmarnock Road. Resulting from so many bank closures, the remaining ones are always busy. I need to queue for ten minutes before having the opportunity to speak to a teller. I explain I'm concerned about transactions on my account and show her my driving license for identification.

She rattles a few keys on her computer then looks cautiously at me. "We've already had an enquiry from the police about this," she whispers, her tone conspiratorial.

"Yes, I'm not surprised. I reported it to them yesterday. My card is missing, so I'd like to put a stop on any payments made using it. Can you also tell me my balance and about any withdrawals in the last week?"

"I can do better. I'll run you a mini statement. Your bank card has already been frozen because the police reported it missing. Would you like me to apply for a new one for you? It will take a few days to come through."

"Yes please," I say. I let out a shocked squeal as I stare at the statement in horror.

Jenny puts her arm round my shoulder. "What's wrong?" she asks.

As of last Friday, there ought to have been a balance of close to £1000 in credit. A rent payment of £500 was due to come out on Monday and then a Council Tax payment later in the week. I see last week's balance was as expected, but two withdrawals of £200 each were made dated last Friday and Saturday and a further charge of £225 was taken off on Saturday. The rent deduction was taken off on Monday, creating an overdraft, then the transaction was reversed the same day and an unauthorised transaction fee of £25 made at the same time. Council Tax of £140 came off on Wednesday, much as expected. My current balance is showing as not much over £200.

"This isn't right," I say, pointing to the rogue deductions. "Can you tell me what they are?"

The teller looks at her screen and replies, "The withdrawals were debit card withdrawals you made using an ATM in town. The £225 was a card payment made to Dixon Retail Services, that would most probably be at a Currys or PC World store."

"I didn't make any of these transactions," I say, my voice defiant.

"I'm sorry. There's nothing I can do," she replies. "If you believe the charges are not genuine, then you need to report it to the card services team." She hands me a leaflet with their information on it.

"Can you give me more precise details of the transactions?" I ask.

"I'm sorry, no. My machine doesn't give any more information. You'll need to take it up with them. Is there anything else I can do?"

I can't say I'm overly enamoured with what she's done so far, although I understand it's not her fault. I'm acutely aware of a growing queue behind me who are shuffling impatiently. "There's nothing more I can do here," I say and march out of the door with Jenny scurrying behind me.

I've calmed down significantly by the time we reach the car and we travel in silence until Jenny finds a parking spot near my flat. "We're still very early," I say. "I don't want to go up, just to sit around waiting."

"We could have a coffee. From what I remember, there's a good café just around the corner," Jenny suggests.

"I think I'm about all coffeed out," I reply. "It's a nice morning. Why don't we have a quiet stroll around the park? I'd feel better being out in the fresh air."

Jenny raises an eyebrow. "If that's what you'd like," she agrees, although she doesn't sound as if she's sold on the idea.

Setting a steady pace, we walk up Langside Avenue, the steep road leading past the side of the derelict building which until recently was the Victoria Infirmary. We then cross Battle Place into Queens Park. I've taken this walk countless times over the years and although I've never had a particular interest in Scottish history, I'm always tickled by the thought that I'm walking over ground where Mary Queen of Scots probably sat in 1568, watching the defeat of her followers in the Battle of Langside. On this occasion, I'm all too aware of the battles I have ahead.

Once in the park, we modify our speed to a leisurely stroll, walking past the Glasshouse in the direction of Shawlands before circuiting back towards Langside Road. We exit the park opposite the New Victoria Hospital and make our way to the flat. When I check my watch, I see there's only a few minutes until my scheduled meeting. I'm about to unlock the building's security door when I hear a car draw up in the restricted parking zone at the corner, followed by a large van.

26 HOURS

A TALL, HEAVILY BUILT WOMAN EXITS THE VEHICLE TO approach me. She has shoulder-length curly black hair framing a round face with rosy cheeks. She has the look of an archetypal farmer's wife. "Briony Chaplin?" she asks. I nod. "I'm Zoe McManus, I believe you're expecting me." She shows me her warrant card then holds out her hand in introduction. Her grip is firm and confident.

I try to match it, as a first step in reclaiming my independence. "This is Jenny Douglas," I say, pointing to my friend.

"Let's make a start. Can you clip the door open, please? The forensic team will follow us up once they've assembled their equipment."

Jenny and I lead the way upstairs but before we reach my flat, Zoe stops us.

"I'd like you to put these on." She hands us each a pair of disposable plastic booties. "I know you've been in already, but we want to minimise any evidence contamination before the technicians do their bit."

We put on the shoe covers before we open the front door.

"Can you please show us around?" Zoe asks.

I take her in and point to each of the rooms, stating the obvious, telling her what each one is, for lack of thinking about anything more meaningful to say. I'm aware the flat could benefit from a good clean. Other than for a short visit last night, I haven't been here for a week and there's a layer of dust over everything. It's untidy, too, with clothes lying around and last night's tea mugs sitting in the sink. What must Margaret and Alesha have thought, seeing this?

"I'm sorry about the mess. I should have cleaned up before you got here."

"Absolutely not," Zoe replies. "We need to check everything over first. We don't want anything disturbed in case it destroys evidence."

The forensic team move in and start collecting samples. I watch as they use great care to strip my bed and bag the bedclothes. They have a miniature vacuum device to collect samples and I see them looking for fingerprints on the phone, door handles and various surfaces. One of them goes through to the bathroom and he appears to be dismantling the plumbing. I see a stunned expression on Jenny's face and realise I must look similarly surprised.

"I've a few things to discuss with you," Zoe says. "It's going to take the guys a while to do their bit here, and they'll be quicker if we leave them undisturbed. We can wait outside, or, if you want, I can take you across to Cathcart Police Station in

Aikenhead Road. It will only take us a few minutes to drive there."

I consider the options. I really don't want to spend more time inside a police station, no matter how friendly and approachable they are. Equally, I don't want to put off this interview; I want it over. "How about we go downstairs and sit in Jenny's car?" The prospect of not having to face my inquisitor is a further attraction.

"We can do, if you like," Zoe replies, "if you're sure you'll be okay with that."

We descend the stairs. Jenny clicks the remote to open the Clio's door.

"We could use my car if you prefer, it's a bit more spacious, a Mondeo."

I look towards Jenny and she shrugs. "Go for it," she says.

At Zoe's invitation, I take the passenger seat while Jenny climbs in the back. Zoe settles into the driver's seat. "I'd like to tape this conversation for our records," she says, lifting a portable device along with a notebook and pen.

"Before we get started, here's your credit card back. We're trying to get more information on your banking, but there doesn't appear to have been anything suspicious happening on this card in the last week."

"Thank you," I say, putting it into my purse. From recollection, I have a credit limit of £1200 which I diligently keep within. The outstanding balance should be a little over £600, which I've yet to pay off for items I'd purchased for the flat. One less thing to worry about, I think.

"We've started looking into the transactions on your bank account," she says.

"I went to my branch this morning," I reply. "What did they tell you?"

She explains everything she'd found so far, which is no more than I'd already discovered.

"Now, I've checked your file and I've listened to your discussion with Paula. However, I'd like you to go through it all again for me, please," Zoe requests.

I sigh. Although it's no less than I expected, the reality of repeating my statement to this new officer leaves me feeling drained merely at the prospect. Nevertheless, I give my statement, including the descriptions of the three men and I answer all her many questions to the best of my ability.

"Thank you, Briony. We're going to do our best to catch whoever's done this to you," Zoe says.

I nod, showing acceptance of her promise, while having my doubts. I don't know what's been done to me, so what chance will they have of catching someone... unless she knows more than she's saying?

"Can I ask you some questions?" I ask.

"Yes, of course."

"Have you received any results from the tests taken yesterday?"

"No, it's too soon," Zoe replies. "They may start filtering through later today, but I expect nothing meaningful until at least Monday."

I close my eyes tight shut, my hand coming up to cover my face.

So many days to wait, before she expects to hear anything! It's the waiting, the waiting and not knowing, which is tearing me apart.

"You said 'questions'. Was there something else you wanted to know?"

"Yes, there was. Can you tell me if there's been any other case like mine, where someone's been abducted for a period of days, then come back not knowing who's taken them or where they've been?"

Zoe looks at me and seems to assess what to say before answering. "I've not come across a situation the same as yours. I've dealt with, or read about, cases where someone's been abducted and been missing for days or even weeks. Often, they've been traumatised, but they have had at least some recollection of who's taken them, or where they've been. I've had other cases where a victim has been drugged or otherwise had a memory loss. Again, sometimes lost or distorted memory can be caused by trauma, but these cases are normally only for one night, or maybe two."

My head drops. I can't maintain eye contact and instead look at my feet. "So, you don't have a pool of likely suspects."

"I'm sorry, no, I can't say we do." She pauses before adding, "We will do our best, though."

Another thought occurs to me. "Do you have my phone, or can you tell me when I'll get it back?"

"It hadn't been returned before I left the station." she says. "I'll check when I get back and I'll give you a call."

I look at her quizzically.

"You gave us the number of..." she looks at her notes, "Margaret Hamilton, where you were staying. Is that still the best one to get you on if you're not home?"

I don't have time to answer before Jenny butts in, "Take my mobile number. Briony's likely to be with me a lot of the time."

"If that's all for just now, I'll head back to the station." She looks at her watch. "It could be another hour or so until the guys finish upstairs. You could either hang about, or I could arrange for them to drop the keys back to you if you tell me where you'll be."

I think through the options, finding it difficult to make any decision.

"I know," Jenny says. "Why don't we go to The Rest for a bite of lunch? It would be a nice treat and it's only a five-minute walk from here. I know it's Friday, but it's early enough that they ought to be able to fit us in." She looks at Zoe. "When your people get finished up, they can phone me there."

"Sounds like a plan," Zoe replies. "I'll let them know."

27 HOURS

THE BATTLEFIELD REST IS ONE OF MY FAVOURITE eateries, serving delicious Italian cuisine. The building is stylish, constructed over one hundred years ago as a waiting room and resting place for the city's trams, opposite the main entrance to the Infirmary. I've read that it was unused, semi-derelict and facing demolition prior to it being turned into a fashionable restaurant, some twenty-five years ago.

Having resolved how we'll kill some time, we walk along Sinclair Drive

"Maybe this will make up for us missing out on our dinner last Friday," Jenny says, then bites her lip thinking she's said the wrong thing.

I doubt anything will ever make up for me not making it to the dinner last Friday, I think, but I say nothing. I don't want to talk about it or make an issue of it; not now, anyway. Jenny and I have always had a rapport. We've felt comfortable talking about anything and everything with each other. Sex, religion, politics, relationships, family, health issues... nothing is barred and typically, we've treated it all with the same disrespect and frivolity.

Once we arrive at the restaurant, we're invited in like old friends and shown to a table.

"Mm, my mouth's watering just reading this," Jenny says, her eyes scanning the lunch menu. "What are you up for, two courses or three?"

As I cast my eyes over the offerings, I remember the conversation I had with Jeffrey before leaving. 'Dinner at 6.30, a pasta bolognaise.' What's more, I've a strong suspicion he'll be a good cook. Much as I love Italian food, I couldn't eat two meals of it today and I don't want to offend Jeffrey by not eating his home-cooked meal. Equally, I don't want to upset Jenny. I'm aware she'd already expressed concern about the influence being exerted by Alesha, Margaret and Jeffrey. I don't want to give her ammunition by explaining they're the reason why I don't want a special lunch with her.

"I'm really not very hungry, I couldn't eat a big meal," I say. "I see they do a lunch promotion, a restricted menu with a single course and soft drink. I'm going for that."

When I see her disappointed expression, I feel obliged to give further explanation. "I'm still a bit out of sorts; I don't have much appetite. But there's no reason why you shouldn't have a proper meal."

Jenny protests but I manage to convince her. She orders an antipasto starter, followed by chicken and salciccia cacciatore accompanied by a glass of Nero d'Avola. I'm happy to select a mushroom omelette, to be washed down by soda water and lime.

By the time the food arrives, I've convinced myself I'm not at all hungry, so I pick at my omelette while Jenny devours her food. The aroma from her main course wafts in my direction, enticing me to relent, but I'm determined, and I resist the temptation.

She's mopping up the last of her sauce with a wedge of bread when her phone rings. I hear her end of the conversation, arranging for my keys to be brought to us and for us to meet the person bringing them outside the restaurant door.

Less than five minutes later, we see a smartly dressed young man approach.

"Miss Chaplin?" he enquires.

"Yes, that's me."

"Here's your keys back. We've finished with your flat. You can go back in now."

He hands me my keys, together with a sheet of paper. "Will you sign for the keys there, please?" He points to a spot on the first page. "Can you also sign this, too?" he produces some more papers. "It's a schedule of items we've taken for lab analysis, where it's more efficient than taking samples. There's a copy for you to keep as well."

Without giving it much thought, I scan a lengthy list of items allocated by location, including laptop computer, various items of bed linen, towels, pens, envelopes, card, money, medicines and a paperback. It pleases me that they're being so diligent. I sign the documents and place my copy plus the keys into my handbag. Before I have a chance to ask any questions, he's turned and jumped back into his van.

"Are you having work done?" a waiter asks. He'd been taking a break, sitting at an outside table, an espresso cup in one hand, a vape device in the other. I've seen him before on several occasions and he's always been chatty in a friendly and flirty sort of way. A bit cheesy, but no menace.

"A new carpet's been fitted," I lie.

He smiles while accompanying us back to our table and on the way he collects the dessert menu. "Sweet or coffee?" he enquires.

We both opt for an Americano.

When we ask for the bill, Jenny insists on paying. "You've hardly eaten a thing," she says, feeling a need to justify her generosity.

We return to the flat expecting to find upheaval, but, to my surprise, it's much cleaner and tidier than how I'd left it when the forensic team arrived. Nevertheless, I feel uncomfortable, even more so than before. It's as if I've been violated. Well, I know that I've almost certainly been violated, but this is different. It's been done by the people who are meant to be protecting me. I'm uncomfortable knowing all my personal belongings, my clothes racks, my underwear drawers, my kitchen and bathroom cabinets, have been inspected and studied by strangers. My bedclothes and my nightwear have been taken away for study, even my shower's drains and my toilet have been dismantled for inspection and reassembled. I feel I don't want to stay in the flat any longer than I have to. Although I haven't really done anything, I feel fatigued. I need to rest soon. I'm having difficulty holding my head up.

Detecting my disquiet, Jenny seeks to comfort me. "Why don't you come back and stay with me?" she asks.

"I don't know, Jenny. Margaret and Jeffrey are expecting me. Besides, I wouldn't want to discuss what's happened with your family."

Seeking to reassure me, she answers, "You needn't worry about that. I've already explained what you've been through so no one will ask you any questions unless you choose to talk about it."

Maybe it was well meant, but now I'm angry. It was up to me and no one else to tell anybody about my problems! Jenny had no right to blab to her mum without asking me first.

I try to tell her, but my eyes fill with tears and I can hardly speak.

Jenny misinterprets my emotion and moves to hug me. "It's alright, Briony. We're like family. We're..."

I push her away. "No, Jenny. You shouldn't have said anything. You've no right. Who else have you told?"

"No-one, I've told no-one else. I only told them because I wanted you to be able to come back with me. My mum thinks of you as a second daughter. She really cares and while she'd do anything she could to help you, she's close enough to understand if you just wanted to be left alone."

I feel guilty for my outburst. My emotions are all over the place. What am I doing, attacking the people closest to me? "I'm sorry," I say. "I'm not myself." Then I add, "I don't want her to see me like this. Could you please come back with me to the Hamiltons'? I think you'll feel happier about them after you get to meet them."

"I told you before, Briony, I'll do anything you need me to, even if it's not what I think best. It's your decision."

29 HOURS

I introduce Jenny to Jeffrey. He shows us into the kitchen. We decline his offer of coffee. Detecting the delicious aroma of home cooking, I inhale the flavours, smelling garlic, basil, oregano and something else I can't place. I see a large Pyrex bowl sitting on a pot stand next to the hob.

"Dinner's mostly prepared. Would you like to join us?" he asks Jenny. "You're welcome to stay. There's plenty to go around. I always make too much and end up having to freeze or throw out what's not used."

"That's most kind of you, Mr Hamilton. I must admit I'm very tempted, but my mum is expecting me home for dinner," she replies.

I suspect she's lying. Jenny has a healthy appetite but, after the lunch she's had, I doubt she'd have room for a pasta dinner. Also, I know she hadn't been keen to come back here. I don't doubt that Margaret and Jeffrey will win her over, but for now, she wants to keep her options open.

Jeffrey turns to me. "Did everything go okay?"

"I suppose." I give him a rough summary of my morning, finishing by saying, "I still don't know very much, and it doesn't look as if I'll find out any time soon."

"I'm afraid that's how it works," Jeffrey replies. "I know it's difficult, but you have no option. You have to be patient."

I chew on my lip, wondering if I dare ask.

"What is it, Briony?" he asks.

"You said last night that you may be able to help me."

"I did, and I meant what I said." Jeffrey examines my face before continuing. "The police will carry out their own enquiries. You've been interviewed by Paula and now by Zoe. It's likely the investigation team might want you to go through everything again for them. For me to investigate, to do it effectively, I'll need to know everything, too. I'll need you to tell me everything you've told them. It's going to be difficult for you. It's hard talking about what you've been through and no doubt it's even harder when you don't know. I must be honest with you, doing it over and over isn't going to be any less of a strain."

I'm about to answer when Jeffrey holds up his hand in a cautioning gesture. "Think about it."

I look at Jenny for reassurance. Her face is impassive. She shrugs.

"If you want me to do this and if I can, I'll work with the police," Jeffrey continues. "Whether they'll want to cooperate with me depends on who's in charge of the investigation. As far as Zoe in concerned, I know her well. We worked together several years ago, and we get on fine. I wouldn't expect any problems, unless her boss was to intervene."

"I thought she was leading the investigation?" I say.

"In practical terms she is, but she's accountable to a more senior officer and that's who'll have the final say. Ideally, we can work together and share information, so we don't end up duplicating or getting under each other's feet. They have access to some resources I don't have and vice versa. There are some things it's easier or more practical for me to do."

"Okay, that makes sense," I say.

"There's something else. Before I start, I need to make clear that I may not find anything and, even if I do, it may not turn out to be anything you'd thank me to hear."

I consider the implications of what he's said and I draw in a breath before speaking. "I understand, but I need to know. I need to find out, whatever it means."

"You're sure?"

"Yes, I'm sure. I may not like it. In fact, I can't come up with any scenario which could in any way be acceptable, but how can I cope without knowing?"

"Do you need some time, or are you ready to start now? It means you must trust me. You must tell me everything you've already told the police."

I close my eyes and my head droops. I turn to look at Jeffrey, but my eyes go out of focus for a second as I consider. "There's no point in waiting," I say. "The sooner we start, the sooner I might get some answers."

"Okay, give me a moment while I get my laptop. I want to take notes."

30 HOURS

"WOULD YOU LIKE TO GO INTO THE LOUNGE?" JEFFREY asks. "You might be more comfortable sitting in an easy chair."

I think it through. "No, I'd prefer to be here, thanks." I don't know why, but there's something reassuring about having a solid table in front of me. I suppose it's like a division separating me from anyone asking questions. Although I know Jeffrey's on my side and it's me who asked him to do this, it's still a defence of sorts.

Jeffrey asks me to run through everything I told Paula and Zoe. Jenny's sitting beside me with her arm around my shoulder. It helps to be held and occasionally I look at her and smile. I try to be as informative as I can, but I find I can't look at Jeffrey while I'm speaking. Instead, I look down at the table or shut my eyes. To make it easier, I try to convince myself that I'm reciting the plot of a book I've read, instead of telling my own story. It works for the most part, but when I talk about the visions, I tremble, and I fail to keep the emotion out of my voice. Jenny squeezes me tighter. I don't know if I'd have been able to do this without her here.

Jeffrey doesn't say a word while I'm talking. He seems to sense I need to get this over with without interruption. However, I can hear the clicking of his keyboard as Jeffrey takes copious notes. Only after I've finished does he ask me to embellish some of my comments and asks me some questions.

"You've done really well," he says. "I know how difficult it must have been."

"Where do we go from here?" I ask.

"First, I want to give Zoe a ring. A courtesy call, at least, to let her know I'm getting involved. I can discuss with her things we might each be able to do. The first thing I'd like to check is what you've told me the bank said about withdrawals from your account. I'll need some more information and, if I get cooperation, it's an easy thing to check. It could be a good place to start."

"What can I do?" I ask.

"At this point, nothing at all. I will ask you to sign a mandate authorising me to access information on your behalf, in case it's needed. For now, you'd be best to find something to distract you. Maybe watch TV or a DVD. We've got quite a collection. I'll show you."

Jeffrey shows Jenny and me back into the lounge. He points to a door in the corner and tells me to open it. Behind the door are floor-to-ceiling shelves, stacked with DVDs and Blu-rays.

"They're all in alphabetical order within genre." He smiles. "Anal, I know. Help yourself to anything you'd like to see. All I ask is that you don't mix them up, as they take ages to sort." He then shows me where the remote controls are for the television, soundbar and player. Jeffrey turns his wheelchair to leave. "You know where the kitchen is if you want anything. I'll be in my office if you need me."

"That's an amazing selection of movies," Jenny says. "What do you fancy?"

"I don't think I could concentrate on a film," I say. "Maybe later."

"Shall we see what's on TV?" Jenny suggests. "I'm not often home in the afternoon so I've no idea what the schedules are like."

"Me neither." I pick up the TV remote and switch it on. It looks like an ancient film is showing, some soppy romance. Having pressed the 'guide' key, I scroll through the dozens of Freeview channels on offer, but I find nothing very enticing.

"Go back to the start," Jenny says. "I think I saw there were some game shows on STV. Nothing very exciting, I know, but it would be a distraction."

"Why not?" I click the programme on, and we sit challenging ourselves to beat the contestants. Many of them appear happy to make fools of themselves by showing excessive enthusiasm in their efforts, all for the chance to win a fairly small prize while they enjoy their fifteen minutes of fame.

Some time later, Jeffrey comes back. He presents me with the mandate he'd mentioned, and I sign it. "I spoke to Zoe. The good news is she's happy to cooperate. The bad news, she's not certain if her boss will approve but, as he's currently on leave, she's prepared to go ahead in the meantime. It's sticking her neck out a bit. She says she owes me a favour because I helped her settle in when she was new to the job. She also confided that she is already working three other enquiries, so an extra pair of hands will no doubt suit her."

My spirits are lifted.

"I've called the card services at your bank," he continues. "I've told them who I am and what I'm doing, and I've told them what we know about your bank account movements. I've made certain they've noted the rogue transactions that are in dispute. If we can prove it wasn't you who made them, then you'll be reimbursed for what was taken out, along with the penalty bank charges for the failed transfer. You may even get a small token payment as compensation. I've to email a scan of your mandate and, once Zoe's given him the okay, they'll give me access to everything they have on the withdrawals."

"That was quick," Jenny says, clearly impressed.

"Don't get too excited. We don't have anything yet, but it's a good step in the right direction. I want to get as much as I can, as quickly as I can, even if I can't use it right away, just in case Zoe's boss revokes my authority."

"Thanks," I say.

Jeffrey takes the document and races back to his office.

"I wonder what he'll find?" I say.

"There's normally a camera built into every ATM. If he can find which ATM was used for the withdrawals, then he might be able to check if there's any film footage," Jenny says.

"Then we'd know who took out the money," I conclude.

I'm excited by the prospect. I try watching more television, but I can't take it in. Time passes oh-so-slowly while we wait to hear more. I frequently look at my watch, expecting it to be later, but on each occasion I'm disappointed to realise only a few minutes have passed.

It feels as if hours have passed by the time Jeffrey next returns. I'm immediately concerned, as his face looks gloomy.

"What did you find?" I ask.

He closes his eyes for a second before speaking. I'm apprehensive. "The two withdrawals were both made from the same ATM. It's located on Great Western Road, not far from Bank Street. In each case, the camera was working well both before and after the transaction on your account, but for some reason it went quite hazy in between. I suspect someone may have tampered with the camera. However, proving it may be another matter. I reckon someone may have put a filter over the lens."

"But..." I start.

"Wait, there's more. Pictures were taken, but they're not as clear as I might have hoped for."

"What did they show?" Jenny asks. By now, I'm too frightened to speak.

"It appears the person withdrawing the money was female, about your height and wearing a blue dress, not dissimilar to the one you told me you had on. She was wearing a jacket with its hood up, so the face wouldn't have been particularly clear even without the distortion."

"Oh my God!" Jenny exclaims.

It takes a moment for Jeffrey's words to sink in. "No! It wasn't me. I didn't withdraw any money, or I'd have known." I'm adamant in my protestations, but how can I be sure? Oh, hell. If I'm doubting myself, what chance is there of making anyone else believe me?

"You don't have to convince me, Briony. I believe you," Jeffrey says. "Besides, it's too much of a coincidence for the film quality to change at those precise points, for the photos to be meaningful."

"But why? And who?" I say.

"The 'who' is the sixty-four-thousand dollars question. As to the…"

Seeing my confused look, Jeffrey explains, "It's an expression, before your time. It dates back to an ancient American game show."

"Go on," I say.

"As to the 'why', I can't answer. Maybe someone is trying to discredit you. If the bank and the police think your complaint is spurious, then it multiplies your problems. What's more, if someone is looking to discredit you, it raises a whole different set of questions."

My brain is swimming with all the possibilities. I'm having difficulty thinking straight.

"You don't have any enemies, do you?" Jeffrey asks.

"Of course not," Jenny cuts in.

"I can't think of anyone who'd want to hurt me. Okay, I can't say I get on with everyone all the time, but for someone to do this, they'd need to really hate me. For them to set up this elaborate identification fiasco must have taken lots of time and planning. Why?"

"Now you're starting to think like a detective," Jeffrey says. "There's something else," he adds.

"What?" I ask, my heart hammering.

"The third payment was a card charge made to Dixon Retail. Do you remember... from what the bank told you?"

I nod.

"Well, I've traced it to a purchase made at their Finnieston store on Dumbarton Road."

My eyes widen. "That's odd. I was in there a couple of weeks ago."

Jeffrey's brows furrow. "Why were you there?"

"Isn't that the time we went out together? You were thinking about buying a new telly for your bedroom. You quite liked one, but decided against it because you wanted to wait until you'd cleared down your credit card," Jenny answers for me and I agree.

Jeffrey looks serious. "By any chance, was the one you didn't buy an LG thirty-two inch, SMART, LED?"

"Yes, how did you know?" I ask.

"You bought it," Jeffrey replies. "That's what the £225 transaction was on your debit card. It was out of stock on the day but it's due to be delivered to you, next week."

"But how could that be? And who could have done this?" I blurt.

"The 'how' is the easy part. Someone either pretended to be you, or said they were buying it for you. They charged the purchase using your card and provided your address for the delivery."

I feel my head throbbing.

"As for the 'who', we're no further forward, but we can now be fairly certain it's someone you know and know well. They must have been aware you'd been considering the purchase. How many people might have known?"

I try to think. "It wasn't a secret. I told Mum and Dad. I may have mentioned it at work, too. In fact, yes, I did, because a few of us were discussing the merits of different manufacturers and who gave best value for money. Anyone could have seen us in the shop, too. I remember we chatted to the sales assistant."

"What about that chap?" Jenny asks.

"What chap?" I ask.

"Don't you remember? The one in the shop. The good-looking one. He was checking out televisions, too, and it wasn't all he was checking out. He started a conversation with you and told you he was a lawyer. He didn't seem to notice that I existed," she added, with a chuckle. "He was chatting you up. Didn't he ask for your number? Don't you remember we joked about him all the way home in the car?"

Racking my brain to visualise the incident, I have a vague recollection, but he didn't make much of an impression on me. It was only a casual conversation, a bit flirty, maybe. I have them all the time. "You don't think..."

"Maybe he's a weirdo and he followed you," Jenny suggests. "Perhaps he's been stalking you ever since."

"I suppose, but it hardly seems likely," I say.

"None of this seems likely," Jeffrey says. "Jenny's right. We need to look at all possibilities."

"Will the shop be able to give you any more information?" I ask.

"I've already tried," Jeffrey answers. "They don't have video surveillance anywhere that would help. They've confirmed the details of the purchase, but it was put through as a standard till transaction on a busy day. The sales person is recorded as Daniel, but neither he nor anyone else has any recollection of seeing you, or of anyone else for that matter."

"Seeing me. You think it was me?" I ask, picking up on what he said.

"No, that isn't what I meant," Jeffrey replies. "I believe what you've told me, but we'll have more of a problem convincing the bank. We have nothing, so far, to convince them it wasn't you who withdrew the money and purchased the TV. Knowing that you'd previously considered buying it makes the argument even more difficult."

"But why?" I ask.

"Everything points to someone messing with your head. By all accounts, they've tried to create problems for you at work, with your property lease and with your finances and that's on top of whatever they've done physically. All of this has happened while your parents are away on holiday. The timing is too much of a coincidence for my liking," Jeffrey says.

"I hadn't looked at it that way," I say

"I can't completely rule out Jenny's mystery man, but I think he's a long shot. I believe that whoever's behind this knows a lot about you and it's all been meticulously planned."

I'm stunned; I don't know what to say. This is all too much, the worst nightmare. My life's in turmoil. I want to turn the clock back and have things return to the way they were.

"Briony, calm down. You're going to be okay." Jenny takes my hand. She looks very concerned. "I don't know who's done this to you or why, but you're safe now. I'm sure whoever's done it will have had their fun and now it's over. You've nothing more to worry about and we'll look after you until you feel better."

I know she doesn't like seeing me upset. This is her trying to make me feel better.

"We're going to get to the bottom of this." Jeffrey, too, seems to be trying to reassure me. "I meant what I said about this having been planned in great detail. But nobody's perfect. He'll have slipped up somewhere. I don't know where, yet, but I'll find it." He smiles at me and, despite all my doubts, I do feel comforted.

Any further thoughts on the matter are interrupted by a ringing phone. Jeffrey returns to his office to answer. I only hear snippets of his conversation. He sounds serious one moment; then there's resounding laughter the next. All becomes clear when he returns.

"Good news, you can have your phone back. Better still, because the duty sergeant is an old friend of mine, he's arranging for a squad car to drop it into Margaret's office in town. He had a car going past the door, anyway. I checked with her. She's just about to pack up for the day, but she'll hang on for a bit so she can collect it and bring it home."

"What was so funny?" I ask, my tone abrupt, the words out my mouth before realising my rudeness.

Jeffrey frowns for a second before answering, "Nothing important. Sam was telling me about the latest admin screw-up."

"Oh," I say. I must be getting paranoid thinking people are laughing at me. "Sorry, I didn't mean to..." My mind goes numb. I can't think what to say.

Jenny stares at me. Her expression is one of concern.

"It's okay, Briony. I know how it is. All your emotions are on the surface," Jeffrey answers.

I feel ashamed. He's making excuses for me. Margaret and Jeffrey have been my saviours. Jeffrey's taking time out of his busy schedule to help me and even makes allowances for my rudeness. What sort of nasty bitch am I? And could I have upset someone so much that they'd do this to me? Is that it? Has someone taken it upon themselves to bring me down, to teach me a lesson?

No, I'm being ridiculous. No doubt there have been occasions when I've said or done something to upset somebody else, but then who hasn't? This is no ordinary act of getting back at someone. I'm trying to rationalise what's happened and the truth is, there's nothing rational about it. Whoever's abducted me, whoever's turned my entire life upside down, must be some kind of serious nutter, a psychopath most likely. Might Jenny be right and he's had his fun and now it's all over? Or is that too simple, too optimistic? Maybe right at this moment he's planning his next move.

"What are you thinking about, Briony? You're looking very serious." Jenny's question interrupts my deliberations.

I open my mouth and I'm on the verge of giving a glib, throwaway answer before it occurs to me that I should be honest. If I keep trying to avoid my issues, the result will be that I'll bottle it all up until I explode. I'll end up having a complete breakdown. I tell them about my thoughts and fears. Jenny hugs me and tells me she's here for me. Jeffrey goes back to his office to further the enquiries he's making on my behalf.

33 HOURS

I LOOK UP, HEARING THE CAR'S TYRES SCRUNCH ACROSS the chips of the driveway. A few moments later, Margaret enters the lounge, closely followed by Alesha and then Jeffrey wheels in. My spirits are lifted. I'm surprised and delighted to see my new friend.

"I hadn't expected to see you again so soon," I blurt.

"I was worried. I've been thinking about you all day," Alesha replies. "I had to leave this morning before I could talk to you. Margaret said I could come back again because she thought it was better for you not to be on your own for a while. Are you okay? Have you remembered anything else?"

"She's not alone. I've been with her all day," Jenny interrupts, before I'm able to answer.

Alesha looks dismayed. "I'm sorry. I didn't mean to cause a problem. I just want to make sure you're okay."

"Don't apologise," I say. "I'm pleased to see you. You've been so kind. I couldn't have managed without you yesterday. It's me who should say sorry for rushing away without talking to you or thanking you properly this morning."

Alesha smiles.

"Jenny came over this morning and has been looking after me. She's taken me all over the place to get things done. I've spoken again to the police. What's more, Jeffrey's started making enquiries. Everyone has been so supportive and helpful. I can't thank you all enough."

Alesha chews on her lip, taking a few seconds while considering whether to speak, then says, "I had a couple of things on this weekend, but I reorganised it so I'm flexible. I've no fixed plans so I could be with you, but only if you want. If you're already sorted, I don't want to be in the way." Alesha glances at Jenny.

"You could never be in the way," I reply.

"I've been thinking. As it's the weekend, it might do you some good to get away from the norm for a few hours. How about I take us down to the coast tomorrow, maybe Troon? A bracing sea breeze might clear your head and we could take time out, maybe have a pub lunch or something." Jenny glances at Alesha and forces a smile. "You could come with."

"That sounds a good idea," Margaret says. "Our kids are visiting us for the afternoon. You're quite welcome to be here and meet them, but I think a day at the seaside sounds more interesting."

Looking around, Margaret sees no dissent. "Settled then. Now, about tonight ..."

"Jenny told us she's having dinner with her mum," Jeffrey says.

"I can stay," Alesha says, without any hesitation.

Jenny pauses for a second. "Yes, I need to pop back and see my mum, although it won't be for long. I can come back by... mmm, nine o'clock. Ten at the latest."

"It's okay, Jenny, you don't need to. I don't want you to have to spoil your plans, particularly as Alesha will be here for me, anyway."

"No, I insist," Jenny replies, "providing it's okay for you." She turns to Margaret and Jeffrey. "I want to be with you, to know you're okay. If I wasn't with you, I'd be worrying all night."

"You're welcome to stay. I can move a camp-bed into the room you girls used last night so the three of you can all be together. I think it would be better for you all being together. If you don't feel able to sleep, you might want to watch videos, take your mind off everything else." Margaret then turns to me. "How are you coping?"

I shrug. "I don't know. It's not like yesterday. I feel a lot better. I don't have any physical aches or pains anymore, but I can't get used to the idea. It's as if my life has changed. It feels like it's not my own anymore. Everything is normal for a moment until I think what's been done to me. Then I feel numb, my brain clouds over and I have a soreness in my head, my body, everywhere."

"It's awful, I know, but what you've described is quite normal," Margaret replies. There's a distant look in her eyes. "It may never go away completely, but it will fade over time. You might want to consider counselling."

I'm certain Margaret is thinking back to her own bad experiences, yet she's talking to me now in a confident and maternal fashion. She has always seemed to me to be so strong, so in control. It had never occurred to me before that her manner may have been masking her own past insecurities. I wonder if this might be my future. If I can only get through these next days and weeks, will I come out of it a strong, confident person, at least on the face of it?

"Well, I don't know about anyone else, but I'm famished and judging from the smell wafting from the kitchen, I won't be disappointed," Margaret says.

"If you can all go get yourselves ready, it'll take me about thirty minutes to finish preparing the pasta and to heat garlic bread," Jeffrey says.

"Just time for a quick shower and let me change from work to relax mode," Margaret says. "Oh, before I forget, I have this for you." She opens her handbag, lifts out my mobile and hands it to me. It's sealed in a polythene bag.

"I'll be off. The sooner I go, the sooner I'll be back." Jenny squeezes my shoulders, gives me a quick peck on the cheek and is out of the door.

I rip open the bag to look at my phone. It's no different from when I handed it over, yet I feel it's not the same. Some unknown person or persons have handled it, they've stripped it and played with its memory. Will it ever feel the same? A bit like me, I guess. No, I must stop thinking like this if I ever hope to get my life back. What is the phone? A cheap silicon chip surrounded by a mix of plastic, metal and a good PR job. Maybe not so cheap when I think about it, although the rest applies. I remember now; I was only partway through checking my voicemails when the battery died. I'd best find out what else I've missed.

While I've been thinking, Jenny's driven away and Margaret and Jeffrey have disappeared, leaving Alesha, now sitting on the couch across from me, appraising me with an anxious look on her face.

"Is everything okay?" she asks.

I look at her, then the phone, then back at her. "Yes, I think so. I'd best check the rest of my messages," I say.

"Before you do, there was something I wanted to tell you"

I'm curious. I turn towards her,

"Two policemen came to the office today. They asked for Stuart and then spoke privately to Margaret and Stuart. Margaret asked me to prepare a list for them of all employees and to include any recent leavers, anyone who may have had a security pass which gave access to our office. Afterwards, they spoke individually to every member of staff who was in and they're planning to come back next week to pick up on any they've missed.

"What did they want to know?" I ask.

"They said that there had been an incident in the building last Saturday afternoon and they wanted to check when everyone left and where they'd been. They had a schedule taken from the building's security system and they were checking information against it."

"Did they say what the incident was?" I ask.

"No, they didn't explain anything. They said it was a routine enquiry."

"Thanks for letting me know. I'd best check my messages now," I say.

"You go ahead. I'm fine here," she says.

I switch on the phone and wait for the screen to come alive. Looking at the icons, I see it's still showing six WhatsApp messages to read but there are two new ones in each of the texts and voicemails. I wonder if the police technician has looked at the messages because they don't appear to have been opened. I remember Paula saying something about cloning the memory.

I check my WhatsApps first and find nothing of importance; one was Jenny trying another route to make contact, while all the others are from friends. They're ones I rarely see yet somehow manage to maintain a dialogue with, supported on the ether. I turn my attention back to the texts and voicemails to find all four are from Mum and Dad, a phone message and a text yesterday and another of each today. Yesterday's communications reiterated what a good time they'd been having, but they were also to remind me of their plans. They tell me they're due to dock in Southampton late this coming Saturday night (tomorrow), disembarking Sunday morning. They're also thinking of spending a couple of days in London, hoping to pick up Sunday matinee tickets for a West End show, ideally *School of Rock*. Their plan is for them then to fly back to Glasgow on Sunday night or Monday morning. Each message ended with a note of surprise at having not heard anything from me and asking if all was okay, then asking me to phone or text them back. Today's call and text were more direct. Arriving this afternoon, they expressed extreme concern and wanted me to get back to them without delay

"Sh... sh... sugar!" I suppress the profanity. They're worried about me. Why didn't I think to message them yesterday?

"What's wrong?" Alesha asks, immediately concerned.

"It's Mum and Dad. It sounds like they're starting to panic because they haven't heard from me. How stupid of me! I meant to message them yesterday, but with everything else going on, it went straight out of my head."

"You'd better contact them now," Alesha says.

"I know. I'm just trying to think what to say. I'm not certain of the best way to handle it."

"The truth might be easiest," Alesha suggests.

"I know I have to tell them – well, as much as I know of the truth, that is, but not yet. Not until after they're back. I need to say something to put their minds at ease for the time being."

"Are you absolutely sure?" she asks.

I give a decisive nod. If only what was happening inside my head was as resolute.

I decide to text. But I abort my first three attempts at trying to find acceptable wording before settling on, *Sorry, I've had a problem and been unable to use my phone for the last couple of days. I'm delighted you've had such a good time and can't wait to hear all about it.* I read it over, then read it aloud for Alesha's reaction. She tilts her head and purses her lips; her face has a noncommittal expression. I press send. It wasn't ideal although I immediately feel relieved at having dealt with it.

"I did tell the truth," I say.

"Just not the whole truth and nothing but the truth. You might want to consider a career in marketing!" Alesha's smirk is mocking.

"And you may want to change to a career in criminal law," I retort.

We're both still laughing when Margaret appears in the doorway. I can see she's happy to find us in good spirits.

"Dinner's ready. Come on through now," she invites.

34 HOURS

I realise Jeffrey was being serious when he talked about making too much to eat at one serving. The table has an enormous ceramic baking tray at its centre, filled to the brim with baked pasta. Steam is rising from the bubbling cheese on top. A large bowl filled with salad is on one side and a plate on the other is covered by slices of the most appealingly aromatic garlic bread I've ever seen.

"Grab a seat. Margaret will dish up," he says.

"This looks amazing," Alesha says.

Jeffrey gives a modest reply. "Don't be too hasty to judge until you taste it."

"Help yourselves to salad and bread. There are serving spoons in the middle and olive oil and balsamic at the side," Margaret announces, while spooning a large serving of pasta onto each of our plates.

"There's water in the jug, but would you like some wine? I've a nice bottle of Primitivo from Puglia," Jeffrey says, pointing to the label. "I think it goes perfectly with pasta."

"I don't believe I've ever had that one," I say. "Can I try just a little, please?" Now that my head's starting to clear, I want to be careful. I don't want to drink much, but perhaps a small glass of wine will help me relax.

The food tastes even better than it looks and I tuck in with enthusiasm. "This is fabulous. I'd love a copy of your recipe if you wouldn't mind. Have you always enjoyed cooking?"

"You couldn't be further from the truth," Jeffrey replies. "I wasn't even able to boil an egg until a few years ago. It all changed after one of the kids bought me a recipe book for Christmas. I tried out a few things and found I really enjoyed cooking."

"And he's a natural, as you can tell," Margaret says, her pride evident.

"Anyhow, I got hooked. A few years ago, I went to an Italian cookery class held at the Caledonian University. The lecturer was excellent, really inspiring. His name was Gary Maclean. You may have seen him on TV. He went on to win at *Master-Chef Professionals.*"

"Did you get this recipe from him?" I ask.

"No, this is one of my own. I've always loved Italian food. What the class gave me was more confidence and an appreciation for how different tastes work together."

"And you made all this yourself," Alesha says, clearly impressed. "How do you do it?"

"Not quite all. I make my own pasta from eggs and flour and I have a special cutting machine to do the shapes. The bolognaise is made from beef mince, passata, onions, peppers, mushrooms, carrots, garlic purée and my own herb mixture. Once it's all prepared, I cover it in a mixture of mozzarella and parmesan before I bake it. As for the garlic bread, I cheat. I bought it in the supermarket, ready to bake."

I love hearing the enthusiasm in Jeffrey's voice as he describes his cooking hobby. The food and wine are delicious and perfectly paired, the company affable. I'm able to enjoy myself without thinking of my own problems.

It hasn't even gone nine o'clock. We're sitting around the table chatting when we hear the doorbell. Margaret goes to answer and comes back with Jenny. The conversation continues, turning from politics and putting the world to right one moment, to music and film the next. It's all so relaxing. Despite claiming not to be hungry, Jenny accepts the offer of a small bowl of pasta. She devours it along with the remaining slices of garlic bread and has some wine from what must have been the end of a second bottle.

We sit around talking some more, until spates of yawning become more prevalent.

36 HOURS

"Has everybody had enough?" Jeffrey asks. Acknowledging our assent, he leads us to the lounge where he offers us our choice of film. While we're choosing, he returns to the kitchen, where he sets to work preparing a tray of snacks in case anyone becomes peckish.

None of us feels like watching anything too heavy. Alesha chooses a rom-com while Jenny picks a low-brow adventure. I'm not particularly interested, but happy to go with the flow. I'm enjoying the company and the camaraderie.

Margaret helps us set up a DVD player in the same bedroom I was in last night. There are now three beds made up for us. I'm happy to be part of the group and, for their sake, I pretend to be enjoying myself as the room is sprinkled with laughter while we watch the films and munch on the snacks.

I really can't get into the movies and, having had a particularly long day, I'm having difficulty keeping my eyes open. I'm starting to doze by midway through the second film. We struggle on to the end before readying ourselves for bed.

44 HOURS

This is all very strange. It's surreal and I know I must be dreaming but I'm drawn to keep watching. I can't rouse myself.

Looking around, I see all the people I know: Mum and Dad, Margaret and Jeffrey, Michael, Alesha and Jenny are all there. Lots of people from my office, too; my boss Stuart Ronson, Dwight, Chrissie and many more, friends from school and university, distant family all standing in a circle around me. All are smiling; they're cheering and applauding.

It makes me happy seeing them, but gradually their features become blurred. They're moving, further away, unclear, fading as they disappear into the distance.

I'm now standing in the room I saw earlier, the one with the large bed and the smell of stale coffee. The room feels cavernous. I don't feel comfortable. Who am I? I wonder. Am I the girl, the one with blonde hair? Michael is here. What's he doing here?

There are other people, too, crowding around me. I recognise the three men, the ones from my visions. This is scary. I don't want to be here. I don't like this at all. I want to leave but I feel powerless to move. I'm surrounded, hands are on me, they're touching me. Now I'm being pushed. I try to bat them away, but it's no use; they're too strong and I fall. It feels like slow motion, falling, falling, before I land on the bed.

I'm lying face-down. Harsh, rough hands hold me down, pressing me into the mattress, tugging at me. I hear fabric ripping and realise they've torn away my clothing. I'm powerless, I can't move. My legs are being forced apart and my hips raised so that I'm kneeling.

I try to resist. No, don't do this. Please don't do this. I can't summon the strength to fight; I can't stop them. I sense movement behind me, warmth touching my skin, something hot and hard. I can't see who it is or what he's doing. Yet I know. *No, please no. Don't do this to me.*

I try to speak, but my face has been pressed into the mattress and it stifles my voice. I yelp as I feel pain, a sharp, piercing pain, more movement and more pain, intense pain, deep within me. I open my mouth to scream but nothing comes out.

No, this can't be happening to me! I want it to stop. I sink my face deeper, pressing into the mattress, whimpering. I feel the strain of weight leaning on my back, a hot, rasping breath on my neck, the feel of skin, legs slapping into my thighs, more pain, pounding me into submission. I want this to stop. I'll do anything to make it stop. I bury my head even deeper. If I can smother myself in the mattress, then it will end.

"Briony, what is it? Are you okay?" I hear Alesha's voice.

"You've been crying in your sleep. Wake up," Jenny says.

I'm being manhandled. I feel hands holding me, pulling my shoulders, turning me.

"Don't touch me! Get away from me. Leave me alone!" I shout, finding my voice at last and slapping them away.

My eyes spring open. Seeing them, I jump backwards. Gradually, I take in the scene and realise where I am. I'm lying in bed, in the upstairs room in Margaret's house. Jenny and Alesha are sitting on the edge of the bed. They look worried.

I haul myself into an upright sitting position. My heart is pounding in my chest; my breathing is laboured. I sense my face is wet. I've been crying. I'm wearing my nightdress; it hasn't been stripped from me. I've had a nightmare, a terrible, terrible nightmare. I try to think, to feel. All my body is sensitive, but there is no genuine pain. It wasn't real.

"It was awful," I whisper.

"You're okay, you're safe. You're here with us," Alesha says.

"It's all right," Jenny says. "We'll look after you." She places a hand cautiously on my shoulder and I lean into her.

I smother my face against her chest, seeking warmth and protection. She places her hand behind my head, holding me to her, cradling me.

I don't know how long I sit like this, with Jenny gently rocking me back and forward. Over time, my breathing returns to normal. My face is getting too warm, leaning against her; I'm aware her nightdress is damp from my tears. I sit up. "Thank you," I say.

"Don't thank me. I'm only glad I was here to help you," she replies.

"Are you feeling any better now?" Alesha asks. "What can we do?"

I still feel dazed. "What time is it?" I ask.

Alesha looks at the clock. "It's early, a quarter to six."

"I'm so sorry for waking you," I say. "I didn't mean to..."

"Don't be ridiculous. That's why we're here, so you're not alone We're here to help and support you," Jenny says.

"I think I'm okay now," I say. "You should try to get some more sleep."

"No, only when we're certain you're okay," Alesha says. "Do you feel able to sleep again yourself?"

I try to think. When I close my eyes, I see the images from my nightmare again. "No, not yet."

"In that case, we'll stay talking until you feel you're able to sleep. We're not going to leave you like this," Alesha says and Jenny nods.

My eyes are welling again, but this time from gratitude.

"Would it help to talk?" Alesha asks.

Interspersed with sobs, I tell them what I dreamt. "It felt so real. Now I know that I must be the girl from the visions I had yesterday. Now I know what's happened to me."

"Oh Briony, I'm so sorry. But we're going to help you. You're going to get through this," Jenny says. She smiles and her expression is full of kindness.

"Briony, it was a nightmare," Alesha says. "What you dreamt was horrible, but just because you dreamt it, doesn't mean it's what you went through in real life. There's such a mixture of things you described... people who don't go together, who can't have been together at the same time. You're obviously fearful and confused about not knowing where you've been, but this nightmare could just be your imagination working overtime. It doesn't mean it's a memory."

I want her to be right, but I really don't know anything.

"Think about it," Alesha says. "Earlier tonight, Jeffrey thought someone was playing mind games with you. Someone you know."

"I don't understand," I say.

"I don't claim to have any answers," Alesha continues, "but how does that fit in with you being violently raped, the way you described?"

"I don't know." I say.

"Is there anyone you know who you can imagine doing that?" Jenny asks.

I try to think.

"Could it be Michael? You said you saw him immediately before you dreamt of the attack," Alesha asks.

I shudder at the thought. I know Michael; well, I thought I knew Michael. He's cheated on me and he's been unfair. Much as I'm angry at the way he's treated me, I can't believe he's capable of doing this. What's more, I know him so well that I'm sure I'd recognise the feel of him touching me. I'd know if it was him. "No, it wasn't Michael. I'm certain."

"If not him, then who? Is there anyone you can think of who's capable of this?" Alesha pursues.

I shake my head, lost for any inspiration.

"Whatever the truth is, you're here with us now and you're safe," Jenny says.

I take comfort from my friends' words and over the last few minutes I've become a lot calmer. The episode has left me exhausted. I need to rest. "It's still the middle of the night. Let's try to get some more sleep," I say.

They agree and each return to their beds, although I'm conscious of their eyes watching me. I know they are worried about me and want to make sure I'm okay. I'm so lucky to have such caring friends, but the truth is, right now there's nothing they can do. They need their rest, too. Even if I consider it from a purely selfish point of view, they must be strong and rested if they are to be able to help me. In any event, I must learn to cope by myself. I want to sleep but I'm afraid to close my eyes, terrified of the nightmare returning. I'm content to rest without sleeping, but I'm aware Jenny and Alesha won't leave me if they think I'm awake. I turn over in bed so they can't see my face and I deliberately inhale and exhale, deeply and evenly, gradually increasing in strength and volume. Before long, I hear similar breathing patterns from them.

I turn over again, lying on my back to stare at the ceiling. I want to restore my energy and I know I need rest. I'm desperate for sleep, but I'm too frightened to close my eyes for more than a few seconds at a time, in case I descend back into the horror. I set myself mental challenges, stupid memory games, trying to keep myself awake.

47 HOURS

I'M AWARE OF THE OLD EXPRESSION CLAIMING THAT A watched kettle never boils, but for me, it's a watched clock which never moves. I stare at the digital clock, willing the numbers to change, but each minute feels like an eternity. Being Saturday morning, I don't expect anyone to want to rise early. I'd set myself a target of lying here until eight-thirty, but no sooner has the clock struck eight than I can't take any more and I slip out of bed. I see Alesha and Jenny are sound asleep and, not wanting to disturb them, I decide not to risk showering yet. Instead, I only splash a handful of water over my face, rinse my mouth and throw on my dressing gown before tiptoeing down the stairs, taking care not to step on the creaky board this time.

My plan was to clear away all the dishes and utensils and tidy up the kitchen from any debris we'd created when we had our delightful dinner last night. Only a small gesture, I know, but I want to do something, anything, to evidence my gratitude. I'm so indebted to Margaret and Jeffrey for their support. My plan is frustrated as I find there is nothing for me to do. Every surface has been cleared and cleaned. The dishwasher has not only been loaded, it's run its cycle and been emptied, with all crockery, cutlery, utensils and glassware returned to their cupboards. I realise Margaret and Jeffrey must have cleared up themselves while we were watching the movies. Something else for me to feel guilty about. I must try to be more considerate and proactive.

I lift a glass, pour some water and sit at the table. Only then do I notice this morning's newspaper, lying at the opposite side, on top of the placemat where Jeffrey normally sits. As I reach across to lift it, I can tell it's been well thumbed. I can't help smiling when I turn to the crossword page to find it's already been completed.

I try looking at the clues. Despite joking with Jeffrey yesterday that I might help him, I've never really got into solving cryptic crosswords and I'd have been useless if he had wanted help. I know each compiler has their own style and it can take a while to get familiar with them. After some minutes examining the clues along with the accompanying answers, I start to recognise a pattern. Maybe this is what being an investigator is all about, I think. You look for clues and try to determine a pattern so you can solve the bigger puzzle.

I'm so absorbed in my study that I don't hear Jeffrey come into the kitchen.

"I think you'll find you're too late. I've done that one already," he says.

I practically jump out of my skin.

"I didn't mean to surprise you."

I regain my composure. "Oh, sorry. I didn't hear you come in. I wasn't going to spoil your crossword, honest. I was only trying..."

He bursts out laughing. "It's okay, don't try to explain. I was only winding you up."

I'm tempted to feign falling apart, to burst into tears, to play him at his own game, but I suspect I couldn't pull it off. Even if it worked, it wouldn't be right. It would be cruel. Instead, I laugh along with him. I'm truthful and I explain that I've been trying to work out the compiler's system.

Jeffrey prepares a pot of tea and offers to serve breakfast. After last night's meal and snacks, I'm still full. I couldn't eat another bite. Truth be told, I feel nauseous at the very thought.

50 HOURS

We sit chatting until we're joined by the others. After a lazy start to the morning, we set off for the coast sometime before 11 a.m.

Traffic is sparse, allowing us to make quick progress and soon we're powering down the M77. Clyde1 is set on the radio and, with road noise making any lyrics indistinguishable, all we can hear is a steady thump, thump from the speakers.

"Do you mind if I switch this off? It's giving me a headache," I ask Jenny.

She glances across at me. "On you go. I'd only put it on to hear if there were any traffic warnings. Are you feeling okay? You're looking a bit pale."

I flip down the sun shield to look in the courtesy mirror. Jenny's correct. My skin looks pale and my attempts to disguise the dark rings around my eyes haven't been too successful, not now that I can see myself in daylight. "I'm fine, a bit tired, maybe because I've not had a lot of sleep."

"We were all up into the early hours watching the movies, then you were disturbed by your nightmare. You seemed to drop off not long after you told us about it, but did you get any real rest?" Alesha asks.

"Not a lot," I confess.

"Well, we're going to have a relaxing day today," Jenny says, "no exertion, no stress and no thinking bad thoughts."

I nod to placate her, wishing, if only it could so simple.

Observing that all the cattle seem to be standing in the fields we're passing, Jenny remarks on it being a good indicator for the day staying dry. Looking out, all I see in the sky are wisps of white cloud and I agree with the prediction.

"Good," she says. "We'll be able to take a gentle walk along the front. Now, what's your preference, Ayr, Prestwick or Troon?"

"I'll leave it up to you," I say. "You're the driver."

"I think Troon," Jenny says. "Although Prestwick's easy for parking, it's very empty at this time of year and Ayr is too spread out. Troon can be quiet, too, but the town usually has a bit of life to it. We should be able to find somewhere within easy reach of both the commercial and the front."

"I'm happy with whatever you choose," Alesha comments. "I don't remember ever visiting any of them."

The road takes us past the entrance to Royal Troon Golf Course and we can see many players taking advantage of the pleasant conditions for a day on the links. We continue into the town centre, where we're successful in locating a vacant space in the car park adjacent to the main street.

Albeit the sun's shining and the air is warm, we're each wearing fleeces to provide some protection against the coastal breeze which, in typical fashion, is blowing up the Clyde. Maybe today it's not quite at hurricane level, but I'd be reluctant to try flying a kite in case it swept me away. Thinking about it, the golfers must find it a challenge beyond the regular hazards of the course.

We struggle to walk at a near forty-five-degree angle, leaning into the wind. We laugh about the conditions as we make our way, passing the shops on Main Street, through a grassed area and onwards towards the beach. All three of us kick off our sandals and carry them, our feet sinking slightly when we venture across the sand and towards the sea. As the tide is out and on the turn, there's a broad expanse of beach before the breakers hit the shore at the waterfront.

I look up and down to see very few souls have braved the conditions. Most of the ones that have are wearing heavy jackets and are accompanied by dogs, playing in the surf, none of whom seem at all fazed by the winds.

After only a few minutes, our adventurous spirit wanes and we seek a bench in a more sheltered spot. There, we sit chatting, looking out to sea. Because of the day's brightness, the views across to the Isle of Arran are spectacular and we can see a few small yachts and dinghies as well as the occasional wind surfer fleeing past, taking advantage of the extra propulsion. Much as the day is unseasonably warm, the water looks distinctly chilly and we can see that those who have braved it look cold, despite their wetsuits.

Jenny was smart to think of this. I am unburdened here, and I feel my head is a lot clearer than it's been, albeit a little weather-beaten.

I couldn't even guess how long we've sat, enjoying one another's company and taking in the scenery, before Jenny suggests going somewhere for a bite to eat.

52 HOURS

There's no shortage of sandwich bars and cafés, but we opt instead for some hot food and seek a bar offering pub grub. Once inside, we see a group of people congregating around the bar while the dining area remains quiet. We select a brightly illuminated table close to the window. A nearby radiator is blasting out heat, so we remove our jackets and hang them over our seats.

After spending time in the salt air, I feel thirsty, but, having consumed more alcohol than I'd intended last night, I stick to soda water and lime, a pint. As Jenny's driving, she too, orders a soft drink and Alesha, not to be different, follows our example. I still don't feel like eating anything very heavy, so I order a bowl of homemade lentil soup, accompanied by a wedge of crusty loaf. Alesha has similar, with the package deal of soup and a half sandwich, while Jenny goes for the works, steak pie with mashed potatoes and peas.

While far from the quality of last night's dinner, we're enjoying our meal. The food is wholesome and satisfying. It's becoming a little more difficult to talk, due to a steady increase in volume from other patrons. Although it all sounds good-humoured, there are half a dozen young men clustered close to a large, wall-mounted television. We can hear the South of England accents and we can see they're dressed in Chelsea Football Club tops. They all seem to be guzzling pints of lager with whisky chasers while exchanging banter with some of the locals.

I spot a wall board announcing Sky Sports coverage scheduled for broadcast this afternoon. Chelsea are due to play a Premiership match, with kick-off in less than an hour. Their support, here, is in strong spirits, quite literally.

Jenny suggests we move on to somewhere less noisy and Alesha and I agree. Having consumed a lot of fluid, I think it a good idea to relieve myself in the ladies before departing and Jenny joins me.

The facilities are clean and smell fresh. Above a row of wash-hand basins, there's a large mirror covering one wall. I take the opportunity to touch up my make-up.

I'm leading the way as we leave the bathroom and walk head-long into a tall, gangly young man, one of the football support-ers. He isn't steady on his feet and staggers into me, hands flailing in the air, seeking support to stop himself falling. Whether or not its intentional, one of his hands cups my right breast and the other grasps the bare skin of my upper arm. His hands are coarse. I can feel the roughness of his skin. In an instant, my mind clouds over. I'm transformed back into my vision. Hands touching me everywhere. Lots of hands, rough hands. It's more than I can cope with. I lash out. As a reflex reaction, I bring my knee up into his groin. I scream, I shout. "Rapist! Don't touch me. Get off me. Leave me alone."

The next moments pass in a blur. I'm not aware of what's happening until I find myself sitting in a chair with Jenny and Alesha on either side, each holding one of my hands, seeking to comfort me. It isn't cold, but my whole body is shivering. I recognise the boy who touched me; he's sitting on the floor propped up against the wall opposite me. His face is chalk white, and he's gulping in breaths while nursing his shoulder. In between us, a man is pacing, a tall, muscular man, holding what looks to be a baseball bat, and he's using it to slap into his hand, as if marking time. He's clearly in control of this situation and I suspect he might be the pub owner or manager.

He looks in my direction. "It's up to you how we handle this. We can call in the police and have him charged with sexual assault. I don't know how he might plead but, in any event, it will be very time-consuming all round." He draws in a deep breath before continuing, "I have my doubts whether you'd be best to do that. It seems to me that this young man has had a bit too much to drink and has stepped over the line." He gives the boy a stern look. "For all I know, he might be a serial offender, one we'd be best to get off the streets. On the other hand, perhaps he's not such a bad lad, and he's made a stupid, clumsy mistake while under the influence. The alternative to calling in the authorities is that we assume he's learned from the error of his ways. Then, provided he's prepared to make a full and unqualified apology, we let him go. But only subject to him and his mates leaving now, and they all get the hell out of our nice little town."

I'm only now coming to grasp what's been going on. It seems that after I called out, this man has come running to my defence, armed with the club. Judging from the terrified state of the boy, he's not been slow to use it. The last thing I need right now is another police complaint and another enquiry.

Although he may have been a bit drunk, and he did manhandle me, I suspect he didn't mean any real harm. Truth be told, I may have overreacted to his touch.

I don't want this to go any further. Speaking slowly, carefully and ever so quietly, I say, "Thank you for your help. I think you're right. It would be best to draw a line under this incident and let's all get on with our lives."

I can see the relief in the young man's face and, judging from the reaction of the barman, he, too, is pleased that it won't go any further. Although he can claim what he did was necessary for my defence, he himself could be at risk of being charged with assault.

The boy tells me how sorry he is and, with an air of great despondency, he leaves the bar, accompanied by his friends. His friends aren't so meek as they push him out of the door, turning to mouth profanities at us all as they go.

"You've clearly had a bit of a shock," the man says. "Hang on there for a minute and I'll get you some hot, sweet tea." He signals to a man standing in front of the serving hatch.

I look up, my eyes tearful. "Thank you, you've been very kind." Although I don't normally take sugar in my tea, I know he means well and I decide against taking issue.

"I'm quite impressed with how you handled yourself there," he says. "Have you had self-defence training? You certainly stopped him in his tracks."

My brows furrow, trying to think what he's talking about. Then, realising, I reply, "Not really. I did go to a couple of classes when I was at Uni, but I haven't thought about it since." There's no way I want to explain why I reacted the way I did and truly, I want to put the whole incident behind me and get out of here.

The tea arrives. Fortunately, it's not too hot so I'm able to drink it down quickly, trying not to gag at its sweetness. "I'd like to go now. I need to get some fresh air. Thank you for all your help," I say to the man, who by now has introduced himself as Billy. It occurs to me that, in the last couple of days, I've done little else other than thank people for their help and kindness. It feels strange, I'm not used to this. Normally, I'm the strong one who other people rely on.

"I'm sorry it happened in the first place," he replies, "I have a zero-tolerance policy to this sort of thing in my pub," thus confirming my suspicions about his position. "In hindsight, I should have realised they were getting too well-oiled. I hadn't expected it because they hadn't drunk all that much in here. They must have started getting tanked up before they came in. I wouldn't have served them had I known."

Jenny and Alesha help me to my feet. I shake hands with Billy, and I thank him again before moving towards the door. He walks ahead and checks up and down the street to make sure the boys are nowhere to be seen before we leave.

"The car's just around the corner," Jenny says. "I'll have you back to Glasgow in no time."

"I'd really like to get some fresh air before being cooped up for the journey," I say.

"Let's get out of town first. I doubt they'd try to bother you again, but I don't think we should take the chance," Alesha suggests.

We jump into the Clio, where Jenny fully opens all the

windows. Only a few minutes later, we pull into the car park overlooking the sea at Prestwick. Although the wind has died down considerably, it's fresh and bracing nevertheless. Unhurriedly, we walk up and down the esplanade. We hear young children in the play park. They're whooping in delight, challenging each other to ever more daring feats on a climbing frame. We stand for a while, watching their games. As we do, I feel a sense of relief. I'm okay, I've come through another ordeal and it hasn't harmed me. The incident in the pub may have only been a misunderstanding, or it could have been a deliberate assault. Whatever it was, I handled it and I survived.

I reassure myself that I'm a fighter and I'll cope with anything. Yet there's a nagging doubt. I wonder, if I'm a fighter, why was I unable to stop whatever happened last week? Worse, why do I not even know what it was?

55 HOURS

THE STRONG WINDS HAVE BROUGHT A PROFUSION OF HEAVY clouds. We're lucky it has remained dry. However, the light is fading and Jenny hates driving in the dark. We're on our way back to Glasgow. Hardly a word's been spoken about what happened in the pub. I think the girls are reluctant to bring it up, thinking I'm too fragile to handle the discussion. Although the Clio's comfortable enough to accommodate the three of us, I don't believe there's space for the elephant.

Uncertain of the best way to raise the subject, I decide to tackle it head-on. "I guess that wasn't the best way to recover from last week's ordeal. It all happened so quickly. I'm lucky Billy was there."

"From what I saw, you had it pretty well covered by yourself," Jenny says.

"Really," Alesha replies. "I saw nothing at all. When I heard you scream, I ran over to see why. It only took a second, but by the time I got there, Billy had it under control with the guy on the ground."

"Not the way I saw it," Jenny says. "You were ahead of me going through the door. The guy made a grab for you and you kneed him in the nuts. I don't know who squealed the loudest." Jenny smiles. "Only joking. I don't know how hard you hit him, because he looked ready to fall over anyway. Billy was there in a flash and walloped his arm. He wasn't going anywhere after that."

So now I know. One less thing to wonder about. I'm starting to feel quite pleased with myself when I hear a buzz from my phone. I take it from my bag and look at the incoming text.

Crazy fucking bitch, is all it shows on screen. Without thinking, I click for more.

It continues, *Just because you're unhappy with your life, don't screw with mine.* I scroll down but there's nothing else. It's from Michael.

I'm stunned. I feel as if someone has punched me in the stomach. I start to hyperventilate.

Alesha leans forward and pulls at my shoulder. "What's wrong?"

Jenny takes one look at me and steers the car to the side of the motorway, coming to a halt on the hard shoulder. She switches on her hazard warning lights.

"What is it?" they both ask. My hands are shaking, and I can't get any words out. Instead, I hold up my phone for them to read.

Finally, finding a tearful voice, I whisper, "This is too much. I don't think I can take any more."

"What a bastard! You're better off without him. You've known that for some time, but why on earth has he sent this to you now?" Jenny says.

Thinking about it, I remember what Paula said. "When I was interviewed by the police on Thursday, I was told they'd arrange for their colleagues in Northumbria to interview Michael," I reply. "I didn't tell her not to. Maybe I should call him to explain."

"You most certainly will not," Jenny says. "You don't owe him a thing after the way he treated you."

"Jenny's right. The last thing you need to do is make excuses to him," Alesha adds.

I don't know what to do. I'm confused. When Paula said she'd have him checked out, I was happy thinking Michael might suffer a bit of aggro. But now I'm not so sure. He hates me, judging from the text he sent and that's not right. I can't ignore the good times we spent together. We were partners, so close for so long. Surely it must mean something? What should I do? My indecision seems to be its own answer as I do nothing.

"Let's get you home," Jenny says. She turns off the hazards, waits for a space in the traffic and pulls back onto the motorway. We go straight to the Hamiltons' house and bundle our way back in.

Margaret and Jeffrey can immediately tell something is wrong, but they wait for us to explain, first about the incident in the pub and then about Michael's text. Their faces are grave.

"You timed your return well," Jeffrey says, forcing a smile. "Our kids just left half an hour ago, so you have all our attention. Come in and sit down. Is there anything I can get you? Tea, coffee, something stronger?"

Hearing the details of Michael's text, Jeffrey says, "Leave this with me. I've a friend in Northumbria Constabulary, one I worked with on several cases. Let's see what I can find out."

In the meantime, Margaret takes us through to the kitchen and prepares some tea.

A few minutes later, I jump to my feet as I see Jeffrey return. "I was lucky. He was on duty and made some enquiries. It's what you thought," he says. "Two of their officers went to visit Michael at his home this afternoon. His new girlfriend was there, wondering what was going on and he wasn't best pleased at her knowing they were speaking to him. They asked him about his whereabouts over the last couple of weeks. The most significant part is that he has a secure alibi, so we can rule him out of any involvement in your abduction. He can prove where he was working, and it was nowhere near to Glasgow.

"When they asked him about his visit, two weeks ago, the time when he met you, the girlfriend went apeshit, even more so when she realised you had been alone together. She was furious because he'd spun her a yarn about being somewhere else. Apparently, he'd told her he was spending the weekend with friends in Birmingham. She said she wasn't prepared to take any more of his lies, she'd had enough and she was walking out on him."

"Oh my God!" I say.

"I think this explains his aggression towards you," Jeffrey continues. "It seems he ranted on about you, accusing you of being obsessed with him and fantasising stories in order to control him."

"But I didn't. He's making it all up," I say.

"He claimed that's why he moved away to Newcastle, just to get away from you. He felt claustrophobic and couldn't stand being with you any longer," Jeffrey continues.

Alesha jumps to my defence. "Well, he's obviously lying, because if that was the case, why would he have wanted to come back to Glasgow to see her?"

"As it happens, the officer thought to ask the same question," Jeffrey says. "Michael put on a good show. He claims he was coming to Glasgow to see family and only met with you because he wanted to get back some CDs you'd borrowed. He said you made him go to your flat to retrieve them and when he was there, you seduced him."

My jaw drops in shock. I can't believe what I'm hearing. Why would he say such a horrible thing? It's not true. It can't be true. For it to be true, I'd need to be deluded, but I'm not, am I? I'd know if I was deluded, wouldn't I?

Now, I'm starting to doubt myself. Could Michael possibly be telling the truth? Might I be some mad psycho bitch who's trying to control and delude everyone, myself included? Was it my madness which frightened Michael away? Was it me who seduced him? For that matter, was the whole episode of my disappearance created and controlled by me for some inexplicable reason? Some of the evidence Jeffrey discovered appears to point to it; the photos at the ATM, the television purchase using my debit card. And what about today, the boy in the pub? Did he really assault me or was it the other way around? My head's starting to hurt. I can hardly think anymore. I must try to concentrate.

It's true I like to be organised, and I like to have things my own way, but who doesn't? Yes, I suppose I do like to feel in control, but not the way Michael was suggesting. Michael liked me to organise him; he often told me so. Left to his own devices, he would faff about and not get anything done. He wanted me to take command, particularly in the bedroom. That doesn't make me a control freak, does it? Oh my God, maybe he's right. I'm a monster! How could I not realise?

I draw in a breath. But wait. I'm getting this all out of proportion. Michael's the one who's at fault here. He's been caught out lying to his girlfriend and he's trying to make excuses. He's a lying, cheating bastard, and he's too much of a coward to take responsibility for his own actions. He's trying to turn this against me to save himself and he doesn't care about the consequences. I hadn't considered him to be so devious before, but then I hadn't realised what a cheat he could be. Maybe he's more cunning and manipulative than I'd considered him capable of. I hadn't thought it in his character, but perhaps he really could be the one who organised my abduction. Jeffrey told me that Michael has an alibi, but he could have arranged the whole thing without even having to be here.

Thinking about this, the pain in my head is intensifying. Why would he do that? What possible motive might he have had? I realise I'm overthinking all of this.

"I need to sit down," I say.

"Of course. Are you okay? You look very unsteady." Alesha guides me back into my chair. Jenny leans in and wraps her arm around my shoulder.

"I feel a bit dizzy and my head hurts. Do you have any paracetamol?" I ask.

A few seconds later, Margaret appears at my side. She hands me two tablets along with a glass of water to wash down the pills.

I gulp them down, nodding my thanks and I'm instantly sorry I moved my head.

"Why has he said such horrible things?" I whisper, voicing my thoughts. "He's lying."

"It's a measure of the man," Jeffrey replies. "I came across it all the time when I was in the Force. Suspects who had lied and then, when their stories fell apart, they would lash out at any convenient target."

"You don't believe him," I say with relief.

"Of course not," Jeffrey replies. "After years of working as a detective, I've become a pretty good judge of character." I see Margaret and Alesha are nodding their agreement.

"I can't believe I've been so stupid," I say.

"What do you mean?" Jenny asks.

"All the time I spent with Michael, I trusted him. Up until the time he left to go to Newcastle, even for quite some time after, I thought we'd be together forever. I loved him and I thought he loved me. I'd have done anything for him. What a fool I've been." Tears are running down my cheeks. I don't want to cry; I want to be strong. He's not worthy of my emotions but I can't help it. It's like a bereavement, I think. I'm upset at the loss of the person I thought I knew.

"You're well shot of him," Jenny says. "You're fortunate to have him out of your life. I know you're upset, but one day you'll come to realise how you've had a lucky escape."

I don't know if I'll ever feel lucky about any of this, I think. I want to put on a brave face. "I'm okay," I say. "I shouldn't let it get to me. It was only because of everything else and then the shock of hearing what Michael said about me. I'm feeling a bit stronger now." I move to stand up. I want to be unrestricted. My knees are a bit jelly-like, unable to take my weight and I sink back into the armchair.

---

62 Hours

It's been a traumatic day – more accurately, it's been a traumatic three days, with one crisis coming after another – but I've survived it. On Thursday, I thought things were so bad that they couldn't get any worse. I've been proved wrong and now I wonder what further horrors might lie ahead. I'm shell-shocked and apprehensive. It feels as though the life I knew is in ruins. Reconsidering, after today's revelations, I now know that the life I thought I knew was a sham. As opposed to it being in ruins, it was never there. If I'd had something which was destroyed, then at least I'd have memories to cherish and comfort me. It's now apparent that any recollections I have from my time with Michael are tarnished. He wasn't the man I thought he was. This is becoming harder to take. The memories I'd regarded as being some of the most important in my life are false and, try as I might, my mind remains blank over the period I was missing.

I'm tired and ready for bed. Alesha and Jenny are with me again, as they were last night. The room is dark, with only a glimmer of light filtering in from the hallway, squeezing around the edges of the door. Much as I'm fearful of having bad dreams, I realise I need to sleep. I rest my head on the pillow and will myself to think of pleasant images: light clouds moving across a clear blue sky, fields of corn blowing in the wind, a picturesque mountain scene. I'm feeling drowsy, my eyelids are fluttering. They feel too heavy to hold open. I close them and my retinas retain the image of the fields. I'm slumbering, head sinking deeper into the pillow.

---

72 Hours

I BECOME AWARE OF MOVEMENT. My eyes are closed, and I struggle to prise them open. When I do, I can see clearly. Although the curtains remain closed, I sense bright daylight beyond, filtering through the drapes.

Jenny is across the room from me, getting herself dressed. I can hear water running.

"Jenny, is it morning?" I ask.

"Oh, sorry, did I wake you? I tried to be quiet. It's almost nine o'clock."

Seeing me gathering my bearings, looking around the room,

Jenny answers the unasked question. "Alesha's in the shower. She'll be out in a few moments and you can get freshened up."

I take a moment to realise that it's now morning and I slept soundly through the night without incident; no nightmares, and no visions. I'm pleasantly surprised. As I'm normally an early riser, I've overslept by comparison.

Some minutes later, we're all sitting in the kitchen. Margaret's standing over the stove this time.

"It's a family tradition, a full cooked breakfast on a Sunday morning. It may not be the healthiest of meals, but a little of what you like does you good. Provided it's only once a week, I think our cholesterol levels can stand it." Margaret sounds in a cheerful mood.

Following yesterday's upset, I had no appetite and couldn't bring myself to eat anything. The last food I ate was at lunchtime in Troon. A delicious smell of grilled bacon is wafting through the air and now I feel ravenous. "No argument from me," I say.

After consuming a hearty meal, I'm midway through my second mug of tea before it occurs to me to check my phone. I see a text from Mum and Dad which was sent late last night: *We've docked at Southampton, too late to phone. We'll call you about 10 tomorrow morning before disembarking.*

I'm delighted to hear from them and to know they'll be home soon. Margaret and Jeffrey have been wonderful hosts and Alesha and Jenny have been very supportive. I can't take any credit away from any of them, but it's not the same as having my own family around me; they're not my mum and dad. I feel a warm glow, knowing I'll soon be reunited with my parents. I check the time, only to see they are due to call in less than ten minutes!

A wave of panic runs through me. What am I going to say to them? I didn't want to spoil their special holiday, so I chose not to tell them about my problems. I'll be speaking to them in a few moments' time and I don't know how to best handle it. I want to tell them everything; well, almost everything. There's no need to upset them with explicit details. However, I'm still of the opinion it can wait until they're home.

I tell the others that my parents are due to call me, and I excuse myself from the table. Margaret asks if I need help, if I'd like her to speak to them, to explain. Much as I appreciate the offer, I politely decline. I must deal with this myself.

I go upstairs to the bedroom to afford myself some privacy. Although I don't have a plan, I answer before the second ring. "Mum, Dad, how are you? How was the holiday?"

"We've had a great time," Mum answers. Judging from the echo, I'm certain she must be on speakerphone. Dad will be listening in, too. "But what's the problem you've been having? We sent lots of messages. You didn't answer for ages and when you did get back to us, you didn't tell us anything. We've been very worried. What's wrong? Are you okay?"

Hearing her voice, knowing how much they care, I almost lose my resolve. Tears are welling in my eyes, but I know I mustn't start to cry. If I do, I might break down completely.

"I'm fine now," I lie. "I hadn't meant to upset you. There's nothing I want to discuss on the phone, but rest assured, I'll tell you everything when I see you."

"I don't like the sound of this. Tell me what's going on." I always find it difficult to keep secrets from Mum. It's almost as if she has a sixth sense, able to read what I'm thinking.

"It's okay, Mum. There's nothing that can't wait. I'll see you soon, won't I?" I swallow, trying to choke back the lump developing in my throat.

I interpret the snort she gives in response as being less than approval, but Dad saves me from any further interrogation.

"The porter will be here in a few minutes to help us disembark and take us to the train. We should be in London by lunchtime," he says. "I spoke to our bank's concierge service," Dad continues. "They were very helpful. They were able to get us tickets for this afternoon's matinee and even at this late stage, they could get us a good discount on the list price They also booked us on the last shuttle up from Heathrow tonight. It'll be a bit of a rush, but worth it. We're due to take off at 8.15 p.m., arriving 9.40. We'll get a cab from the airport, so we expect to be home about 10.30."

"Call me back once you're at Heathrow," I say. I wonder if Jenny might be prepared to take me in her car to meet them on their arrival. I don't want to say anything yet as I haven't had an opportunity to ask her. Also, I don't want to panic them by letting them see how anxious I am to see them.

The call over, I return to the kitchen and tell everyone what's been said.

"What are your plans, Briony? You're welcome to stay on here as long as you'd like, but you said you were going to move back in with your parents for a while. Do you want to give them time to get used to being home first?" Margaret asks.

I think through the possibilities. I know Mum and Dad will

only have just returned from holiday and won't have settled back home properly. However, once I've told them everything, and they have had the chance to absorb the information, I'm sure they won't want me to be anywhere else. They'll want me to be with them, where they can look after me. I'm certain they won't want me staying anywhere else.

"I really appreciate your offer and I'm so grateful to you for inviting me in and taking such good care of me." I look around at Jenny and Alesha. "For taking care of us," I correct. "I know Mum and Dad will want me to be with them and I think it would be the best solution."

"I understand," Margaret says, "but I'll leave the room made up for you just in case. It gives you options. Do you have any plans for today?"

"I hadn't thought about it until now," I say. Then, after a moment's consideration, I add, "I'd been hoping my memory might have returned, but nothing has come back. I haven't tried doing anything to trigger it. Are you still willing to drive me about?" I look at Jenny.

"Yes, of course. I'll do everything I can to help, but are you sure? Wouldn't you be better leaving well alone and allowing yourself a chance to heal?" she replies.

Maybe she's right, but whatever the risk, I can't go on like this. "I can't just do nothing. I need to know. What I'd like is for you to take me to all the places I know I could have been during those missing hours. I want to start at my office. It's the last place I know I was, before the blank period. Once there, I could walk in the direction of Alfredo's, to see if it brings any recollection back to me." I look at Jenny to see if she appears willing.

"I'll come, too, if you want," Alesha offers.

I smile to show my appreciation. "After doing that, I'd like to go to the ATMs where my money was withdrawn. I'm certain it wasn't me who took it, but it wouldn't do any harm for me to check it out, to see if it seems at all familiar. Similarly, I want to go to Currys. I don't know if there's much point going there, as I know I was in the store the week before, when I first looked at TVs, but it's worth a try, if you wouldn't mind taking me."

Jenny's face is serious, but nevertheless she nods.

"One other place I want to check is Central Station, as it's the first place I was when I returned to reality."

"I think you have a very good plan. There could be any number of things you might see which could be a catalyst to bringing your memory back," Jeffrey says. "Of course, the police should have already checked out all these places and tried checking if there were any closed-circuit television recordings, but you'll be looking at it from a different perspective."

"When can we go?" I ask Jenny.

She shrugs. "Why not now. We don't have anything else we need to do."

"I don't think you have my numbers saved on your phone in case you want to contact me," Jeffrey says. "Key them in now. In the meantime, I've a few lines of enquiry I'd like to follow."

74 HOURS

Despite it being Sunday, we're faced by traffic delays resulting from street closures because of a charity-sponsored fun run in aid of Dementia UK. The irony is not lost on me. It takes the best part of an hour for us to reach the city centre and find suitable parking near to my office.

We get out, lock up and feed a parking meter. Approaching the front of the building, my nerves are on edge. I haven't ever studied the building before, but I am doing so now; I'm hoping it might offer me some clue. The facade is modern, and it looks to be made from coloured, pre-formed concrete sections and glass. The red colour provides a warm impression, and it blends well with some of the older red sandstone buildings predominant in this part of town. Taking time to gaze up and down the multi-storeys, I'm lost looking for inspiration.

"Let's try inside. I'd like to speak to the security guard," I suggest, and Alesha and Jenny are quick to follow.

I march up to the desk. As it's the weekend, there's only one man on duty to provide service for the occasional workers putting in extra hours. He looks very young; I get the impression he can only recently have left high school. Before I have a chance to speak, he addresses me. "Good morning, Miss Chaplin. I haven't seen much of you lately."

I'm instantly thrown. He recognises me and knows my name. I'm certain that we haven't ever spoken before, although he looks vaguely familiar to me. He's not one of the regulars I speak to on my way in and out of the building.

I'm a little tongue-tied until Alesha comes to my aid. "Hello, Alec. We were wondering if you may be able to help us. Do you remember when I spoke to you on Thursday, I asked you to check your records for a week last Friday, to see when Briony Chaplin left for the night?"

Spotting Alesha, his face melts and takes on the look of a love-struck puppy.

"Y-y-yes, of course, M-M-Miss Forest," he stammers. "I can even remember my answer. It was 7.23 pm."

Seeing her amazement, he stutters his explanation. "I-I-I've a g-g-good memory. Not only that, a couple of police officers were in asking questions. It wasn't m-me, it was Big Campbell who spoke to them. After he let them see the register, they asked to look at video footage of the front door to confirm it, but it didn't show anything. They checked it thoroughly, looking before and after the time Miss Chaplin was signed out, but she wasn't on it."

Realising he's captured our attention, he continues, in a conspiratorial voice, "Of course, she could have left by one of the other exits, maybe the one in the underground car park.

Although we've got security cameras down there, they wouldn't show someone walking out."

It makes perfect sense. Most times I'll use the main entrance. Whenever I'm walking and coming from or going to the station, it's the quickest way. There are many times, though, when I've used the car park. Any time I've gone out to meet a client and been with someone who was driving, it's the obvious route. But there have been other times. If I've been meeting someone, or staying in town for some reason, I'd often use it if it provided a shorter walk to where I was going. There have also been a couple of occasions when I've been leaving at the same time as someone else who was using that exit and because we'd been chatting, I'd go the same way.

I explain my thinking to Alesha and Jenny.

"What direction is Alfredo's from here?" Jenny asks.

I take a moment to work out my bearings before I point towards the west. It's probably a little bit shorter leaving through the basement, but it would be marginal. I doubt I'd make a conscious decision to go that way, for all the difference it would make.

"Did anyone else leave at the same time as me?" I ask.

Alec consults his screen. "As I said before, you were at 7.23. Starting from seven o'clock, Grant Bowman and Celia Hanson both left five minutes before you."

Seeing my mystified expression, he explains, "They work for MacArthur's, the accountancy firm on the eighth floor. Then Dwight Collier from your office was at 7.29. Do you want any more?"

"No, that will do, thanks. Can you tell me who was on duty around the time I left? Maybe I could arrange to speak to them," I ask.

Again, Alec consults his screen. "Campbell did the Friday evening shift. He won't be back on duty until tomorrow morning, although I doubt if he'll be able to help you."

"Why not?" Alesha asks.

He manages his sweetest smile to her, which personally I find a bit creepy. "Although Campbell will have been here, he'd have been in the back room on his break at that time. The police asked him the same question. We always take our evening break around then."

Jenny cuts in, sounding quite agitated. "How on earth can you quote the time people come and go with such accuracy when you don't see them?"

"Oh, that's easy," Alec replies. "We don't actually sign people in and out. They show their identity passes to the scanner, and it records the time of coming or going on the system, linked to the same computer I've been using to answer your questions." He taps the top of the screen.

"So, all you know is the time a card has been presented to the scanner. You can't actually tell for certain if someone has arrived or left," I say.

Alec looks perplexed.

"Anyone could scan someone else's ID to create a record and, unless you saw them, you wouldn't know any different," I explain.

"Yes, but why would they do that?" he asks.

Ignoring his question, I ask, "Would it be okay if we left through the basement? I'd like to take a look in the car park."

His brows furrow, but nevertheless he agrees. "Yes, no problem, but you won't find anything down there. The building's almost empty today, less than half a dozen cars."

We walk over towards the elevator but, before pressing the button, I decide to call Jeffrey to tell him what I've discovered.

"Damned good detective work. If you ever get fed up with marketing, I'm sure I could find you a job," he says. "What do you plan to do next?"

"I've no recollection of leaving the building, irrespective of which exit I used. Judging by the records, I don't appear to have left with anyone, but I can't rely on them. I could have taken the shortcut through the basement, or gone in someone's car. I'm going to look in the car park and then try walking out through the basement exit towards Alfredo's."

"As good a plan as I can think of," Jeffrey says. "Good luck."

75 HOURS

After descending in the lift, we take our time
wandering around the basement. It's familiar to me from the
previous times I've been through it, but it generates no specific
memories. Accompanied by Alesha and Jenny, I experiment
with walking out using both the vehicle and pedestrian exits,
but again no recollections are stirred. I follow the road until it
joins up to the one which I'd have taken had I left by the main
door. I try doubling back before resuming the walk to Alfredo's,
but all is to no avail. We arrive at the bar as it's starting to fill
with lunchtime trade.

I recognise Antonio clearing a table. He's a waiter I've seen
there often. He looks away as I approach.

"Hold on a moment," I call. "I'd like a word. I want to ask you
about..."

His eyes dart around the room. "I've no time just now. We're
too busy. Can you come back later, or maybe another day?" He
turns away, moving towards the bar.

I touch his arm. "Please help me?" I plead, but he doesn't react. Walking away, I feel dejected. I've almost reached the door when Antonio calls me back.

"I'm sorry, "he says. "I heard about what happened. Are you okay now?"

I manage a shrug. "I'm trying to find out where I was..."

He interrupts. "I can't stop to talk right now, but there's nothing I can tell you, anyhow. The police have been in asking questions and no one remembers seeing you that night. They've taken away our security videos."

I manage a weak smile. "Thanks, anyway."

Following the flying start I made talking to Alec, I'm disappointed because I haven't been able to maintain the momentum. However, I'm reassured from my enquiries at both locations by the knowledge of the efforts being made by the police. It's clear they're taking the enquiry seriously.

Now, having less purpose, we saunter back to Jenny's car, only then realising that it's ten minutes beyond the point when her parking ticket expired. We're lucky. On this occasion, there are no wardens about.

After we feed the postcode we've been given for the ATM into Jenny's satnav, we head across town to the west end. We reach the general location only to find we have to drive in ever-increasing circles, looking for somewhere safe to leave the car. Eventually, we find a parking spot in Otago Street, near to the Glasgow University Union and we make our way back to Great Western Road. The area feels familiar to me from my student days, as I have many friends who rented flats near to this location.

77 HOURS

Once we locate the ATM, Alesha and Jenny stand at the corner while I walk up and down the street in close proximity to it. I look all around me, trying to absorb the atmosphere... trying to remember if I've been here.

"I don't recollect this ATM as being one I've ever used." I note it has no features to distinguish it from any other. I see an antiquarian bookshop on the opposite side of the road. It's very distinctive.

"I recognise the bookstore. I know I've seen it before. I can't quite figure out why, but there's something about this vicinity that's familiar."

"What is it? Do you think you've been here recently?" Alesha asks.

"I don't think so," I reply.

I'm racking my brain, trying to remember. Alesha and Jenny

are looking around them for inspiration, but there's nothing they can say or do to help.

I feel this nagging doubt eating away at me, and I don't want to leave until I can work out what it is.

"There are lots of cafés nearby. Let's drop into one, so we can sit in to have a cold drink while you think it over," Alesha suggests.

"Good idea," I reply.

We sit in silence, sipping our drinks. Some time passes before I start to make sense of it. There's not only one, but two times I can recollect having been here in the relatively recent past. It took me a while to realise, because it was dark on both occasions, but the more I think about it, the more certain I am about the location.

"I remember an occasion when I, as one of the team, went to make a presentation to a potential new client in Aberdeen. We left early in the morning, returning well into the evening. Stuart Ronson was driving a large BMW, a seven series, I think," I say.

"You're right. He drives an X7. I had to renew his road tax last week," Alesha says.

I nod. "He dropped each of us home after what had been a very long day. I was the last to leave because my flat was closest to where he lives. I remember we stopped near here for someone to get out. But who was it?" I try to recollect who else was involved in the presentation. "I worked closely with Chrissie on the project, but she had something else on and didn't go to Aberdeen. It was Dwight or Allison. One of them got out of the car here, and the other was dropped in Cardonald. But which was which? I think it was Dwight who was here, and Allison and her husband live in Cardonald."

"I think you're right, because Allison does live on the South Side," Alesha agrees.

"There's something else. I remember walking along this street with Michael. It must have been months ago, back in the spring or maybe even last winter, as I remember there was frost on the ground. We were on our way to a party being held by a relative of his. Michael referred to him as a cousin, but they weren't truly related. It's starting to come back to me now, with clarity," I say.

Both Alesha and Jenny turn towards me, listening intently.

"They'd grown up together, like brothers, he'd said. Their respective parents were close friends and neighbours, and because they'd called each other's parents 'auntie and uncle', they felt that made them cousins. Over the years, the families drifted apart geographically, and their friendship didn't remain as close, but they'd kept in contact, which was why we'd been invited to the party." I close my eyes, trying to concentrate.

"His name was... Billy, or was it Bobby? Something starting with a 'B'. No, neither one is right – it was Barry. Yes, the more I think, the more certain I am. Barry, that's it. Nothing registers with me as a surname."

"Go on," Jenny coaxes.

"I recollect speaking to Michael, saying the bookshop looked interesting, and I told him I wanted to return at a time when it would be open. I do remember walking past here to go to his flat. I can picture it now. Oakfield Avenue. Yes, he lived in a flat in Oakfield Avenue, on the second floor. He wasn't renting, either. He'd only recently completed the purchase. It was a housewarming party."

I close my eyes and I can picture him now; clean shaven, with cropped, fair-coloured hair, medium height and stocky; no, not stocky, he was in truth rather plump. He had a round face and wore tortoiseshell-framed glasses.

"I didn't take to him at all. He was smarmy and arrogant, worked in insurance, if I remember correctly. When Michael introduced us, Barry insisted on kissing me on both cheeks. His face was sweaty, as were his hands holding my arms. He kept hold of me for an uncomfortably long time. He said something stupid to Michael, faking a North of England accent. Something like, 'Looks like you've got a good 'un there.' I remember him leering. He made some very suggestive remarks to me. I didn't think it appropriate. I would never have thought it appropriate from him, but to do so within seconds of meeting me was particularly wrong. It gave me the creeps, a feeling like... I can't put it into words. Anyhow, I don't think I'd have felt safe alone in his company."

"Did anything happen?" Alesha asks.

"No. I was with Michael and there were lots of other people there, so I spent the evening avoiding Barry and instead mixed with others. I didn't think too much more about him at the time. Afterwards, I spoke to Michael. I told him I didn't like Barry, but he made light of it, trying to convince me he was a good guy and I'd get used to his humour. In any event, I never saw him again."

I haven't had any reason to think about Barry for months. Now, I'm near his flat. My previous discomfort with him seems even more pronounced when combined with my growing doubts about Michael.

"The idea of the ATM being only a two-minute walk from Barry's flat is too much of a coincidence for my liking. Is it possible Michael and his 'pervy' cousin have been responsible for my troubles?" I shudder, feeling my skin crawl at the very prospect.

"I'd like to tell Jeffrey about Barry. I don't know how I can find out more about him without asking Michael, although I'm confident Jeffrey will have his ways."

"It will be more difficult without a surname," Jenny says, "but how many people with the name Barry will have purchased a second-floor flat in Oakfield Avenue last winter or spring?"

"I wonder if details might be available from the Land Register?" I conjecture. Although he may only have been joking, Jeffrey was right; I'm now starting to think like a detective. Maybe I'll wait to see what else I can find before speaking to him.

"I remember you talking to me after the party and telling me about it," Jenny says. "You were upset at the time. Wasn't it the cause of a big fight you had with Michael? It was in February. I know because it was about the same time as my birthday and I had been trying to plan a night out with you, but you weren't available the first night I chose because you already had arrangements to go out with Michael."

"Oh God! You're right. We did have a big falling out over it. It's one of the very few times we ever had a serious argument. I'd wanted to leave the party early, but Michael said it would be rude and he insisted we stay on. I'd accused Barry of being the rude one and I felt Michael was taking his side. We didn't speak to each other for nearly a week before he apologised."

"How awful," Alesha says.

"I hadn't made a connection before, but it was less than four weeks later when Michael told me about his new job and moving to Newcastle."

My eyes glaze over as I think about all the possible implications. Could that party be the source of all my problems? If it was Michael and Barry who organised my abduction, what on earth was their motive? Are they mad, or is it something vindictive?

I'm roused from my deliberations by Alesha's question, "What would you like to do now?"

I bring myself back to the here and now. "There's nothing more I can do now. Let's move on and check out the Currys store."

78 HOURS

We trudge back to the car and then drive across to Finnieston. I remember coming here with Jenny before. However, when I walk through the automatic doors of the shop, something strikes me as odd. I have a perplexed expression as I look around me.

"What is it, Briony? Is there something wrong?" Alesha asks.

"I know I've been here before, but it seems different somehow," I reply. "It is the same shop, isn't it?" I ask Jenny.

"Yes, it is," Jenny replies. "I don't know what you mean."

An elderly sales assistant is walking past, and I stop him. "This may sound a stupid question, but has something changed about this store recently?" I ask.

"Very observant of you, young lady. We did a bit of a refit and changed around the layout."

"How long ago?" I ask.

He pauses for a moment, thinking. "A week last Wednesday, eleven days ago. Most of the work was done overnight, but we had to close for part of Thursday morning so there was no danger to the public while it was going on."

"I was right," I say. "The change was made after I was in here with Jenny, but before the television purchase was made."

"What difference does it make?" Jenny asks.

"None, I suppose. It's just reassuring to know I'm not going mad," I say.

"I didn't notice anything different," Jenny says.

"I guess it's from the work I do," I reply. "I notice these sorts of things. Effective marketing relies on good display and product placement." It's only a small thing, but I'm pleased that my thinking powers seem to be getting back to normal.

"Is there anything I can help you with," the man asks.

I tell him about wanting more information about my television purchase.

"Mm, don't know if there's anything I can do. Hold on a minute and I'll get the manager."

While waiting, we pass some time perusing the latest tablets and netbooks. Almost ten minutes pass before we're approached by a very smartly dressed young man. "I'm sorry to have kept you waiting, but I was on a phone call and couldn't get away." He leads us to an area separated from the main showroom by acoustic screens, thus providing some privacy.

After I explain what I'm looking for, he replies, "You do know the police are involved?"

"Yes, of course. I was the one who called them," I tell him.

"Well, there's nothing more I can tell you that you don't already know. We've made enquiries and no one has any recollection of the transaction. The police have taken away our copies of the security tapes. They're wasting their time, because we'd already checked when they first made the enquiry, and there wasn't anything relevant on them."

"As there's nothing more you can tell me, I won't take up any more of your time," I say.

"Before you go, can I ask you a question?" he asks.

I nod.

"The police told me you're claiming someone else made the purchase using your card."

"Yes, it wasn't me."

"Does that mean you don't want the television?"

"That's correct," I reply.

"Well, in that case, would you like us to cancel the delivery? It would be a lot simpler than you having to return it."

It makes perfect sense. Why didn't I think of it myself? Maybe my thinking is still a bit warped. "Yes, please."

"If you have the payment card with you, then I can reverse the transaction."

Damn, I don't have the card and I don't have any idea what's happened to it. Besides, I remember, the bank was going to put a stop on the account. "Is there another way? My card is missing," I say.

"There is," he says, "but it's a lot more complicated." We take forty minutes to complete the paperwork to formally cancel my purchase and to arrange for a rebate of my payment to be sent to me by cheque to my parents' address. I'm grateful, delighted to have recovered some of my money, although I'm feeling slightly cross-eyed by the end of the process.

80 HOURS

CENTRAL STATION IS OUR LAST PLANNED STOP. I'M BOTH exhilarated by what I've achieved and exhausted by the effort of it all. I don't expect to be here for long as I don't think I'll learn much. If it's anything like the other locations, the police will have already requested any video footage of the concourse from Thursday morning. I doubt there'll be anyone here for me to talk to, so my main purpose is to see if the experience of standing or walking through the station is enough to bring any recollection.

As we think we'll be in and out in a few minutes, Jenny agrees to park near the Union Street entrance and wait with the car while Alesha and I go to look.

We climb the stairs and take a few steps forward, then stop to look around. It's late Sunday afternoon and there are not many people about. A lot of the sales stands are closed. I know the station well as, when living with my parents in Giffnock, the train was my main mode of transport into town. Since I moved into the flat, I've more often used a bus. I look around me, seeing the clock, the shell, the destination screens, the hot food outlets and the shops. All look the same as normal, less busy, less frantic, but normal. I examine the floor; the tiles where I slipped are now dry, the bench I hurt my leg on looks the same. I see nothing to trigger any memory of how I arrived here on Thursday. I walk to the exit I used on Monday, then return the way I've come. My memory is clear of being in the station on Thursday. I remember the slippery surface, falling, hurting myself and breaking my shoe, then staggering away. But it all starts here. There's no recollection whatsoever of anything before.

Although I hadn't expected to find anything, I'm disappointed to confirm my prediction. With Alesha in tow, I return to Jenny and the car.

We travel back to the Hamiltons' house and, on the way, I ask Jenny if she'd mind doing the airport pick-up. She almost seems pleased to be asked, which makes us both happy.

I'm keen to tell Jeffrey about Barry and about my further concerns regarding Michael, but before I get a chance, he tells he has his own information to impart, and he wants to speak to me privately. I'm immediately alert because he doesn't appear to want Alesha or Jenny to know. What can it be? As they already know so much, I expect the news to be significant for him to want to reveal it to me with them not present.

We go into his office and he asks me to sit down.

"I've made a fair bit of progress," he says. "First of all, I think I've found your rapists."

It's lucky he told me to sit first because, had I been standing, I might have collapsed. My jaw drops and I feel hollow inside.

"Really? You've found them? Have you told the police so they can pick them up?"

"I haven't said anything to anyone yet, not even Margaret. I wanted to check with you first, to make certain I have the right guys."

I'm stunned and I feel sick. "Who are they?" I ask.

"Well, first, I want you to relax," he says. "It's not what you may think. I did an online search using the descriptions you gave me, and I think I've found who it was. If you're feeling strong enough, I'd like to show you some video footage I downloaded. Be warned, it's not for the faint-hearted." His face is grim.

How do I know if I can take this? I don't know what effect it will have on me, but I can't say no. I need to find out. I nod my head and say, "Please let me see it," my voice barely more than a whisper.

As Jeffrey's fingers fly across his keyboard, his screen comes to life. I look with increasing shock at what it reveals, a sick feeling deep in my stomach. It's as if Jeffrey has somehow managed to capture the visions which have taunted me. The three men. The girl lying naked on the bed. The men are undressing, touching her, instructing her, manoeuvring and abusing her, hurting her. I know and dread what comes next. I've experienced it in my nightmares and maybe not only in my nightmares. I don't want to see any more. I turn away, my mouth dry, my stomach retching.

With a mounting feeling of panic, a thought comes into my head: how did Jeffrey find this? As he said he searched online, then it must be available to anyone who knows how to look for it, or anyone who frequents this type of material. With growing trepidation, I again wonder if the girl is me. Could these be pictures of men having sex with me? Has someone video-recorded it and are they available freely to anyone who knows how to find them on the internet? Pictures of me being violated, penetrated, raped and brutalised. I think I'm going to faint, and I tighten my grip on the arms of the chair. My vision is blurring, my eyes fill with tears. Much as it disgusts me, I must look back at the screen to see if it really is me, but by the time I do, the screen is already blank.

Jeffrey takes my hand. "I'm sorry I had to show you that. Are these the men, the ones from your visions?"

I nod my head. "The girl, is it me?" I blurt, in between sobs.

"Good God, no! Why would you think that?" he replies.

"My visions, I told you about them. My fear has been that they're flashes of memory of what's been done to me. The girl looks very like me. How can you be so sure?"

"Oh, Briony, I'm sorry. I thought you understood. This girl isn't you. It can't be. The video was posted online months ago, long before you went missing."

I exhale heavily, only now realising my breath had been held. I feel mystified.

"I had a theory, and it's proved to be right. I didn't want to say anything to you to start with, in case I was wrong, because I was afraid to create false hope. That's why I waited until I knew more. One doubt I had was because of the clarity of your visions when you had no other memories. The marks on your wrists and ankles suggested you'd been restrained, and this added to the possibility. You said that after your medical examination you were told there was no evidence of violent sex and I thought that unlikely, if you'd been the subject in your vision."

He pauses to ensure I'm following what he's saying. "Taking these things together, I thought a likely scenario could be if they had tied you into a chair and forced you to watch pornographic images. I checked online, using the descriptions you'd given me, and I managed to track down the ones I showed you, and a lot more which are similar." He squeezes my hand, offering reassurance. "When I started talking to you just now, I said I was going to show you the video footage. Because I was so excited to have found them and I needed you to confirm I had the right ones, I didn't properly explain what I'd found. I'm sorry. I didn't mean to upset you."

I'm still in shock but overcome with relief. "So the girl isn't me. She's some other victim, poor girl."

"She might even be a willing participant or an actress," Jeffrey says. "She didn't look distressed, although it's fairly certain she's been drugged. Whether of her own choosing or not, we can't know. The same men were in other films, too, with different girls. I showed you this one because it was the closest in description to what you'd told me you'd seen. The films were all posted to a website hosted in Florida. They violate our sense of decency. However, strictly speaking, they are not illegal unless we can prove the girls were abused against their will. In any case, it's outside the jurisdiction of our own police to investigate films made in the USA, even if they did have the resources or the motivation to follow them up."

I feel as if a giant weight has been lifted from my shoulders. "So, it wasn't me," I repeat. "I wasn't gang-raped."

"It definitely wasn't you in the videos," Jeffrey corrects. "I can't say for certain that you haven't been sexually assaulted. Perhaps the medical report will be able to tell you more – or, better still, if you get your memory back. I don't think it was accidental that you were shown films involving a girl who might easily be mistaken for you."

"But why?" I ask.

"Whoever abducted you and showed you these videos must have been trying to make you doubt whether anything had happened to you. Worse still, there could be an implied threat. Until we get to the bottom of this, you need to be very careful."

Although I am relieved to know the visions weren't about me, Jeffrey's words hit me hard. I'm not too much further forward, because I still don't know what happened to me and I now have further confirmation of someone messing with my head. I place my hands over my face. "Why would someone do this to me?"

"We don't know yet, Briony, but we are making progress. We're going to find out."

Jeffrey passes me some tissues. I wipe away my tears and blow my nose. It occurs to me that I must look quite a state, eyes red and runny makeup, but I don't care.

"If you're okay, Briony, I've other things to talk to you about... unrelated things. Do you want to take a break, maybe get a cup of tea or something?"

"No, I'll be okay. I want to keep going. I just need a minute or two to get used to the idea. Maybe I'll get a glass of water."

"You can get some from the kitchen, or I have bottled water here, if you like."

I accept the bottle with gratitude.

81 HOURS

Now that I've started, I'd rather keep going. I tell Jeffrey about my recollection of the party and my suspicions of Barry and Michael perhaps being involved.

"Very interesting," Jeffrey says. "I must do some more digging. Northumbria Police said they'd checked Michael's alibi. I'd like them to double-check in case they've missed something."

"Is there anything else?" I ask

Normally Jeffrey is very decisive but, on this occasion, he turns away; he looks uncertain. "What is it?" I persist.

"I'm not certain if this is the best time," he says.

"You have to, now you've started," I say

"I don't have all the information yet," he says.

"Tell me what you know, I insist," I continue.

Jeffrey purses his lips, considering. "Okay, but please remember I'm at an early stage in this. I received a call this afternoon from a PC Firestone. She works in Zoe's team. She'd been given the task to research the background on your birth parents."

"Yes, what about them?" I ask. I don't know what's coming but, from Jeffrey's serious expression, I suspect I'm not going to like it. Do I want to hear this? Until now, I've avoided looking into my birth family. I realise this will be a turning point. Once I learn something, I can no longer choose to ignore it.

"When you were asked about your birth parents, you told Paula that your mother gave you up for adoption shortly after your birth because she had a terminal condition," Jeffrey says.

"Yes, I told her that, because it was true. At least, that's what I've always been led to believe."

"This may come as a shock, then, because it's not true," Jeffrey says.

"What? How?" I ask.

"It's true your mother gave you up for adoption shortly after your birth and she died within a year afterwards. However, it wasn't from a terminal illness. Not one showing on her medical records," Jeffrey says.

"What then?" I ask.

"I'm sorry to tell you, it was a suicide. She took her own life," he says.

"But why? Maybe she knew she was going to die, anyhow and didn't want to suffer a slow, painful death," I suggest.

"Perhaps you're right," he says, although his demeanour implies otherwise. "Until now, we've seen nothing to suggest she had any physical impairment, although Firestone is making further enquiries. We do know she had been diagnosed with clinical depression."

I realise Jeffrey is trying to be kind, but my interpretation of what he's really saying is, my mother had mental health issues. What are the implications? Might I, too, have issues which I've inherited? Paula asked me about family; she wanted to know if there was any history of dementia. I'd dismissed the possibility of it being significant to my memory gap, but now... but now I can't be so sure. Might my disappearance have nothing to do with Michael and Barry – or anyone else, for that matter? Could it be more innocent than I'd suspected? Could it all be down to me? Is it possible I have a mental health problem which has been the cause?

But wait, I'm overreacting. Jeffrey found the videos of the abuses which were in my visions. I didn't make them up. Surely it proves there was someone else involved who inflicted them on me? There can't be any other explanation. Not unless I have some sort of multiple personality disorder. I'm going to drive myself insane thinking through these possibilities. Of course, I might already be mad. Although I feel sure I'm not insane, isn't it true any mad person would claim the same? This isn't good. I'm descending into a malaise and I can't afford to if I'm going to get any answers. I need to shake myself out of this. I need to find out more about my birth mother.

"Is there anything else you can tell me about her?"

Jeffrey looks pensive. "No, there isn't. I'm sorry."

"You're holding out on me. There's more," I accuse.

"I have no more information for you about your mother," he replies.

Somehow, I know he's not telling me everything. I suspect he's not prepared to lie, but neither is he telling me the whole truth. "There's something else, isn't there? What is it?"

Jeffrey looks at the floor. He can't meet my gaze.

"What is it?" I persist, my voice becoming shrill.

"Okay, I'll tell you, but it could mean nothing. In fact, I think there's been a mistake. Wrong information may have been keyed into the data register. We've been trying to have it rechecked. We won't know for certain until tomorrow," he says.

I pull at his arm. "Please, Jeffrey, tell me."

"Firestone told me the first thing she did was pull a copy of your original birth certificate," he pauses.

"Yes, go on."

"It lists your father on the birth certificate," he says.

"Of course," I reply. "A birth certificate will normally state who the father is. So, tell me. Who is my biological father?"

Jeffrey looks straight at me. "Your father, Arthur James Chaplin. He's the one who's listed as your father on your original birth certificate."

"It can't be! He's my adoptive father, not my biological one." My mouth gapes in astonishment. Although my eyes are open wide, I can't see anything. I'm staring at nothingness. I do the mental arithmetic. "I'm now twenty-five years old. Only this week, Mum and Dad celebrated their thirtieth anniversary. They'd been married for more than four years by the time I was born, three and a half years when I was conceived."

They have always been such a close couple. They do everything together. It has never occurred to me that Dad could have had a fling with someone else; that he could have fathered a child with them.

"Yes, we made the same calculation. It could be an innocent mistake made when the records were updated for your adoption and the wrong box was filled in. It's Sunday. We'll check with the Registrar once their office is open. The other obvious route is to speak to your father, but we know he's not back home yet after his holiday and it's not the sort of question we'd want to ask without seeing him."

"I'll be seeing him tonight," I say.

"I really don't think you should say..." Jeffrey starts.

"I don't know if I can wait until tomorrow. I don't know if I'll be able to ask him, either," I say.

I feel very tired. I'm leaden. As Jeffrey says, someone may have made an administrative error, but what if it's true? How could Dad, the man I've always known as my dad, as my adoptive dad, actually be my birth father? If it's true, then why wouldn't he have told me? What could it mean? Does Mum know? If so, what does she think about it? If not, then what effect will it have if the news comes out? Surely, it must be a mistake? Oh my God, this is all too much to take in.

"Briony, are you okay? I didn't mean for you to hear all of this, not all at once. It must have come as a shock. After the day you've already had, maybe you should get a lie-down. A rest might help you come to terms with it all. Get a rest now, there's plenty of time before your parents arrive home. We have cold cuts available for supper so you can eat anytime you want," Jeffrey says.

"I don't know," I say. "I think I need to keep going. If I lie down now, I'm not sure I'll want to get up. What time is it now?" I check, to see it's already gone six. I want Jenny to take me to collect my parents from Glasgow Airport. As their flight isn't due to land until 9.40, we won't need to leave for hours.

"Does anyone else know any of this?" I ask.

"I haven't told anyone about the videos and your birth parents. Firestone will have completed a report of what she's working on, but Zoe's the only one who'll see it for now."

"Please don't say anything to anyone, not even Margaret. I don't want anyone to know any of it until I find out the truth," I ask.

"Of course I won't, it's your private business," Jeffrey says.

"But what can we say? They're going to be curious. They'll want to know what we've been talking about all this time," I say.

"Fair point. We can tell them I've been outlining to you the police investigation procedures, and how the enquiry will move forward. We can truthfully say I've passed on information received so far on their enquiries into your birth parents, albeit they haven't got anything conclusive," he suggests.

"It might work, but what if they ask why you had to see me alone?"

"They may wonder, but I very much doubt they'd ask the question. I know Margaret certainly won't." Jeffrey appears to be considering something for a second. "Even if someone does ask, then I can tell them it's a matter of professional ethics. You are technically my client, and if I'm passing information from an investigation on to a client, then it has to be on a one-to-one basis unless the client has specifically requested otherwise."

81.5 HOURS

Before leaving Jeffrey's office, I lift a mirror to check and touch up my make-up. I don't want it to look too obvious that I've been crying. I step into the hall and Jeffrey follows. As I can hear the television playing in the lounge, I expect to find everyone there. When I go in, I find Margaret draped across a couch, a paperback in her hand, paying scant attention to the news programme playing in the background. I look around but nobody else is there.

Hearing me enter the room, she closes her book and places it on the coffee table beside her. "Alesha's off home. As she didn't want to interrupt you, she asked me to say goodbye for her. The girls were saying how Jenny was planning to take you to the airport and thought if Alesha went home, she'd have a chance to catch up with her boyfriend for a bit before the weekend was over. Jenny's giving her a lift. I think she was going to see someone, too, before coming back for you."

"Boyfriend? I didn't know Alesha had a boyfriend. She hadn't said anything to me."

"Oh yes," Margaret replies. "They've been an item for several months now."

It hadn't occurred to me. Until three days ago, I hardly knew Alesha existed and in this short period of time she's become a close friend and confidant. She's been unbelievably kind and caring and I don't know how I'd have managed without her support. She's been with me, hearing me confide so many of my most intimate secrets. Now, thinking about it, I know next to nothing about her.

It came as a surprise when Margaret told me she had a boyfriend. I never thought to ask her, to ask her about anything, in fact. She mentioned parents, but I don't know if she has siblings, about her education, anything. It's all been about me. I've been so selfish. This isn't like me, either, I think. Normally, I take a keen interest in other people, particularly in my friends and their lives. Some people might even accuse me of being nosy, because I like to know what's going on, I like to be helpful and supportive. This time, Alesha has been the supportive one and I've been weak and self-obsessed. Maybe the last few days have been unusual, but if I'm going to get my life back, then I need to act normally again, to stop being a victim. To start with, I ought to call her and thank her for all her help. But I can't even make that start, because I don't have her number. What's more, if she's finally getting some time to herself, some private time to catch up with her boyfriend, then I shouldn't be intruding, or I'd only be compounding my felony.

"How long ago did they leave?" I ask.

"Not long, about twenty minutes, I think," Margaret replies.

If she left for home only twenty minutes ago, then I shouldn't be interrupting anything. "Do you have her mobile number?" I ask.

Margaret gives me her number and I feed it into my phone's memory. I call her to thank her for all her help. I apologise, sincerely, asking her to forgive my selfishness and I promise to be a better friend to her.

She bats aside my apology, claiming to understand the trauma I've been through and promising for us to get together again soon. We wish one another a pleasant evening.

The call ends. I'm left, phone in hand, wondering what traumas Alesha may have suffered to make her so understanding. I want to be a good friend to her. For this to be the case, I know I shouldn't intrude. I need to leave her to do the talking, if and when she chooses.

83 HOURS

On his arrival at Heathrow, Dad phones to tell me how much he and Mum enjoyed the show. "A perfect way to end our holiday," he says. He confirms their flight is shown as being on schedule and tells me it will be easiest for them to book a cab to take them home. He has the number of a reliable local company. I tell him no, insisting I'll be there for them with Jenny at the arrivals gate.

Dad relents. "If you insist on coming to collect us, then we'd be very grateful. However, airport parking can cost a small fortune. The best way is if you stay outside the perimeter until after we've landed. I'll phone you once we've collected our cases and you can then head to the pick-up point. We should then arrive there at about the same time. Doing it this way only costs a couple of quid instead of needing to take the proverbial remortgage on your house. The only problem is, you're only allowed to stop there for a few minutes."

"Sounds like a plan," I reply. I've no sooner finished the call before Jenny arrives back at the Hamiltons'. "I'd like to leave early so I can go to my flat and collect some clothes," I say. "I also want to pick up some groceries; essentials like milk, bread and butter, so the fridge won't be empty for them coming back. I know it will be late, but they might fancy some tea and toast after all their travelling."

"Not a problem," Jenny replies. "We drive past Sainsbury's, so you can drop in on the way."

I collect my belongings from the bedroom and go to say goodbye to Jeffrey and Margaret. My eyes are welling up as I hug each of them in turn, clinging on, not certain I ever want to let go. "I can't thank you enough," I say, and I truly mean it.

"It doesn't need to be a big emotional goodbye," Jeffrey says. "You're always welcome to visit us. What's more, we've a lot to follow up on and we're almost certainly going to be talking tomorrow. I'm sure you'll be seeing Margaret soon. You're a lot stronger now and once you've a few more things sorted out, you'll be ready to return to work."

I dab my eyes with a tissue as we drive away. Although sorry to be leaving the comfort and security provided by the Hamiltons, I'm happy at the prospect of being with my mum and dad. Happy, yes, but also apprehensive.

84 HOURS

Having collected some shopping and fresh clothes, we're now driving towards Paisley on our way to the airport. Somewhat belatedly, I remember the volume of luggage Mum and Dad packed for the cruise.

"Will we able to get everything in?" I ask Jenny, after explaining my concern.

"If their packing was within the baggage allowance they were permitted to fly with, then I'm certain I won't have a problem fitting it in the boot. In anticipation, I emptied everything I didn't need to be carrying when I went home. Let's face it, if the worst comes to the worst, then we can always put a bag on the front seat, and you can travel in the back, between your folks."

Although Mum is average in size, Dad's a big man, six-foot-three tall, eighteen stone and muscular from working out. I'd expected he'd sit in the front. I wouldn't relish being crushed in the back between him and Mum. "I'm sorry for panicking," I say. "You'd think I had enough problems to sort out, without looking for ones that don't exist."

Jenny takes her hand off the steering wheel long enough to give my arm a squeeze. "You're going to be all right. Trust me."

As I didn't want to risk arriving late, I insisted we left early. Consequently, we arrive at the airport a full fifteen minutes before the plane is due to land. We follow Dad's instructions to find a place to wait and park adjacent to a filling station. Jenny switches off the engine. I decline her offer to play some music as I feel tense and don't want to risk aggravating a headache. Instead, we sit in silence, watching traffic come and go.

85 HOURS

When I use my phone to check online, I find the plane has arrived, on time. By ten o'clock, I'm fearing there may be a problem... perhaps, they may have missed their flight. Then Dad's call comes through. "It took ages for them to unload our luggage, but we have it now. We'll be out in a few minutes. Do you know where to go?"

Jenny's already restarted the car and we take time to reach the pick-up point. I'm out of the car, looking, and sure enough, I catch sight of them a couple of minutes later. Even from a distance, I can see they're looking well and happy, although tired from a long day of travelling. Both are well tanned and, with Dad's boyish face and Mum's trim figure, they appear much younger than their fifty-two years. Dad's pushing a luggage trolley weighed down by two large, hard-shell cases plus a cabin bag. Mum is walking alongside, pulling her own small, wheeled case.

Seeing them, all my intentions for a composed greeting evaporate. Like a toddler being 'rescued' by their parents after a first day at nursery, I run to embrace them, almost bowling them over, throwing my arms around Mum's neck and hugging her close.

"Oh Mum, I'm so happy to see you," I say. Dad stops the trolley and turns towards me. I pull him into our family hug.

"I'm happy to see you, too," Dad says in a jocular voice.

Mum is more circumspect. "Much as I'm delighted with you being happy to see us, these displays of emotion aren't like you. What's wrong, Briony?"

We hear Jenny's voice calling to us, "Hurry up, you lot! I'm only allowed to stop here for ten minutes and we're already half-way through."

Mum reluctantly releases me, although her face is grave and her eyes don't leave my face. Dad keeps one arm around my shoulder as he resumes pushing the luggage to the car. Jenny is already out, opening the tailgate. Effortlessly, Dad slings the cases into the boot, squeezing them into the small space, where anyone of lesser stature would have struggled to manoeuvre them.

The car loaded, Dad takes the front seat beside Jenny and I sit in the back beside Mum.

The moment the car is in motion, Mum resumes her interrogation of me.

Although this is not how I'd have wanted to tell them, I start to explain about my memory gap and 'waking' on Thursday with no idea of where I'd been, or what had happened in the previous week.

Although Dad is sitting in front, he has turned in his seat and is leaning into the back to hear what I'm saying. "How can you not know what's happened to you for the best part of a week?" he asks. "There's more to this. There's something you're not telling us."

"I've no solid recollection of anything for all those days. I remember being at work on Friday, then everything is hazy until Thursday morning. When I try to think about it, my mind is blank. The police are investigating and..."

"You couldn't have taken anything, a drug of some type?" Mum asks.

"I don't do drugs," I snap. "All the evidence points to me being abducted. I can only imagine that someone may have done it to me."

"You must know something. Why would anyone do this to you?" Dad says. He looks shocked. "Have you been molested? Has someone..." He can't bring himself to say what he dreads.

"I don't know. I had a forensic medical examination on Thursday, but the results aren't back yet."

"Tell them about your visions," Jenny says, taking the conversation somewhere I don't want to go right now.

I shoot her a shrivelling look, although I'm wasting my time as her attention is on the road. "No, I don't want to. Not now," I reply

"What visions? What's this all about?" Dad pursues.

"I've no proper memories of what happened last week, but when I try to think about it, I do get some images in my head. It's difficult for me to talk about it. Can we wait until we're home to discuss this, please?"

"Why didn't you tell us sooner? We could have helped. We could have been here for you. You shouldn't have had to face this on your own," Mum says.

"I told her she should call you," Jenny says.

I'm irritated. "Please stay out of this, Jenny. It's hard enough for me to deal with, without you telling me what I should and shouldn't have done." Turning to Mum, I reply, "I wanted to tell you, truly I did. I wanted to have you beside me. But I knew there was nothing you'd be able to do which could have changed what I had to go through, and I didn't want to spoil your celebration. You'd been planning your holiday for ages and, from what I've heard, you've had a great time." I manage a weak smile. "What would have been the point in ruining it for you, when it wouldn't have made a difference?"

"I feel awful to think we were away having a good time while you were suffering," Mum says.

"But would you have felt any better if you'd been suffering along with me?"

"We could have held you and given you support. We could have helped you," she replies.

"I know, but it wouldn't have changed anything," I say. "Besides, I wasn't alone. I had Jenny and Alesha and I had Margaret and Jeffrey."

"Who's Alesha, Margaret and Jeffrey? I haven't heard you mention them before," Dad asks.

"Alesha is a girl who works in my office. She's become a very close friend. She's been very supportive. Margaret Hamilton is my boss at work. After she heard about my problem, she insisted I come and stay with her and her husband until you got home. They let Jenny and Alesha stay with me, too."

"You told us before about a boss called Margaret at your work, who you couldn't stand. It can't be the same person, can it?" Dad asks.

"Actually, it is. I'd misjudged her before. She's really kind and..."

"Why would she want you to stay with her? Is she something to do with you going missing? And what about this Jeffrey fellow?" Dad asks.

"Jeffrey's her husband. He's a retired police officer and now he's an independent private detective. He offered to help me investigate what happened."

"I don't understand," Mum says. "Why would you want to go to live at their house?"

"Please stop quizzing me. I'll tell you everything... everything I know, but please let me do it in my own way." I start to cry.

"Oh Briony, I'm sorry. I didn't mean to upset you. I'm just so shocked. I want to help you every way I can. It's all so difficult to take in." She releases her seat belt and moves closer to me, cradling my head to her bosom. It feels good to have my mum to hold on to.

Amid sobs, I start to explain how I didn't feel comfortable in my flat, how Margaret came to see me and offered to look after me. I tell them how kind and generous both she and Jeffrey have been. "They said you could call and speak to them any time, if it would help."

86 HOURS

We're travelling through Giffnock. Nearly home. Jenny turns off Fenwick Road onto Merryburn Avenue and after a short distance she pulls to a halt in front of our driveway.

We all disembark and use our combined efforts to lug the cases to the front door. Only after I see Dad struggling to open up, pushing against a barrier of mail which has arrived while they were on holiday, do I remember my dishonoured promise to check the house every couple of days. I've let them down. I do have a reasonable explanation to excuse my failure for a large part of the time. However, I chide myself for not thinking to come round prior to doing the airport pick-up. Too late to do anything about it now. Although Mum and Dad say nothing, I hope they're not too disappointed in me.

After we deposit the baggage in the hall, we all sink into chairs in the lounge. Mum is certainly pleased when I produce the shopping I'd purchased earlier. "Thanks for doing that, luv," she says. "I think we could all use a nice cup of tea."

"Jenny, I really appreciate you taking me to collect Mum and Dad from the airport. You've been incredibly supportive when I've needed you over the last few days. I know you've been my best friend for more than ten years, but you've certainly proved yourself recently," I say. "It's nearly eleven now, and I know you have an early start in the morning. I don't want to be even more of a burden than I've already been. Would you like to get away?"

I catch her exchanging furtive glances with Mum and Dad. No doubt she's checking they're okay looking after me without her help.

She stifles a yawn. "Yes, you're right. I really should get going. Let me know how you get on tomorrow." I stand to hug her before she leaves. Mum, too, embraces her before she reaches the door and Dad expresses his gratitude.

"Tea for three then," Mum says, picking up the bag of groceries I'd brought in.

Over the next two or more hours, I tell Mum and Dad about my last four days. Dad again asks about the visions. I hadn't wanted to discuss it in the car and I still don't. However, I give a bland indication of the content without going into graphic detail and then I explain to them what Jeffrey found and our realisation that someone appears to have targeted me. Without mentioning the weekend I spent with him, I tell them, too, about my concerns regarding Michael and his friend, Barry, also telling them about the debit card transactions and the coincidental location of the ATM.

Whether it's as a result of the late hour, exhaustion from travelling or hearing about my ordeal, I can't judge, but I'm certain

Mum and Dad's tans have faded already. Dad's face looks positively pale.

89 HOURS

We're all exhausted, and I haven't even started to ask about my birth certificate. I wanted to speak to Dad, alone in the first instance, but so far, we haven't had the opportunity. It will need to wait for another day as I suspect none of us has the strength or commitment to tackle it now.

I go to my bedroom. It's the same one I used from childhood up until the time I moved into my flat. It hasn't altered; it still has the same boy-band posters on the wall, unchanged since my teens, the same cuddly toys on my bed and on a shelf. I wash, get changed and tuck the quilt around myself. It's only a few minutes before Mum comes to check on me. "Call me if there's anything you need. It doesn't matter about the time, just call me," she says.

Although I feel very tired, I sleep fitfully. I don't know how much time has passed but I can hear voices, arguing. I hear Mum's voice. "Calm down, Arthur. You're being ridiculous."

Dad is saying, "I tell you, I'm going to find that boy and wring his neck. I'll make him sorry he'd ever met this family. I'll kill him."

Mum again. "Enough, Arthur! Shush now. You don't want Briony to hear you."

I try to hear more, but there's nothing.

I doze off again. The images come back into my mind. The three men again. Odious as they are, they don't seem as threatening now that I know the visions are derived from seeing videos. I don't know if it's because I'm seeing them with greater clarity, or if it's my new knowledge filling in the gaps, but the images are framed now and I'm watching them on a television screen. I'm also getting more of an impression of the room I was in. The same pictures I saw before; the wall-mounted television, the computer workstation, the table and chairs, the heavy drapes. This must be the room I was held in, kept strapped to a chair while I was made to watch the pornographic videos. Again, I look at the table; I see the box holding bottles, the edge of a label: 'something pharmaceuticals', it says. I can't make out anything else.

I must have nodded off again. I wake feeling uneasy, as if I'm being watched. I switch on the bedside lamp, noticing it's 5.14am, and see rows of eyes watching me. It's the shelf holding my childhood dolls and they're all facing towards me. Why have I kept them? I should have thrown them out or given them away. I'm an adult. What am I doing with my room stacked with toys? I'm twenty-five years old, for God's sake. I haven't played with them in years, not since primary school, most likely.

Dad never likes throwing away anything, so I must have inherited the trait from him. It might even be in my genes if he's my biological father. Not getting rid of them is one thing; but keeping them sitting on a shelf is too much. I want to clear them out, the dolls, the posters, all the other keepsakes, but it's the middle of the night. I'll do it in the morning, but for now, I can stop them watching me. Wearily, I drag myself from bed and clear everything off the shelf, placing the toys on the floor in the corner of my room, all carefully positioned to face the wall.

95 HOURS

FOLLOWING MY NOCTURNAL ACTIVITY, I MUST HAVE SLEPT soundly because I wake at 8.15 feeling well rested. I can't hear any activity in the house, so, not wanting to wake my parents, I tiptoe through to the bathroom to wash away any remaining drowsiness before returning to my room to put on jeans and a sweatshirt. I sneak downstairs to the kitchen and flick on the kettle so I can make tea.

Before it has time to boil, Dad appears behind me. He looks fresh and rested, his colour restored. He closes the door quietly and whispers, "Your mum isn't awake yet. I'm sorry about last night. I came on a bit strong. I shouldn't have. It's because what you told us came as such a shock."

I'm uncertain whether he's talking about the interrogation I was given by him and Mum, or his threatening outbursts later on. It doesn't matter much, so I shrug in response.

"Did you get any sleep?" he asks. "I heard you moving about in the middle of the night."

"Surprisingly good," I reply and explain about moving the toys.

"I guess they've had their day," he says. "If you're certain you're finished with them, then I can get a box so we can move them to the garage. Either you can pack them away or I can do it. If you like, we can choose some new décor and we'll give the room a complete facelift. That's if you're planning to move back home."

I enjoyed having my independence, so I'm not sure how long I'll want to stay. For the time being, I'd rather avoid a deep discussion about my plans when I don't have any. "That would be good," I say, "although, with the toys, I might want to take the next step and give them away. There are lots of charity shops which would be grateful to have them."

"They're yours to do what you want with, but are you certain you don't want to hang onto them?" Seeing my curious expression, he adds, "For the future, for your own kids if you choose to have any." As an afterthought, he smiles and says, "I quite fancy being a granddad."

"*Daaad!*" I elongate the word to express my exasperation.

He smiles. "It doesn't matter what age you are, you'll always be my little girl." He takes me in his arms, resting my head against his shoulder, rocking me back and forth. "You know your mum and I love you and we'd do anything to make you happy."

I'm content, cradled in his strong arms, feeling safe and protected. After a few seconds, though, I break away. "Dad, I've something to ask you. Can we sit down and talk, please?"

"This sounds serious. Of course you can. You can talk to me about anything you want, anytime you like."

We sit facing one another across the kitchen table. I'm thinking about how best to express myself. I look down at the table cover, unable to maintain eye contact.

"Come on, girl, out with it." He can see my hesitancy.

I start cautiously. "As part of the police investigation, they have to check into my background, my parentage."

"So?"

"They looked out my original birth certificate. Now this might all be a stupid administration error, but they said..., they said you were listed as my biological father.,." I pause to look up at his face. "Is it true?"

In the space of a few seconds, Dad's appearance changes. His shoulders drop, his face seems to crumple and takes on an ashen colour. It's as if he's ageing in front of my eyes. "I always wondered if we'd have this conversation one day. I think it might be best to wait for your mother before we continue."

I guess that means 'yes'. "I didn't know if it would be true and then I thought, if it *was* true, Mum might not know. That's why I wanted to speak to you alone to start with."

Dad nods but says nothing. With impeccable timing, we hear footsteps, then Mum comes into the kitchen.

Dad tells her about my question. She purses her lips. "I see the kettle's been boiled. Let's pour some tea and then we can sit down and talk this through."

Tea! Mum's perfect answer and remedy for everything, I think. I can't see it helping much with this. "What is there to talk through?" I ask. "It's a simple enough question."

Mum's busying herself preparing a pot of tea. She has her back to me as she's talking. "It's not so simple. It happened a long time ago."

"I'm aged twenty-five, so it must have happened twenty-six years ago, by my reckoning," I accuse.

Mum ignores my verbal assault. "We want you to understand. We should have told you before but there was never a right time."

I'm frustrated. I want answers and they're not coming quickly enough. When Mum turns, placing the teapot and cups on the table, I can see great sadness on her face. There are tears in her eyes. I didn't want it to be like this. I regret being so aggressive.

We all sit and sip at our beverage before Mum finally starts.

"Your father and I love children. When we were first married, we planned to have a big family, but it was not to be. I had a late-stage miscarriage a year after we were married. Six months later, I was diagnosed with an ectopic pregnancy. There were complications. I had..." Mum pauses to dab at her tears with a tissue and I feel my eyes filling up, too.

"I needed surgery. I nearly died. It left me unable to conceive."

I reach across to take Mum's hand, to hold it between mine. "I knew you were unable to have children, but you never explained why."

"Your dad and I have never stopped loving each other, but we went through a rough patch. Looking back, I realise we were both low, dealing with our own grief, but it was the darkest period of our lives."

Dad takes Mum's other hand and holds it to his mouth,

kissing her fingers. "It was awful. During that period, we were existing, not living," he says. "I was out of my mind at the time. I felt like I'd lost everything. I was stupid, too. There was a girl who worked in the same office as me and we liked each other. What can I say? There's no excuse. We had an affair."

"My mother, my biological mother?"

Dad gives a curt nod. "Her name was Theresa, Theresa Conway. Anyhow, she got pregnant. When she told me, she said she wouldn't have a termination, but she didn't want to keep the child. I offered to help her so she could bring you up herself. I said I'd give her money, but she said no. She wanted to have you adopted. That's when I confessed everything to your mum."

"At first, I thought I wanted to kill her," Mum says. "Here was I, trying and almost losing my life wanting to become a mother to your father's baby and then she comes along, prepared to give birth and give the child away. Then I started to think, maybe it's meant to be... God's way of making up for my infertility."

I'm taken aback. I've never thought of Mum as religious and hearing her talk in these terms seems strange to me.

"We talked it through. Your dad introduced me to Theresa, and she agreed we could organise a private adoption. We gave her support through her pregnancy and shortly after you were born, we completed the paperwork and paid her a sum of money. She handed you over to us."

"You bought me!" I say, astonished.

"No, no, it wasn't like that at all," Mum says. "She had already decided to have you adopted. We just made the process easier for her."

"What happened to her?" I ask.

"From what I've heard, she suffered from depression. She mixed with a bad crowd and started taking drugs," Mum says.

"What! My biological mother was a junkie?"

"That's not the case, Briony. She wasn't on drugs before you were born. It was something she went through. It happened much later," Mum says.

"It couldn't have been very much later. She didn't live much longer," I say.

Mum looks stunned that I know. She looks as if she's about to question me, then pauses. "She went downhill very rapidly."

"Why have you not told me any of this before?" I ask.

"We wanted to, but we just never found the right time," Mum says, repeating her earlier claim.

"You told me she had a terminal illness," I say.

"I suppose in a way she had," Dad replies. "That's what being a drug addict can be."

"Save me from the sermon, please. You told me she gave me up because she had a terminal illness. It's what I told the police, but they corrected me."

"I'm sorry," Mum says. "It was a white lie we told when you were too young to understand the truth. You are right, though, we should have corrected it when you became older."

"But Dad, why did you not let me know you were my birth father?"

Mum answers for him. "That was my fault. We wanted to adopt you together, to be equal as parents. I didn't want you to think of your dad as your dad and for me only to be your step-mum."

So now I know the truth.

I need some time on my own. I go back to my bedroom to lie on the bed. I think through the new information I've learned. Poor Mum and Dad. What a terrible time they must have had. Two failed pregnancies culminating in infertility; it must have torn them apart. As for my birth mother, she must have gone through horrors. How sad that I never had the opportunity to know her. I'd like to find out more about her. It occurs to me that I didn't ask if she had family. Maybe I have uncles, aunts or grandparents I haven't met, who could tell me about her. The discomfort I felt when I learned of her mental health problems are magnified now I've heard about her drug issues. The prospect of any inherited weakness is concerning, particularly with my memory gap becoming no clearer.

I'm both pleased to know more about my origins, and disappointed. What a pity Mum and Dad couldn't have told me all of this when I was younger, instead of waiting until it's forced from them while I'm struggling to cope with my current issues.

97 HOURS

It's now nearly ten o'clock in the morning. I decide to call Jeffrey to tell him what I've discovered. I want him to know my birth certificate was correct, to save him and the police from wasting time rechecking with the Registrar.

I pick my phone off the bedside table where I'd left it and see I have a missed call and a voicemail. The call was from Michael. My brow furrows. What on earth can he be calling me for? More verbal abuse, perhaps?

I check my voicemail, but as soon as I hear his voice, I terminate the call. I'm about to delete it, but I change my mind. It's just possible it could be evidence, I think. I see from the screen that I have one unread text. It's also from Michael. Persistent, I think. I'm now curious enough to open the message.

I'm sorry. I said stupid things. I didn't mean them. I was angry because the police arrived at a bad time and they didn't tell me what it was about. I didn't know what had happened to you and thought it was you having a go at me. Are you okay? Please let's talk.

I chew on my lip, thinking. What's going on? Why the sudden change of attitude? Is there any truth in what he's saying? Is he truly sorry, or is this some sort of smokescreen to try to stop me suspecting him? If that was his intention, then it hasn't worked as I'm now even more suspicious of him. I want to know what he's up to, but there's no way I'm going to call him back. Perhaps Jeffrey can find out. I was about to call him, anyway.

Jeffrey answers on the first ring. "I'm pleased you called, as I wanted to talk to you and didn't want to phone too early."

I tell him about my parents' revelations and hear his sigh. "How do you feel about it?" he asks.

"I'm pretty shell-shocked, to tell you the truth. Okay, I can understand their motives and I know they've been through their own hell, but to let me reach this stage of my life without telling me... for the news to come out the way it has... So much of my life is a lie. It leaves me feeling... I don't know... betrayed, I guess is the best way to put it."

"I sympathise with you. It must have been a shock, but try not to be too hard on them. True, they should have handled things better and been more upfront with you, but does it make any real difference to how you feel about them? They're the same parents who've loved and cared for you all your life. They still love you and want what's best for you."

"I suppose. I just need to get used to the idea. However, it's also made me determined. If I can ever get over all this mess with my own life, I want to find out more about my birth mother. I want to know if I have any other family out there whom I've never met."

"I think you're right," Jeffrey says. "It will help you come to terms with it all. I might be able to help."

"You said you wanted to call me," I say. "Have you any news?"

"Yes, I do, sort of," he replies. "Nothing definitive. After we spoke yesterday about Michael and his alibi, I called my mate in Northumbria to check out what they did. He looked into what had happened and came back to me, last night. It appears there was a bit of a screw-up."

My heart takes a leap. "What do you mean?"

"Most of what I was told before is correct, but not complete. It seems the officers who went to see him on Saturday arrived just as he and his girlfriend were leaving his flat. They told him they needed to speak to him and asked to go inside. He was dismissive. He said he was in a hurry and wanted to know what it was about before agreeing to anything."

"Yes, he can be quite impatient, particularly if stressed," I say.

"Ordinarily, they would have suggested speaking to him privately, but he was the one who was insistent on doing it there and then, apparently. They asked him about his whereabouts in the previous week and he gave them his work itinerary which showed he was nowhere near Glasgow. He volunteered his boss's number so it could be confirmed. Your name had been mentioned when he'd asked what it was all about and he went berserk. He said he hadn't seen you for months. After they called him out on his lie and asked him about the preceding weekend, the girlfriend started shouting at him and he went off on the rant about you."

"Okay, but what's different to what you told me before?" I ask.

"The checking they did is what's different. His boss confirmed his work itinerary, from last Monday until Friday, starting late morning on Monday in Sunderland. They didn't ask him about the time between the Friday evening and Monday morning."

"Oh God," is all I can say.

"They followed up this morning, to ask about the previous weekend. They went back to his house at eight o'clock and caught him before he left for work. He admitted leaving work at lunchtime on the Friday. He said he left early because he had a sore throat and he was afraid he might be coming down with something. He said he spent the weekend in his flat, with his girlfriend being there most of the time. They've tried to corroborate his claim by speaking to the girlfriend – or perhaps ex-girlfriend may be more accurate. However, he hasn't seen her since Saturday and she's not at home or answering her phone. They tried checking with his neighbours, too, but without success. The bottom line is, he has no one to confirm his story."

I tell Jeffrey about the attempted phone call from Michael this morning and about the text.

"Ah! When explaining the reason for their follow-up visit, they told him the investigation resulted from your disappearance between Friday, a week back, and Thursday," Jeffrey explains. "From what I've been told, he showed concern. Whether he was feigning it or not, we can only guess."

"I don't want to speak to him," I say.

"There's no reason why you should have to. There's a way you can block his number if you want. I can show you how, the next time I see you."

"Yes, I think I'd like to do that," I say. "So, where to now?"

"I put in a call to Zoe to see if she's had any results. She was in a meeting. I'm expecting her to call back when she gets my message," Jeffrey says.

"I'd best go make my peace with Mum and Dad. They'll be wondering what's happened to me. Let me know when you hear anything."

———

Seconds after I hang up, my phone rings again. It's Jenny.

"Hi, Briony. I'm just calling to see how you are this morning."

We chat away for several minutes, agreeing to meet up later in the week. The conversation contains nothing of significance. I'm hoping this is an indication of me getting back to normality.

Speaking to Jenny acts as a prompt for me to give Alesha a call. Am I putting off going back downstairs, I wonder? I suppose I am, but it's also true that I want to nurture this new friendship and now is a good time to call, as Alesha's likely to be on her coffee break.

As with Jenny, we don't discuss my recent problems, instead talking about more mundane topics: music, film and holidays. I have more of a spring in my step as I descend the stairs.

98 HOURS

Mum and Dad are both in the kitchen. Dad's sitting at the table, working his way through a mountain of mail, mostly junk, filing it into designated piles: to pay, to retain, to read later and to bin. Mum has her head inside the larder, a notepad and pen in hand, making a shopping list.

Turning and seeing me, she says, "I was about to call you. We ran down the food store before we went on holiday. I'm going to Morrisons to stock up. I wanted to ask if there's anything you'd like me to buy. If you've nothing better to do, you might want to join me, then you can choose the stuff you like for yourself."

I realise I don't have anything at all I need to do, except maybe to phone Margaret. There's no point in me moping around at home. I need to be at work, to have something practical to occupy my mind. I'll ask her if I can go back tomorrow. "Thanks, Mum, I'd like to. I'll just go and change."

Before leaving the room, I hear my phone ring again. When I look at the screen, I see Jeffrey is calling. While taking the stairs two at a time, rushing back to my bedroom, I press to accept the call.

"Have you heard back from Zoe?" I ask, dispensing with the usual pleasantries in my eagerness.

"She did call. There isn't a lot so far. It seems we're being drip-fed the results."

"What has she told you?" I ask.

"It's quite odd," Jeffrey says. "The first results back are the last checks they made. There's nothing yet from your medical examination. She's chasing it up. However, she has received some provisional information from your flat."

"Really? Is there anything significant?" I ask.

"I don't know yet. It depends what it leads to. They've collected a lot of prints and DNA samples, but they haven't yet run them to find matches."

I'm excited. "You said they found a lot. Does that prove someone's been in my flat? The person who took me?"

"Don't get ahead of yourself. It proves a number of people have been in your flat, which doesn't necessarily mean there was anyone who shouldn't have been there. The next step is for them to catalogue what they have, then eliminate those you'd have expected to be there to see what, if anything, we're left with."

My initial elation has deflated a bit. "So, was that it?"

"No, she told me they've now dusted the pill bottles, the envelope and the money for prints. There weren't many prints and the only ones they found were yours, so we're no further forward there, but you can have them all back. It was the first I knew about the money."

"What envelope and money?" I ask.

"The two lots of two hundred pounds taken from the ATM. She told me you'd signed the inventory of what was taken from the flat."

"What? I don't understand." I remember back to the forensics officer returning my flat keys to me outside the restaurant and giving me a piece of paper. I explain it to Jeffrey while fishing through my handbag. Reading the inventory, I see 'envelope and money' listed, noted as taken from a clothes drawer in my wardrobe. It hadn't registered with me before. I'd only scanned the list and hadn't thought about it. If anything, I'd thought that when they'd written 'money', it could have been some loose change. I hadn't dreamt they'd found the money taken from the ATM. I explain my thinking to Jeffrey.

"She told me it was in a drawer where you keep knitwear. It was hidden at the bottom underneath the clothing and your bank card was there in the envelope, too."

"I can't believe it!" I say. This means all the money taken from my bank is accounted for. "But why? Why would someone do this?"

"There's more, Briony. One of the pill bottles contained the steroids you told us about, but another was labelled aspirin and it actually contained tabs of ecstasy."

"That can't be right! I don't do drugs. I've been offered them often enough, but it's not my thing." I'm frantic at the thought of drugs being found in my apartment. "They must have been planted."

"There's something else. When they were in the flat, the forensics boys noticed that you have SMART meters."

"Yes," I say. "They'd been installed before I'd moved in."

"They checked with your utility supplier – Scottish Power, I think she said – and they have a historical trace of electricity and gas usage. It gives a very strong suggestion that someone has been using the flat at night."

"I don't understand," I say.

"They can track what power has been used and when. They checked the timer on your boiler and noted when it was on and, from the gas usage, they can see when it was firing. Then, by matching it to a trace of electricity usage, they can see what power was used and when it was used. They didn't come across anything else which ran off a timer. Taking an educated guess, based on what they've found, there has been occasional use of lights, television and computer, together with heavy spikes which they'd associate with your electric shower."

I'm speechless, my emotions wavering between shock and amazement at their technical know-how.

"Are you still there, Briony?" Jeffrey asks.

The spell is broken. "Yes, of course. I'm sorry. I was quite taken aback. What you're telling me is they know someone has been living in my flat." I think through the implications. "Do they think it was me? Do they believe I've been taking drugs and hallucinated the whole thing, or that I'm having some sort of breakdown?"

"It's not what they're saying, although, to be honest, I don't think they've ruled out any possibilities." Jeffrey says.

And you? I think. *What do you believe?*

Not for the first time, I'm filled with self-doubt. I'm not much closer to knowing what happened to me during those missing hours, and there's now mounting evidence to suggest, nothing was inflicted on me. Could I have had some sort of mental aberration? Might I have acted in a strange manner without realising it and be left with no recollection? I didn't go to work on Monday, Tuesday or Wednesday. Might I have withdrawn the money and ordered the television? But why would I do such a thing and why would I go all the way across town for that purpose? It sounds unbelievably strange, but is it any less likely than the alternative? Why would anyone abduct me and then fabricate evidence to make everyone doubt my sanity, myself included? Even if someone could have had a motive to do it, how could they pull it off in practice? It's inconceivable to me and the more I think about it, the sorer my head feels.

I hear Mum calling upstairs to ask if I'm ready to go out. I was meant to be getting ready, until Jeffrey's call came in and created this chaos. I wonder if I'd be better to stay home. But why? I've nothing to do here. I can't keep myself cooped up. No, I must face reality sometime and the sooner, the better. "Just coming," I shout back, before quickly changing and going to meet her.

99 HOURS

I feel better outside the house. I push the shopping trolley around the store while Mum collects items, scoring them off her list.

We round the top of the dairy aisle and are moving in the direction of the delicatessen when I hear a voice calling me.

"Briony, is it you?"

I turn to look at the woman walking towards me. It's Mrs Douglas, Jenny's mum. I force a smile.

"I haven't seen you for ages. How are you?" Mrs Douglas asks and continues without waiting for an answer. "I wouldn't have expected to see you in here at this time on a Monday. What is it? Are you having a day off?"

Why would she be asking about what she already knows? I wonder. Last Thursday, when Jenny asked me to stay with her, she told me she had told her mum about me being abducted, although she said she'd made her promise not to question me.

Has Mrs Douglas forgotten already? It's hardly the sort of thing someone would forget, but maybe that's it. Or could she be pretending? Whatever, her question seems genuine.

"Hello, Mrs Douglas, I'm pleased to see you again. This is my mum. I don't know if you'll remember one another because it's been so long. She and Dad are just back after their holiday, so I took the day off to help them settle back in." This little white lie is close to the truth so should be the easiest to pull off, I think.

Mum and Mrs Douglas greet each other warmly while I hang back.

"You're so lucky to have such a considerate daughter," Mrs Douglas says, smiling towards me. "I hardly ever get to see my Jenny these days."

"Oh, why's that?" Mum asks, and I, too, wonder what she's talking about, as I remember that Jenny left the Hamiltons' on Saturday evening to have dinner with her mum.

"You know, young people these days. Technically, she still lives at home but she's rarely there now. What with her working at the pharmacy during the day and then helping her brother build his hypnotherapy practice, she's kept very busy. Even then, I used to see a lot of her in between, particularly at meal-times," she sniggers. "But these last few months, since she's taken up with her boyfriend, she's rarely home, day or night."

I gulp in amazement. *Boyfriend?* What boyfriend? What's this about? I wonder.

Looking at me, she continues, "I expect you see a lot more of her than I do these days, don't you? I think the only way I'm likely to be sure I'll see her is if I book an appointment at the clinic." Mrs Douglas cackles at her own joke.

I'm finding it hard to take in what I'm hearing. Jenny has had a boyfriend for months and she hasn't told me about it. She's been living with him most of the time, if I'm to believe what Mrs Douglas has said. Why? Why wouldn't she have said? What's the reason for her secrecy? We're meant to be best friends, after all. If it was months ago, then it may have started about the same time as my break-up from Michael. Jenny knew I was upset at the time; maybe she was trying to protect my feelings and not talk about her new relationship because she thought I was hurting. She's always been very considerate that way. But, if months have passed, why has she not told me since? Is it like Mum and Dad withholding information thinking they're protecting me and then never managing to find a right time to tell me the truth?

"Briony, close your mouth before you catch a fly in it," Mum says, giving my arm a nudge. "Mrs Douglas asked you a question."

"What?" I ask, shaking myself out of my stunned silence.

"I said, 'I expect you see a lot more of her than I do these days.' Isn't that right?" she repeats.

"I've seen quite a bit of her over the last weekend, although that's been quite unusual," I reply, with complete honesty. I want to know more, but I don't want her to realise I'm probing for information.

"Do you like him, at least?" I ask.

"I haven't actually met him, though not for the want of trying. I've asked Jenny to bring him for tea, just so I can get to see him, but they've always been too busy doing their own things. They met at a friend's work do, I think. You'd have thought he might have wanted to meet her family, but I know some of these Americans can be a bit strange."

He's from America! I'm starting to learn more. I smile, encouraging her to continue.

"I guess Jenny is afraid I'm going to embarrass her. I can never remember his name right. How is it you pronounce it? Dwain, Dwade, Dweeb?"

"Dwight?" I suggest, a reflex reaction.

"Yes, of course. Dwight, that's it. You would think I'd manage to remember. Wasn't there an American president with the same name?"

"Yes, Eisenhower," Mum replies.

I'm now even more gobsmacked. Jenny's mystery boyfriend is Dwight. My Dwight, the one who works in my office. Well, I'm assuming it's the same one. How many other American men called Dwight live and work in Glasgow? I say 'men', because if it is my Dwight, he's a lot older than us; he must be well into his thirties. Jenny's been quick to tell me about other boyfriends she's had, as I have her. It's what best friends do. So why has she kept her relationship with Dwight a secret from me? Is she afraid I'd disapprove, maybe because of his age, or is there another reason? No, it can't be an age thing. Jenny's often dated guys much older than herself. Is it because he works in the same office as I do, and she feels some need to keep us unconnected? Jenny's like me, she always wants to have everything organised the way she likes.

But how did they get together in the first place? Mrs Douglas said she thought they'd met at a friend's office do. Thinking about it, I must have been the friend. I remember inviting

Jenny to a night out not long after I joined Archers. The company was paying for everything and we were each allowed to bring a partner or friend. It was after my split from Michael, so I'd asked Jenny. There's not a lot I can recollect about the night. Because I was new, I didn't know many of the people and I was desperate to make a good impression. I don't think Margaret was there, although I spent a lot of the evening talking to the director, Stuart Ronson. I do know Jenny was there because we booked a taxi to travel in together, but I can't remember spending any time with her.

Did I abandon her to her own devices? Did she meet Dwight there and form a friendship without me ever realising? Neither of them has mentioned anything about it to me since. If I abandoned Jenny in the company of people she didn't know, then it would have been very wrong of me, but unintentional. Perhaps Jenny was annoyed and didn't say. Maybe she thought it unforgivable.

"Briony! Briony, are you with us?" Mum again interrupts my deliberations.

"Yes, what is it?" I ask.

"Mrs Douglas just asked you what you thought of Dwight. Are you feeling okay? You've gone a bit pale and you don't appear to follow what we're talking about."

"Oh, I'm sorry. But no, I'm fine, honestly. I'm just a bit tired because I didn't sleep much." Then, turning to Mrs Douglas, I say, "As for Dwight, I do know him a bit, because he works in the same office as me. He's always seemed an okay sort of guy, but I can't remember ever being out socially with him and Jenny."

We chat for a couple of minutes more before Mum makes our

excuses and we move on, Mum explaining that she'd due back home to meet Dad.

Once we're out of earshot, Mum again asks if I'm okay, saying I looked strained.

I explain to her my surprise at discovering that Jenny having a serious boyfriend who works in my office and this being the first I've heard of it.

"I thought she was your closest friend," Mum says.

"I did, too. I need to call her as soon as we get home. I want to find out what this is all about."

We collect the rest of the items on Mum's list. Mum says she wants to buy a large bouquet to give as a gift to Margaret and Jeffrey, a small thank-you for taking such good care of me, she explains. We check out the shopping, and drive back to the house. I help with the unpacking before dashing upstairs, wanting to phone Jenny. I hear Mum's words echoing in my ears. "I'll put together a tuna salad for you. Will you come back down for it or would you like it in your room?"

"I'll be back down," I reply, then sit on my bed and focus on my call to Jenny. I dial her number.

"Hi Briony, are you okay?" she asks. I'm aware it seems everyone is asking me the same question these days.

Although I want information, I know I need to approach this carefully. "I went shopping with Mum and we bumped into your mum at Morrisons."

"Oh," she replies and her voice sounds apprehensive.

"Yes, she was telling me you're hardly ever home these days. She said you have a new boyfriend."

There's silence.

"Jenny, are you there?"

"Yes." Her voice sounds dry.

"She said your boyfriend is American... that his name is Dwight. Is it the same Dwight I work with, the one from Archers?"

"Yes."

"Jenny, why didn't you tell me? I'm happy for you, of course. But I don't understand. How can you be going out with one of my work colleagues and not tell me? How come neither of you said anything? You've been together for months, from what she told me."

There's a short pause, then Jenny replies, her tone cold. "Not everything has to be about you, Briony. Listen, I'm at work. I can't talk now. Let's discuss this another time." The phone goes dead.

I remain sitting, looking at the disconnected handset for some moments. What did she mean by her comment? She said not everything's about me. Has there been something going on in her life that I don't know about? Something where I've not been caring enough to notice or ask about? Or is she accusing me of being selfish? I can't deny I've been self-obsessed during these last few days, but isn't that understandable after what I've been through? Maybe I'm just making excuses.

Maybe she's saying that I'm always selfish. I'm not narcissistic, am I? How would I know if I was? Surely the mere fact of me questioning whether I could be, ensures I'm not. But have I been a good friend? I've known Jenny for years. We've been very close friends and done everything together for as long as I can remember. We've socialised, we've helped each other. We've been there for each other... or have we? Have I grown complacent and expected Jenny's friendship and support without always being there for her, too?

These last few days, Jenny's been my rock. She's ferried me around wherever I've wanted to go, and she's asked for nothing. Not only these last few days, either, but back when I had my break-up with Michael, she was there to help and comfort me. She was the first person I turned to, two weeks ago, after the weekend Michael came back to Glasgow, when I'd felt bereft. What have I ever done for her? I can think of all sorts of things we've done together where we've been mutually supportive; studying, socialising, choosing clothes, lots of good times. But, try as I might, I don't recollect any occasion where Jenny has relied on me the way I have on her. Has there been a time where she's needed my help and I've not been there, or simply not noticed?

I try harder to analyse our relationship. For years, we've been close and socialised regularly, only now, when I really think about it, I can see there has been a distinct cooling off in the last year or so. When I was with Michael, I had less time for her, but surely that's only to be expected? There have been times when each of us have had boyfriends, which have distracted our attention from one another. Sometimes we've double-dated, but more often we've done our own thing and talked together regularly, either in person or on the phone. I think back to the last boyfriend Jenny told me about. It must be well over a year ago. That was a long time before she met Dwight. Most unusual! I frown, thinking deeply. Is that when she stopped telling me things? Did she stop confiding in me because she thought I was selfish and only interested in myself?

"Briony, are you okay up there? Aren't you coming down for lunch?" I've been so wrapped up in my thoughts, I'd forgotten Mum had expected me to come down to eat. I walk down the stairs, deeply troubled.

101 HOURS

I ENTER THE KITCHEN TO FIND MUM AND DAD WAITING for me. The table is set with a plate at each setting containing a boiled egg, cut in half, slices of smoked salmon and a mound of mixed tuna with mayonnaise. Bowls in the centre of the table hold mixed green leaves, tomatoes and an assortment of pre-prepared salad mixes from the deli.

Dad's holding a bottle of Merlot and a corkscrew. "This is my last chance to have a 'wee swally' with my lunch for a while. I'm back to work from tomorrow."

"That reminds me, I want to call Margaret to ask if I can start back," I say.

"Are you sure you want to do that, Briony? I don't know if you're ready yet. You've seemed quite distracted today," Mum says.

"No, I appreciate your concern, but I don't want to feel trapped. I couldn't stand being cooped up at home all day. I don't know how you do it, Mum." The words are no sooner out of my mouth than I already regret them, seeing Mum's face fall.

"I'm sorry, I didn't mean... What I meant was, I need to be working so I have something to take my mind off what I've been through." As an exercise in damage limitation, my level of success is barely discernible. I chide myself for my insensitivity. I must try to become more careful and think before I speak.

As I realise this, I'm struck by the concern that my thoughtless insensitivity may not be a new thing triggered by my abduction. Is this the real me? Am I guilty of riding roughshod over other people's emotions? Can it be true I'm so selfish? This could be why Jenny has stopped confiding in me. Her parting words were, 'not everything has to be about you.' Is this symptomatic of how I've treated my family, friends and colleagues? I could have mistreated someone so badly, they've wanted revenge. Could this be the reason for my abduction?

"I'm sorry, Mum, I'm really sorry. It's not what I meant to say. You were right when you said I've been a bit distracted. My head is still a bit confused and words aren't coming out the way I intend."

"The point I was making, Briony, is if you're not thinking straight, it may not be a good idea to be in work. You could do more harm than good," Mum says.

"I do see what you mean, but I want to speak to Margaret. I'd like to ask if there's anything I can do so I can feel useful and so I can get back to normal, even if the process is gradual."

Mum shrugs and Dad adds, "If you're sure."

———

JUDGING FROM MARGARET'S TONE, she's pleased to hear from me. She listens to my request and says she'll get back to me. Fifteen minutes later, she calls me. "I've spoken to Stuart and we're in agreement over what we can do. We've a project which has newly come in and there needs to be a lot of research done to kick-start it. It's all desk-based, by phone and computer. It's relatively junior work but we're confident it will be something you can easily cope with so you can ease your way back in."

"It sounds perfect," I say.

"We think it would be best if you broke into it slowly, so you can see how well you're coping. To begin with, we'd like you to work part-time. Come in tomorrow at ten and put in a few hours, say until two or three. Then we can take it from there."

104 HOURS

Late afternoon, I receive another call from Jeffrey. "I have some more information," he starts, "some good, some not so good."

I'm apprehensive. "Start with the bad bit first. I need to get it over with. Then anything else can only water it down."

"Okay. Zoe said the technicians have finished with your computer and you can have it back."

"That doesn't sound so bad," I say, wondering whether to feel relieved.

"It's not. It's what they found on it that's not so good."

I try to remember if there's anything I've done on the computer which could be problematic. Although I occasionally use it for work, for me, its main purpose is for social networking and accessing YouTube. I occasionally play games, but I don't gamble, and it holds no interest for me to access illegal sites. Then a recollection comes back to me and I feel a lurch in my stomach. I've occasionally downloaded films or music videos. Maybe the bad news Jeffrey has is that I've breached some copyright and I'm going to be prosecuted. "Go on," I say, fearing what I'm about to hear.

"The technicians have been able to access the machine's log and trace when it's been used. It appears that it was switched on and used overnight on the Friday, Saturday and Sunday of the time you were missing. On each of those occasions, it was used to access porn websites, including the videos with the three men."

"Oh my God," is the only thing I manage to say.

"The not-so-good news is that Zoe's having to give serious consideration to you being the only one in your home watching it."

I breathe deeply, trying to calm myself. "You said there was also some good news," I say.

"First of all, an update on the testing done in your flat. They've found matches in some of the prints and DNA to you, as expected, but also to Jenny, Alesha and someone who's a close match to you, which we expect might be your father. We also have unmatched data for another two females, perhaps Margaret and your adoptive mum and two other men, so far unidentified. For elimination purposes, can you tell us everyone else who's been in your flat recently?"

Pointlessly, I nod at the telephone, a feeling of disappointment running through me. "Over what time period?" I ask.

"Fingerprints will have been erased the last time you gave the place a good clean. Similarly, with DNA on bed linen, although some traces might last longer. For that purpose mainly, we need to know about who's had reason to be there in, say, the last week or two."

I try to think when I last cleaned the flat. To my shame, it was a while ago, a few days before the weekend Michael visited. It had been my intention to do a thorough clean the following weekend, but it didn't happen. I changed the bed linen after Michael left, but the old sheets and pillowcases were left in the laundry basket. The rest of the place, too, hasn't even had a dust.

Somewhat embarrassed, I explain this to Jeffrey and list Alesha, Jenny and Margaret from last Thursday, with Jenny returning on Sunday, Michael from the previous weekend and Mum and Dad from the day before, as Dad had been there to help me hang curtains. I can't think of any others.

"If our assumptions are correct, there's one other male to be traced." I can visualise Jeffrey's shrug at the other end of the phone before he speaks again. "There's something else. I've done a bit of research into your birth mother."

"Already!" I'm stunned. "What have you found?"

"I've traced a number of relatives who're still alive. You have a grandmother who lives in Ireland and an uncle in Mussel-burgh, near Edinburgh. The uncle is married and has two daughters."

"I have another family! Can I get to see them?" I'm enthralled at the prospect.

"So far, all I've done is trace them. At this stage, we don't know if they'd want to see you. They may not even know you exist."

"How can I find out? I want to meet them," I say, without hesitation.

"I can try to make contact," Jeffrey says. "I don't know how it will go, so don't get too excited, not yet. It doesn't always work out like an episode of *Long Lost Family* and I'm no Nicky Campbell."

"Oh, do you see yourself as being more like Davina McCall?" I quip.

Jeffrey chuckles and before ending the call, he says, "Let me see what I can do."

———

I SPEND the rest of the day in my parents' company. Mum has made a hearty dinner. Then, after eating, we watch a lot of rubbish on television. Magazine programmes, soaps and the start of a new box set series provide most of the entertainment, with *University Challenge* supplying my only mental stimulation of the night. Achieving seven correct answers within the thirty minutes, I'm pleased to surpass my average performance as well as beating the combined score of Mum and Dad. Maybe I'm being unfair; perhaps the other programmes weren't so bad, but the quiz show was the only thing which came close to holding my attention.

The rest of the evening, I've sat watching the screen and occasionally chatting. However, most of my attention has been devoted to more introspection and doubting my own behaviour, interspersed with fantasising about the new family relationships I could make if I'm able to unite with my biological mother's family.

118 HOURS

LAST NIGHT, MY SLEEP WAS UNSETTLED, AND I'VE HAD another tiring day. I go to bed early. Following my request, Dad has removed all my toys and posters to the garage. The room is very stark; it feels cold and clinical. Although it's what I asked for, I'm now doubting the wisdom of removing everything at once. Perhaps I should have retained some pictures, or even my favourite childhood teddy. Too late now. I suppose I'll get used to it or, even better, regain the strength and confidence to be independent again and have my own flat.

I drift in and out of sleep, my dreams sharing the same doubts and hopes as my earlier distractions.

I awaken at seven o'clock, hearing Dad's alarm go off next door. I turn over, trying to steal another hour of sleep but to no avail. Being a big man, Dad isn't too light on his feet. Even had I been able to ignore the noise of the shower and of him clomping about, the intermittent berating Mum dishes out to him, hushing him and directing him to be quieter and more considerate, is inescapable.

I lie in bed, staring at the ceiling, or counting the geometric patterns woven into the drapes, trying to relax. Eight o'clock comes and goes. Then I hear the noise of the front door closing. Enough is enough. I get up, wash and dress to ready myself for work. By the time I reach the kitchen, Mum has already prepared the table: juices, fresh fruit, cereal, cold meats, cheeses and pastries. It's more lavish than you'd find offered for breakfast in many hotels. Following yesterday's meals, I swear she's trying to fatten me up! I either need to get my own place or I'll have to say something to stop her, but, with her being so thoughtful, I don't want to appear ungrateful or unkind.

I drink some juice, then pour a cup of tea and nibble on some toast.

"I must leave soon, so I can catch my train," I say.

"I can drive you in if you'd like," Mum suggests.

"Thanks, I appreciate the offer, but it doesn't make sense for you to spend half your morning stuck in city traffic," I reply. "The train takes no time, and the walk to and from the station will help to clear my head." In truth, I'm feeling a bit stifled, but I'm trying to be more careful, so I don't hurt her feelings.

Once I arrive at the office, Alesha rushes over to hug me before Margaret sees me and shows me to one of the private rooms. It's equipped with a computer and a phone. She hands me a file containing details of the new client and his requirements. She tells me that all the other staff have been informed that I'm coming back after being unwell for a few days. The excuse sounds lame, but it will have to do.

I feel as though I'm back in the real world and I'm thoroughly enjoying it. As midday arrives, I feel ready for a coffee. I walk through to the cloakroom which we affectionately refer to as our kitchen because it has a worktop, a fridge and a microwave for communal use. I flip the switch on the kettle then turn around, only to find I'm facing Dwight.

"I'm pleased to see you back. Are you feeling better now?" he says. He looks sincere.

I'm confused. Surely he knows the truth about my absence? Has Jenny not told him? Maybe I'm misjudging her, and she's kept my secret, even from her boyfriend. If so, how has she explained to him all the time she spent with me?

"A lot better, thank you." Having him here and now in front of me, I can't stop myself asking. "I've only just found out you're going out with Jenny. Why didn't you tell me?"

He smiles and replies, "Now, there's a question," before turning and walking back into the main office.

I want to pursue him, to quiz him, but now, in front of all my work colleagues, is not the right time.

I go back to my research and the day continues without me being aware of the time passing. It's almost three o'clock when the door opens, and Margaret comes in. I look at the clock, then back at her. "I've really enjoyed being back, but do you think I've done enough for my first day?" I ask.

126 HOURS

Margaret checks her watch, then looks at the paperwork I've prepared, before replying, "Yes, you seem to have achieved a lot, but I came to see you for a different reason."

I look at her, curious now.

"I'd like you to come through to my office. Jeffrey called to say he has a lot more information to give you. He suggested you might want to have me with you when you hear it. If you like, we could use the conference phone as it has a speaker and microphone facility. There's no pressure, it's up to you."

"What's he found out?" I ask.

"I've no idea, Briony. He hasn't told me anything. It's your news, so he'll only confide in me if it's what you want. He did say he thought you'd benefit from having some support. The alternative is you could wait until tonight and come around to our house with your parents."

"I don't want to wait until tonight. I want to know now," I say. Without knowing what he'll have to say, I'm uncertain whether it would be easier or harder to hear important news with my parents present. Mum can get very emotional at times and it's not uncommon for Dad to fly off into a rage when things aren't going his way.

"He can call you to this room if you prefer and it will be private, or you can come to my office if you'd like me to sit in."

This is a dilemma. I normally cherish my privacy, but I don't know what I'm going to hear. In the short time I've known him, I've come to trust Jeffrey's judgement. If he's suggested I should be accompanied, he must have a reason. Margaret, too, has been a lifesaver for me. "Thank you, I'll come into your office," I say.

————

No sooner have we entered the office than Margaret closes the door firmly and places a *Do Not Disturb* notice in its window. I'm very apprehensive as I wait for the call to connect. What can be so disturbing about what Jeffrey has to tell me that he thinks I should have Margaret to support me? I sit on a chair and cross my legs, then I uncross them and stand up. I sit again, my foot tapping the floor, my hands shaking; I can't settle.

Margaret engages speakerphone mode and presses a button for autodial. Jeffrey answers almost immediately.

"I'm in my office on speaker and Briony is beside me," Margaret says.

"I know it was my recommendation, but before I start, I need you to confirm you're happy for me to speak to you in front of Margaret."

"Yes, yes, please go on," I say Now my knees are trembling, too.

"Okay, thanks. Briony, I have the results of your medical examination. There's quite a lot I have to tell you."

"Yes?"

"To start with, there's confirmation of what you've already been told and of what we've suspected."

"What in particular?" I ask.

"Okay, there was no physical evidence of violent sex or rape. I'm sorry, but I need to be more explicit. There was no bruising or abrasions, either internally or in the vicinity of your vagina, anus, mouth or throat."

I inhale deeply and hold my breath.

"Because of the length of time you were missing, it's not possible to totally eliminate that you've been sexually assaulted without violence during the first day or two, as it wouldn't necessarily have left any evidence which would have endured until your examination."

I breathe out in a rush as if someone has punched me in the stomach. It's not bad news, but neither can it fully put my mind at ease.

"There's evidence of restraints being used to hold your ankles, wrists and neck. They weren't heavy-duty, more the lightweight type of thing sold to bondage fetishists or sometimes in joke shops. You've also been wearing earplugs to prevent you from hearing. It could have been so you wouldn't be able to pick up on background noises, so as not to identify your location or hear people's voices. This fits with what you commented when you spoke about your visions of the videos. You said they were silent, but we know from the internet versions that there was a soundtrack. My guess is that the reason was for sensory deprivation. It may have been intended to cause you more disorientation and confusion."

I nod my head.

"Unsurprisingly, nail scrapings found skin fragments which were identified as Jenny's. We expected that, because we know you'd gripped her hand tightly during your police interview not long before the medical. However, there were no traces of DNA anywhere on your body. It looks as if this is because you'd been thoroughly washed using a non-bio, fragrance-free detergent. It wasn't a standard shower gel or cosmetic, it was something more specialist. It seems you'd been given the equivalent of a bed bath and probably more than once. We haven't located the exact product yet as it appears to be quite unusual, maybe something like a surgical wash. This means that once we find it, we might be able to narrow down the supply chain quite significantly."

The thought of my entire body being meticulously hand-washed by some unknown person or persons is abhorrent to me. The vision, or recollection, of hands, lots of hands, touching me all over, comes back into my mind. This could well be the explanation. I squirm at the thought. My breathing is now coming in short, sharp bursts. I can't get enough air into my lungs.

Margaret reaches across to take gentle hold of my hand. "Would you like some water to drink?" she asks. She lifts a bottle of Evian from her desk and hands it to me. I see the wisdom of Jeffrey's suggestion to have her with me.

"Now, to get onto the meatier side of what's been discovered, we have your blood results. They found traces of three different drugs at various levels. GHB, GBL and ketamine. The abbreviations stand for gamma-hydroxybutyric acid and gamma-butyrolactone, if you want to know the chemistry. All three are known to be commonly used as date-rape drugs and it's just possible they may have been used individually, or as a cocktail to make you unaware of what had happened to you. Also, you said in your interview that you'd been taking steroids for a sports injury. The interaction of chemicals could also have a quite unpredictable affect."

"Does this prove that I wasn't lying?" I ask.

"Nobody has accused you of lying," Jeffrey says. "Okay, maybe there have been one or two doubts about the authenticity or interpretation of some of what you've reported, but no one has put that down to you lying, or trying to mislead."

"Instead, you've been uncertain about my sanity."

"It's not like that, Briony. Let's not go there. However, if I may continue, there is one other very significant finding from your blood test."

Hasn't he already covered everything? I try to think what it can be.

"Briony, your test results show that you are pregnant."

"What! You can't be serious," I respond.

"There's no doubt about it," Jeffrey replies.

Oh my! With everything else I've been worried about, I didn't see this coming. I raise my hands, covering my face

"I must have been raped," I whisper. "You said before that it couldn't be ruled out. Oh God, I'm carrying a rapist's child."

"No, Briony, that's highly unlikely to be the case. In fact it's virtually impossible. Judging from your tested HCG levels, the foetus is almost certainly older than one week."

"The only person I've been with is Michael, the previous week-end," I say. "I'd been on the pill when we'd been a couple, but I stopped taking it after he moved away. When we met two weeks ago, I hadn't expected us to end up sleeping together. Now I remember, it was impulsive, we didn't use a condom. Michael has to be the father."

I'm stunned. I can't speak. My head's spinning, my thinking is jumping in cartwheels at the thought of a living being growing inside me. My egg, fertilised by Michael's seed. This isn't what I wanted. When Michael and I were a couple and I thought we had a future together, he'd often spoken about wanting a family. I'd dismissed the idea. I wasn't ready. I had my future and my career mapped out in my head and children weren't part of it. Now, I'm in uncharted territory. I'm alone, single, having parted from Michael and now, after what was effectively a one-night stand, I'm expecting a baby; his baby.

Aware of my distress, Margaret takes my hand and clasps it in hers. "Tell me what you're thinking?" she asks. "It could help to talk."

My thoughts are jumbled. My first consideration is, do I want to keep it? "It must be very early in my pregnancy. I could have an abortion. I haven't ever seriously considered becoming a mother. Whether it was because I felt I was too young, or for other reasons, I haven't categorised myself as mother material. But for me to abort a foetus – no, the idea is unthinkable. It's not a foetus, it's a baby! It's growing inside me and it was created out of the love I shared with Michael. Yes, I can't deny I did love Michael. Okay, it didn't last, and we split up, but even if our reunion was short and unsustainable, it was nevertheless an act of love which created this baby."

"You've only just heard the news. You don't have to decide anything right now," Jeffrey says.

I'm certain. I won't change my mind about this. I need to consider the practicalities of raising a child. "My biological mother must have gone through the same dilemma. She chose to have me adopted. From the little I know of her, it wasn't much later that her life went downhill. Perhaps she couldn't live with the decision she had made. In any event, I'm determined I will not follow in her footsteps. Maybe it's only minutes since I received the news, but I know my own mind. I not only want to give birth, but I want to raise my baby. I don't know what Mum and Dad will say. No doubt, they'll be appalled, but I hope they love me enough to support me. Whether or not they will, I'm adamant, I will raise my own child."

"I'm sure they'll stand by you, but I want you to know that Jeffrey and I will give you all the help we can," Margaret says. She opens her arms to envelop me in a hug. "What about Michael?"

I consider the question. "It was clear from his text on Saturday and from what he told the police, what he thinks about me. He hates me. Okay, he tried coming back to me this morning to smooth things over, but I'm unclear of his motives."

I need to know he wasn't involved in my abduction, because if he was, then it's a game-changer. I need to leave the police and Jeffrey to carry out their investigations. What I do know for certain is that Michael walked out on me when he moved to Newcastle and again after our weekend reunion. He deserves no place in my life now.

"There's another consideration," I say. "Doesn't my child have a right to know who his or her father is? My own recent experience has taught me a lesson. I went for years loving and trusting my adoptive parents and thinking I didn't need to know more. Now the door has been opened the way it has, I feel let down because I wasn't told the truth. If for no other reason, I crave to learn more."

"I understand," Margaret says.

I continue. "I never had an opportunity to know my birth mother and I don't want to inflict the same issues on my child by hiding the truth of his or her father, or, for that matter by hiding the truth *from* his or her father. Michael must be told. He may or may not want to know. He may or may not want to have a place in my baby's life. If he does, we need to find a way to manage."

Time is passing and I'm lost in my thoughts. There are too many things to consider and I'm overthinking the situation. It's too soon for me to try to find an answer for every consideration. If I'm not to drown, I need to take it slower and not try to solve every issue all at once.

"Are you still there, Briony?" Jeffrey asks.

"Yes, I'm here. I'm sorry. I was trying to think."

"I've nothing else to tell you just now. I'll go now because I've some other things to chase up. Margaret will look after you."

Tears are running down my cheeks.

Margaret hands me a tissue and holds me close, cradling my head against her shoulder. "Are you very upset?

"No, that's the strange thing," I say. "I didn't think I'd ever say this, but I'm happy. I'm actually happy to be pregnant."

Margaret offers to drive me home and to come in with me to meet my parents, giving me moral support when I tell them the news.

128 HOURS

It's after five o'clock before we arrive back. Dad has come home from work only minutes before. Mum and Dad are delighted to meet Margaret and they invite her in, taking us all into the lounge.

"You've saved me a trip. I wanted to give you these." Mum produces the large bouquet and presents it to Margaret. "It's only a small token of our gratitude, for looking after our girl. We would have come home sooner if only we'd known. You have to understand, she's very precious to us."

Margaret takes the flowers. "Thank you. This was very kind of you. However, I'll have you know she's precious to us, too. She a lovely girl, very talented and she's a credit to you both," Margaret replies.

"Careful, she'll be getting a big head with all these compliments," Mum says.

"Mum, Dad, please sit down. I've got something I want to talk to you about," I say.

"What is it? Have the police found out what happened?" Mum's eagerness is palpable.

"No, it has nothing to do with that," I say. "It's very personal."

"In that case, shouldn't you wait until Margaret has left?" Dad asks. "I mean no disrespect," he adds, looking at her.

"No, I'd like her to stay. She was with me when I found out, so it isn't news to her."

Mum and Dad both look perplexed. They sit down together in silence, waiting for me to speak.

I look to Margaret, seeking her moral support. She gives me a reassuring nod. I take a deep breath before I start, as I want to get my whole admission out without pausing. "I hope you will not be disappointed in me. This isn't something I planned or wanted to happen, but I've just found out I'm pregnant."

I see Mum's eyes well up. "Does this have anything to do with your abduction? Is it the result of you being raped?"

"No, I already told you, it has nothing to do with it," I say

Without thinking, Dad jumps to his feet and his quick-fire response explodes from him. "What were you thinking of, girl? This is a serious matter! You're not married or in a relationship. What on earth have you been up to? Do you even know who the father is?"

It doesn't surprise me that they are disappointed in me, but I feel hurt and my emotions flare on hearing Dad's rant. Who knows, maybe I've inherited his temper. "I don't think it takes a genius to know what I've been up to. But, after your admission to me yesterday morning, I think it a bit rich for you to be trying to claim any moral high ground."

Seeing Mum's tears, I regret my outburst. Dad sits back down, deflated

"I'm sorry for reacting the way I did," I say. "You deserve a proper explanation."

I go on to tell them about me being celibate for months prior to my weekend together with Michael. I mention I haven't yet told him, but irrespective of that, I see no future with him. I continue explaining to them how I don't want to follow the example of my biological mother. I've made the decision to raise my child. Amidst Dad's protestations of what types of torture he'd like to inflict on Michael, they accept my decision and say they'll stand by me and give me whatever help and support they can.

I couldn't have hoped for a better outcome. We all know it won't be easy for any of us. However, working together and helping each other will ensure the best possible result.

Her strength and support having again proved invaluable, Margaret leaves to go back home.

129 HOURS

Mᴜᴍ ᴀɴᴅ Dᴀᴅ ᴡᴀɴᴛ ᴛᴏ ᴄᴏɴᴛɪɴᴜᴇ ᴛʜᴇ ᴄᴏɴᴠᴇʀsᴀᴛɪᴏɴ so they can start to make plans. However, I excuse myself as I feel I ought to call Michael.

I go to my bedroom to call his number.

Before he has a chance to speak, I introduce myself using his words. "Michael, this is the crazy fucking bitch."

"Briony, I didn't mean it. Listen, I'm so glad you called. I've been desperate to speak to you. I need to explain, but first I want to know you're okay."

"A lot has been going on. There's something I want to talk to you about," I say.

Michael starts, "Before you do, please listen to me. I'd like to..."

As I need to get this over with, I don't want a long conversation. He needs to hear my news, so I break in. "No, let me speak first. It's important." I give him no opportunity to interrupt. "Do you remember our weekend together, two weeks ago? I've just found out that I'm pregnant."

"And it's mine?" he asks.

"Of course it's yours! I've not been with anyone else."

There's no hesitation. "That's wonderful news! You know I've always wanted us to have a family."

"Wait a minute, Michael. You've got this wrong. We're not having a family. I'm having a baby and, much as I have my doubts, I reckoned you had a right to know."

"But we have to be together. This is what I've always wanted," Michael says. "The only reason I took the move to Newcastle was because you weren't prepared to commit. You told me you didn't want a family and you even sent Jenny to reinforce the point by telling me you'd always put your career ahead of everything else. You were happy with our relationship as it was, but didn't want it to go any further."

I remember well the many conversations between us when I'd been adamant that I wasn't ready to start a family, yet. I'm more unclear as to the rest of what he's saying. "Listen, Michael, I phoned because I thought you ought to hear the news from me. I'm not ready to talk any more just yet. Let's give ourselves a day or two to let the news sink in, then talk again."

I return downstairs to find Mum has prepared dinner. I don't have any appetite, but she insists that I must have some nourishment, now that I'm eating for two.

I manage a mouthful before I'm saved by hearing my phone ring and seeing Jeffrey's name come up on the screen.

"Briony, can you tell me where we might be able to get hold of

Jenny?" he asks. He tells me she's not answering her mobile and they've already tried her home, the pharmacy and her brother's clinic without success.

"What's this about?" I ask.

"I'll give you the whole story later, but for now, please give me any information you can. We want to move quickly."

When I suggest contacting her boyfriend, he asks if I know his details.

"I don't, but Margaret does. He works in our office. His name is Dwight Collier. I only found out about it myself today. Please tell me why you need to speak to her?"

"We want to bring her in for questioning right away. I can't talk now. I want to find Dwight's details and pass them on to Zoe, then I'll call you straight back to explain."

Why would they want to talk to Jenny, I wonder? Could she be at risk, or is there something they believe she might know? Whatever it is, it sounds serious.

I'm impatient, wanting to know. I pace up and down my room.

Ten minutes pass and I wonder if I ought to call Jeffrey back. No, I shouldn't, he said he'd call me as soon as he could.

I see the light flash on my mobile and I press to answer before it's properly started to ring.

"What is it, Jeffrey?"

"Margaret didn't have the information to hand, so she had to look it up. I've passed Dwight's address on to Zoe and she's sending a car there to check it out. They'll pick her up if she's there."

"But why?"

"I don't know yet exactly how. However, I can tell you that Jenny has been involved in your abduction."

My legs feel weak, as if they're about to give way. I collapse onto my bedside chair. "But why? How?"

"I've had some suspicions for a while, but didn't want to say in case I'd got it wrong. We now have the evidence to bring her in and question her."

"What evidence?"

"From the forensics results, we know she's been in your flat," he says.

"Of course she has," I reply. "Last Thursday, I sent her there to pick up a change of clothes for me. She drove me back there after I had my medical examination, although she didn't come in. Then on Friday we both went there before Zoe arrived with the technicians. Again, on Sunday I was there with her before going to the airport."

"It was more than that, Briony. She didn't only visit the flat. The evidence suggests it was more like she was living there."

"But she couldn't be! I'd have known."

"A lot of the fingerprints and DNA can be explained as you've said. However, there's some which can't and that's why we need to speak to her."

"What in particular?"

"Let me go through some of the evidence. Her prints on the keys of your laptop were suspicious, but not too damning.

However, what we found in the bathroom and bedroom clinches it."

"What?"

"There were hair follicles and DNA traces in the shower, which proves she's used it. What's more, there were traces on your toothbrush. The evidence points to her living in your flat as if she was you, perhaps pretending to be you and, taken together with the SMART meter evidence, we think it was through the nights of the weekend you were missing."

I try to think of an explanation. When was the last time Jenny stayed over in my flat? In fact, has she ever? Is there a rational explanation of why she would have used my shower? I don't think so, and certainly not my toothbrush. A cold shiver runs down my back.

"There's more. She's been sleeping in your bed, although 'sleeping' might not be the most accurate terminology."

"I'm sorry, I don't..."

"Your sheets have been recently changed. The ones on the bed had been freshly laundered. Even so, we found her DNA traces on the mattress. We found the used sheets in your laundry basket along with a second set, the ones you told us about, which you'd changed yourself."

This can't be happening. Why would Jenny have done this?

"It's no more than a guess at present, but, putting all the pieces of the jigsaw together, I reckon she's stayed in your flat and for some reason pretended she was you. She's used your bathroom, your shower and even your toothbrush. And she's most likely lain on your bed watching pornography, using your computer."

"Why? Why has she done this to me?"

"I don't know, Briony. From my experience, I've seen cases where people have pretended to take on someone else's life out of sheer jealousy. I'm going to go now. I hope to know more once Jenny's been picked up. I'll call you back later."

130 HOURS

I CAN'T JUDGE HOW LONG I SIT IN THE CHAIR, MY EYES gazing at nothingness. I feel totally drained; my body leaden. Jenny's been my best friend for years. We've done everything together. How could she have done this? She's smart and successful, so why would she be jealous of me? My mouth is dry; I need to get water. My steps are heavy as I walk downstairs to the kitchen.

"Briony, are you okay?" Mum comes out of the lounge to meet me. I hear a medical drama playing in the background. "Oh my God! What's wrong? Your face is chalk white," she says. She draws me into the lounge and sits me down on the sofa, reaching for the remote to turn off the television.

Dad comes and sits alongside, putting his arm around my shoulder. "What's wrong, pet? Has something happened? Do you need a doctor?"

I summon the energy to repeat what Jeffrey's told me.

There's silence. Mum is hugging me close. Dad stands up and starts to pace up and down, his breathing laboured.

"Why would she do this to you?" Mum asks, repeating the question I've been asking myself over and over since I heard the news.

It starts as a whisper, gradually getting louder, Dad's voice. "I'm sorry, I'm so, so sorry."

In unison, Mum and I turn to look at him.

"It's my fault. It's all my fault. It should never have happened. You have to forgive me," he continues. His shoulders are slumped and he's staring at the floor, his hands balled into fists and he's pacing. He's sobbing. I haven't ever seen Dad cry before.

"What are you saying, Arthur?" Mum asks, her voice caustic.

I feel as if I can't breathe. I need to find out more even though I know it's something I won't want to hear.

"I had an affair," Dad blurts, in between great gulps of air.

"What are you saying?" Mum asks again. "Out with it."

Dad collapses into an armchair, leaning forward, his head low, hands clasped on top. "It started more than a year ago." He glances up towards me. "You girls had been for a night out and came home after drinking quite a lot. I offered to drive Jenny home. On the way, as we were driving past the park, she asked me to stop the car." Dad pauses, his breath catching in a sob before continuing. "I did stop, because I thought she may have been feeling unwell and I didn't want to risk her throwing up inside the car. I misjudged the situation because she wasn't so drunk... I didn't expect it... she turned and kissed me. She came on to me."

I'm speechless.

"What are you saying, Arthur? You and Jenny?" Mum shrieks.

"I didn't mean for it to happen. I guess I was flattered. A young girl wanting me. It made me feel young again. You have to understand."

"With Jenny? She's your daughter's age! She was your daughter's best friend. Young, you're not. You're just a sad old bastard taking advantage of a child. You can't justify that!"

Mum's standing, shrieking. Her fingers are stretched, her nails extended. She looks as though she's ready to scratch his eyes out. I'm sitting rooted to the spot. This seems unreal, as if I'm watching some terrible drama on television.

"She was the one who started it," Dad says, thinking it somehow makes matters better. "Like I said, we had an affair. It went on for about three months, but I put a stop to it."

"You're actually looking for credit for stopping something you should never have been doing?" I can almost taste the venom in Mum's accusation.

"No, I didn't mean it like that," Dad says. "Jenny wanted us to go on. She wanted me to leave you and take up with her. I told her, no. I wouldn't ever do that. I told her I couldn't do it to you, and I couldn't do it to Briony.

"She was furious. She ranted about how Briony had always had everything – a nice home, her family, her security, all the toys and games and belongings she could possibly have wanted as a child. She, Jenny, didn't even have a father, she said. I tried to placate her. I even offered her money. She spat it back at me. She said she'd find a way to get even. I knew she was angry, and I thought it was an idle threat. I didn't believe she meant to do anything. I didn't see her again until last night. I'd thought her words were meaningless, spoken in the heat of the moment, and afterwards it had all been forgotten."

Is this real, or am I having some sort of awful nightmare? Dad admitting he had an affair with my best friend, telling me Jenny has always resented me? I shake my head, to try to clear it, but nothing changes.

Dad looks at me. "When we came back from holiday and heard about what had happened to you, I remembered her threat and I did have one or two doubts. I dismissed them because I didn't believe Jenny could be capable of such an awful thing. I was wrong. She must have been planning this for months. Please believe me. I had no idea this would happen."

Dad reaches across to touch Mum's shoulder. "Listen, love…"

She jumps aside. "Don't touch me! Get away from me. I don't want to see you. I can't stand the sight of you. Get out! Get out of this house."

"I've nowhere else to go," Dad pleads.

"Maybe you should have thought of that before now… before you started screwing around with a child," Mum says.

"She's not a child. She's in her mid-twenties, for God's sake. I'm not a paedo. She…" Dad realises he's wasting his breath. He instead turns to me, his eyes pleading. "Please, Briony. We're flesh and blood."

If he'd consciously searched for the worst thing he could say, he couldn't have angered me more. Appealing, using our genetic relationship, within such a short time of confessing it, disgusts me. Using it, hoping it will make me side with him against Mum, is repulsive. I turn away. I can't stand to look at him. I could never forgive what he's done, and I certainly can't condone the consequences of his actions.

131 HOURS

After Dad leaves the room, Mum turns to me and holds me close. "I'm sorry, Briony. I feel I'm to blame."

"How could you be?" I ask. "It had nothing to do with you." I bury my head into her shoulder.

"I should have realised. He's always had a wandering eye. I pretended it didn't bother me. I should have faced up to him before now," she says

"It wouldn't have been so bad if it was only his eye which wandered," I say, trying to lighten the mood by introducing a hint of dark humour.

Mum gives me an indulgent smile. "I'm certain there have been other times. I didn't challenge him when I should have. I didn't question his philandering, thinking it was only a temporary aberration and he'd soon tire and come back to me. Not for one moment did I suspect he'd take up with a girl half his age, and worse, one we all knew so well."

Mum and I spend the rest of the evening comforting one other. I want to call Jeffrey to let him know what appears to have been Jenny's motive, but I don't want to leave Mum alone. She tells me to go ahead and I compromise by calling from the lounge with Mum in the room.

"We have still to work out the details, but it's all starting to make sense," Jeffrey says. "Being a pharmacist, Jenny will have had access to any number of drugs. Zoe has made a request for a search warrant for Dwight Collier's flat, which they hope to have processed before they go there looking for her. They'll no doubt want to check her mother's house, too, as it's Jenny's legal residence, and maybe Philip's clinic as well, because Jenny worked there. As she had your keys, she'll have had free access to your flat anytime she liked. She must have planted the ecstasy tablets in your bathroom cabinet. She'll have hidden the money which she stole from the ATM, along with your bank card, in your wardrobe drawer."

"But why?" I ask. "Why would she steal the money only to hide it back in my flat?"

"I have a possible theory," Jeffrey replies. "I don't believe she ever intended to keep the money. She only took it to build on your level of panic and to make your story sound unreliable to the police. The same applies to the ecstasy. She must have known you'd soon find out your card was missing and that money was gone out of your account. She'll have realised you'd try to research what had happened to it, and if the police were involved, then they'd check the security cameras. She'd think once they'd seen the footage, which made it appear as if you were the one who withdrew it, then your credibility would have been totally shot. You might even doubt your own sanity."

"It worked, too. I wondered whether I'd had some sort of breakdown and imagined the whole thing, or worse, made it happen myself."

"I believe her whole scheme went wrong right from the outset," Jeffrey says. "I think she expected you to go to pieces as soon as you realised you had more than a five-day memory block. She'll have thought the first thing you would have done would be to call her and ask for help. She'd then have been able to direct how it all went. She might have been planning to talk you out of calling the police, or thought she'd go with you to undermine your confidence all the way."

"But I didn't call her right away."

"No, you didn't, because you had Alesha helping you. You had genuine support and sound advice from someone who cared for you. Even when Jenny was able to get involved, any effect she had was diluted by Alesha and then further, by Margaret and me."

"So, it was Alesha who saved me."

"Yes, I believe so," Jeffrey says. "If it hadn't been for her intervention, there's no telling how you might have ended up. Listen, I must go, as I'd like to keep this line free in case Zoe phones. I promise I'll call if I hear anything."

134 HOURS

TIME PASSES SLOWLY. I START TO DOUBT WHETHER I'LL hear from Jeffrey this evening. It's approaching ten o'clock when my mobile comes alive again, showing an incoming call.

"Yes?" I start, tentatively.

"We've got her!" Jeffrey says, the triumph evident in his tone.

"What happened?" I can scarcely breathe, I'm so tense with excitement.

"Zoe went to Dwight's flat along with a full team, forensics in tow. When they told Jenny they wanted to take her in for questioning, she clammed up, didn't say a word. Two of Zoe's officers led her away. However, when Zoe showed the search warrant to Dwight, he just fell apart and admitted his part in the whole scheme."

"Wow!" is all I can think of to say.

"His only request was for us not to let his uncle find out."

"What's this uncle got to do with it?" I ask.

"His biggest fear is of his uncle being disappointed in him and pulling him back to the States. He hasn't worked out yet that he could well be facing a long prison term. In any event, we don't have to tell the uncle. The media will most likely do it for us."

"Oh my God! I hadn't considered the media. Am I going to have to relive everything again through the news?"

"To be honest, Briony, it's not something we have any control over. No doubt the Procurator Fiscal will want to bring charges. We've already got enough evidence to convict them of kidnap, even if Dwight hadn't confessed. There'll be more, too, because we haven't even started to trace Jenny's car's movements and her phone locations and, of course, any forensics results from the search. How much news coverage the case will attract will depend on whether Jenny and Dwight try to put up any defence."

"What did Dwight say?"

"He told us it was all Jenny's idea. She'd talked him into becoming involved. She set up to meet you on the Friday evening to ensure you'd stay working late. She gave him pills and she told him to dissolve them into your coffee after everyone else had left, when you were alone with him, working. As soon as you were completely out of it, he took your ID card to register the two of you out of the building a few minutes apart, once he knew no one was watching. He then went back to your office and carried you down to the car park, using the lift. He bundled you into the boot of his car and then took you to his flat. You were correct, by the way. His flat is less than one hundred yards from the ATM used to withdraw your money."

"But why did they do it?" I ask.

"We already suspected Jenny's motives from what your father said. Dwight has told us she said she always felt her life was out of control and she resented the stability you had. Her aim was to turn it around, so it forced you to live with the same doubts and uncertainty she'd always experienced."

"What about Dwight?"

"Apparently, he knew Stuart and Margaret had recognised your potential as soon as you started with Archers, whilst they didn't rate him at all. He has an inflated opinion of his own ability and put it down to them resenting the fact that his uncle arranged for him to have a senior post in Glasgow. It was sheer chance when Jenny teamed up with him at the party and they realised they considered you to be a common enemy. She came up with the plan of how you could be discredited and at the same time Dwight would showcase his own ability. It didn't quite work out the way they planned it, though, because Dwight flopped when he was given the opportunity to present his ideas."

I'm shaking my head, finding it difficult to take in all I'm hearing.

"Jenny's plan had been to keep you incapacitated, not just over the weekend but until after the presentation on Tuesday. She planned to use a mixture of drugs and hypnotherapy, supplemented by falsely implanted memories like the porn films, to get you confused so you wouldn't know the truth from fantasy."

"I remember now, not long after she started helping her brother in his clinic, she told me she was learning how to do hypnosis. There was an evening when, for fun, she tried out her new skills on me. She made me eat an onion, making me think it was an apple. After hearing what I'd done, I wouldn't let her experiment on me again."

"Well, it appears that was another of your requests she didn't take any notice of," Jeffrey says. "They've still to go through the formal interviews, so we expect a lot more detail to come out. Dwight said he was terrified because Jenny left you alone with him during the times when she went to your flat. It seems he had quite a shock on the Friday night, because you had a violent reaction to the drugs she'd administered. At one point, you were fitting and he was afraid you'd die, but after a while you settled down. Dwight said he wanted to abandon the plan, but Jenny insisted they were already in too deep and they had to go ahead."

"Will there be any lasting damage?" I ask.

"I wouldn't have thought so, but I'm no expert. I think you'd be best to speak to your doctor, to be on the safe side. You'll need to make an appointment anyhow, because of your pregnancy."

"What about the drugs?" I ask. "Could they have affected my baby/"

"Again, I think you should speak to your doctor. It's never a good idea to take drugs or alcohol during pregnancy, as some can trigger a miscarriage, but that risk may be low because they should be out of your system by now. I'm not aware of any direct correlation between these drugs and birth defects, but you'd better seek professional advice."

"I'll call first thing tomorrow to make an appointment," I say.

"Dwight knew about the cash withdrawals and the television purchase. He told us Jenny had dressed in your clothes to do it.

He said the reason she'd gone over to your flat was to plant evidence."

"What about the porn videos?" I ask.

"Apparently, he came up with them. It was a website he'd become partial to when he'd been in the States and it seems Jenny was turned on by them. She loved the idea of implanting the images in your head."

"Did he say who she was trying to hurt most, me or Dad?"

"Dwight only knew she was trying to get back at you. He didn't mention your father, other than to say Jenny had hoped you would call them immediately so their holiday would be ruined."

"It's over," I say. "I can't believe how much has happened in the last week."

"I've a curious fact which may interest you," Jeffrey says.

"What is it?"

"The time you were missing extended from somewhere between seven and eight o'clock on Friday evening, until sometime between eight and nine on Thursday morning. It equates to an hour longer than five and a half days – one hundred and thirty-three hours, to be more precise. The time it's taken to come up with the answers is from the same time on Thursday morning until Dwight's confession at about nine-forty this evening, just over five and a half days – one hundred and thirty-three hours. It's identical."

EPILOGUE – 133 DAYS (3196 HOURS

THURSDAY AFTERNOON

I'm sitting in Mum's car, waiting to make my way home from the pre-natal care unit of the Queen Elizabeth University Hospital. I feel euphoric as I have just undergone my twenty-week scan as they've found no abnormalities. It was a delight to see my baby, but what's more important is the scan has looked in detail at my baby's bones, heart, brain, spinal cord, face, kidneys and abdomen, allowing the sonographer to check for eleven rare conditions. Although nothing is ever guaranteed, I feel reassured having reached this stage in my pregnancy without the slightest indication of any problems.

My family doctor has been wonderful. When I went to see him to discuss my pregnancy, he was very caring and understanding. He was reassuring, saying the risk was slight, due to it only being temporary and limited exposure. However, he warned me about possible side effects of the drugs Jenny had inflicted on me; miscarriage, premature birth and heart defects being the most common. He's given me frequent check-ups and I've felt stronger and more confident with the passing of each day.

My twenty-week scan is significant. Everything is okay so far and my baby appears well-formed and a normal size for this stage. I say 'baby' because I've not let them tell me yet whether it will be a boy or girl, fearful of becoming even more attached. Another few weeks and I'll feel confident enough to know. Mum's dying to find out. She's been obsessively knitting, using neutral colours, but she's keen to switch to blue or pink. I think having my baby to think about has helped her fill the void in her life now Dad's gone.

Although my instincts say blue, there have been too many things in the last year where my instincts have been unreliable for me to consider it a safe bet.

Despite all the evidence which I've been made aware of, I have no further memories of the time I was kept sedated by Jenny and Dwight. My underwear was discovered in Dwight's house, believed to have been hidden away by him as a trophy. Throughout her questioning, Jenny has remained silent. However, resulting from Dwight's confession, I know they kept me bound and naked for most of the time and forced me to watch pornography. He claims everything was Jenny's idea. Under interrogation, he's admitted to keeping me in that state as a hostage and to him and Jenny washing me all over on a daily basis. It means the recollections I had of hands touching me everywhere were genuine. They must have been Dwight's hands and Jenny's hands.

He's been adamant no one else was involved. He claims not to have abused me in any other way. I want to believe him, but how can I ever be sure? Jenny's mission was to inflict uncertainty and havoc into my life. I may never know for certain what happened during those awful 133 hours, but I won't let it destroy me. I have my baby to think of. I won't let her win.

I've been well and my therapist is happy with my progress. The nightmares are becoming less frequent and less intense. Often, when I visualise the three men carrying out their abuse, it's Jenny's face I see on the girl and Dad replaces one of the men.

Dad keeps trying to contact me, wanting to know how I am. I've blocked his number from my phone, but he still tries to find alternative ways to call. I can't forgive him for what he's done to Mum and to me. I suppose there will come a time when I may feel I can talk to him, but I don't see it coming any time soon. It won't be for his sake or even for mine, but if my child has a grandfather, perhaps they ought to get to meet. I've heard through the grapevine Dad has a new girlfriend: she's only a few years older than me. Leopards don't change their spots, I think.

I'm very happy working at Archers and I get to see Alesha and Margaret on almost a daily basis. I was given a promotion when a vacancy arose for a more senior role following Dwight handing in his notice. It may be a euphemism to say he gave his notice, as he could hardly continue working from his cell in Barlinnie prison. It's unclear how long it will take until his case is called to court, but, as a wealthy foreign national who owns a yacht, he was considered to have a high risk of absconding and he's been detained in custody. I haven't seen or heard anything from Jenny. If I never see her again, it will be too soon, yet I know there's a high likelihood of having to face her in court. Pleading guilty and making life easy for me is not in her nature.

Dwight's Uncle Carlton came to visit our office. Although a shrewd businessman, he seemed very personable and it became all too clear that Dwight had been sent to us to get him far away from their head office. Having exhausted his family responsibilities, Carlton felt entitled to wash his hands of him.

I talk to Jeffrey on a regular basis. I read somewhere that friendships formed in adversity are the most genuine and durable. I wouldn't argue the point.

Thanks to Jeffrey's research, I've been able to contact my birth mother's family. He wrote to, and then telephoned, her brother, my Uncle Sean. He's arranged for us to meet and set it up for a time when Sean's mother, my grandmother, would visit from Ireland. I don't know what to expect and I'm quaking at the prospect. Saturday is the day and Alesha has agreed to come with me. She has become such a good friend and she always gives me confidence. We're going to travel by train through to Edinburgh. As we thought it would be best to have a first meeting on neutral territory, we've arranged to meet at a coffee shop on Princes Street. Although she thought it best not to be present for the first meeting, Mum has encouraged me to make the trip. She's told me, if it goes well, she'd like to invite my new family back to our house. I'm relieved she feels comfortable with the prospect.

I'm brought back to the present when I hear Mum start the engine. I look around to see Michael approaching, carrying a magnificent bouquet and sporting a broad smile. We'd been waiting for him to come out to the car park and I'd mistakenly assumed he'd detoured to the toilet, but now I know he's been to the florist. Michael insisted on attending my scan, desperate to see images of his baby. He's been successful in transferring back to Glasgow, so he could be close, while retaining his promoted status. He's desperate for us to rekindle our relationship; he wants us to be a couple, a family. I can't deny the temptation and I won't rule out the possibility, but I want to take things slowly. I now know Jenny's lies and interference played no small part in my relationship with Michael failing. The poisoned seeds she sewed caused Michael to believe we had no future together and resulted in his move to Newcastle. However, I find it hard to forgive him for shacking up with a new girlfriend so quickly and then for not telling me, prior to the weekend we spent together. Perhaps the revelation of Dad's lies and deception is colouring my judgement, but I'm in no hurry to be tied into a relationship. For now, I'm happy with how things are.

135 DAYS (3244 HOURS)

SATURDAY AFTERNOON

As the train leaves Haymarket, I become increasingly apprehensive with there now being only five minutes travelling time to Waverley, Edinburgh's main station. So far, Alesha has done a marvellous job of keeping the conversation going so I'll be too preoccupied to think of what's ahead. During the journey, we've made plans for a night out for the four of us – Alesha, her boyfriend, Calum, Michael and me. We're going out for a meal and then a movie at Springfield Quay. Much as I love Indian food, I've vetoed curry because I'm suffering enough heartburn with my pregnancy without adding spicy food to the equation.

I'm up, standing at the doors even before the train comes to a halt, but I need to wait impatiently for them to open. Much as I'm eager to move quickly, I don't want to risk a fall. I take care walking, with Alesha taking my arm, as we climb the steep ramp then walk round to Princes Street. Seeing the Starbucks sign, Alesha steps ahead to hold open the door for me.

The moment I step through, I'm practically smothered by Cath

Conway, my grandmother, drawing me to her and weeping. "When I saw you walking along, I thought I was seeing things," she says. "I'd have known you anywhere. You're the spitting image of my Theresa."

Neither Cath nor Sean knew I existed until Jeffrey contacted them. They welcome me with open arms, quite literally. I'm overcome with joy. I feel I've turned a corner with the expectation of new life, genuine new friends and the addition of a whole new family.

Witnessing our reunion, Alesha says she will leave us to it, but I'm not prepared to let her go. She's like family, too, I feel. Thinking about my experiences of recent weeks, Alesha, Margaret and Jeffrey are more than family.

END

Dear reader,

We hope you enjoyed reading *133 Hours*. Please take a moment to leave a review in Amazon, even if it's a short one. Your opinion is important to us.

Discover more books by Zach Abrams at https://www. nextchapter.pub/authors/zach-abrams-scottish-mystery-crime-author-glasgow

Want to know when one of our books is free or discounted for Kindle? Join the newsletter at http://eepurl.com/bqqB3H

Best regards,

Zach Abrams and the Next Chapter Team

You might also like:
Source by Zach Abrams

To read the first chapter for free, head to:
https://www.nextchapter.pub/books/source

BIOGRAPHY

Zach Abrams is a writer of thrillers and crime novels. He lives in Scotland but spends much of the year in the Languedoc region of France.

Having an unusually varied education and work history, Zach was equipped with an extensive range of life experiences to draw on when developing his characters and stories. Following a science degree, a management post-grad and a professional accountancy qualification, he spent many years working as a CFO, business director and consultant in a range of industries as varied as transport, ostrich farming, manufacturing and public service.

Although having considerable experience of writing reports, letters and presentations, it's only fairly recently he started creative writing of novels - "a much more honourable type of fiction," he claims.

Prior to '133 Hours', he has six novels published plus his collaboration with Elly Grant on a book of short stories and a non-fiction business guide book. So far there are four tartan noir books in his Alex Warren Murder Mystery series, set in his hometown of Glasgow, Scotland.

The first is 'Made a Killing'. This British Police Procedural features Detective Chief Inspector Alex Warren as the senior investigating officer, assisted by female detective Sergeant

Sandra McKinnon and supported by a team of detectives, scene of crime technicians and other specialists. They carry out their investigation after the discovery of the corpse of a much-hated criminal, found with an elephant tusk impaled in his chest. Besides the main murder investigation, the team research a range of other criminal activities including financial crime, fraud, blackmail and extortion. Away from the crime investigation, there's family drama as well as a touch of romance and more than a sprinkling of humour. Readers familiar with the geography of Scotland, and Glasgow in particular, may well recognise locations as the detectives tread their weary path on their way to researching the crimes to solve the mystery.

The second in the series, 'A Measure of Trouble,' sees Alex's team seek the murderer of a CEO, killed within the cask room of his own whisky distillery. There's no shortage of suspects. Investigations lead them to interview the victim's family, employees and colleagues as they consider the varied motives of greed, revenge, adultery and nationalism.

The third, 'Written to Death,' begins with the mysterious death of a successful author, the murder taking place on stage during a writers' group meeting. Alex and Sandra are swamped with work as they must deal with a second enquiry, this one into organised crime, and it runs in parallel with the main murder investigation.

The fourth, 'Offender of the Faith,' follows the investigation after a young Asian girl was sexually assaulted and murdered in the home she shared with her Scottish boyfriend. With Sandra off work on maternity leave, imminently due to give birth, Alex and his team require to use kid gloves to handle the ultra-sensitive investigation with both the victim and her boyfriend's families brought under intense scrutiny. Potential motives of racism, islamophobia, hate, jealousy and honour killing all have to be considered. But who is behind the killing... and what is the real reason?

These are fast moving, gripping, murder mystery novels set in and around the tough, crime-ridden streets of Glasgow.

Zach's first novel was 'Ring Fenced', an unusually themed psychological thriller. It's a crime story with a difference, following one man's obsession with power and control. The main character, Benjamin, uses five separate personae to independently control the different divisions of his life. The story shows how he juggles the five separate existences and follows what happens when the barriers break down. The anti-hero, Benjamin, was nominated and shortlisted in the category of best villain in the 2013 eFestival of Words.

Zach's quirky thriller, 'Source; A Fast-Paced Financial Crime Thriller' centres on financial crime. It sees three investigative journalists travelling across the UK, Spain and into France. They suspect economic terrorism as they research corruption and sabotage in the banking sector. Resulting from their investigations, they face personal threats and all the time they're trying to cope with their own fraught private lives. Despite the weighty subject matter, it's a light and amusing read with plenty of humour, family drama and romance.

A collaboration with Elly Grant produced 'Twists and Turns,' a book of short stories, which range from flash fiction to a novella. They all have mystery and an element of the unexpected, with content ranging from Gothic horror to mild comedy.

All of Zach's books can be purchased from Amazon as eBooks and paperbacks. Audiobook versions of both Ring Fenced and

Made a Killing are already available and the other titles are in progress.

Alike his central character in 'Ring Fenced,' (Benjamin Short), Zach Abrams completed his education in Scotland and went on to a career in accountancy, business and finance. Married with two children, he plays no instruments but has an eclectic taste in music, although not as obsessive as Benjamin. Unlike Benjamin, he does not maintain mistresses, write pornography and (sadly) does not have ownership of a mega internet distributor. He is not a sociopath (at least by his own reckoning) and all versions of his life are aware of and freely communicate with each other. More in keeping with 'Alex Warren', Zach was raised in Glasgow and has spent many years working in Central Scotland.

Printed in Poland
by Amazon Fulfillment
Poland Sp. z o.o., Wrocław

53614690R00186